" TARF

AUTHOR'S NOTE

Small towns-and families- are often full of stories, legends and conjecture. This book is a work of fiction, however. Any similarities the reader might find with actual people or events are purely coincidental.

INTRODUCTION

My father, Conway Duque was a beautiful man to behold. God had graced him with unearthly charm, the keenest wit and the smile and sun-streaked hair of a teen idol. He operated with fluid confidence and was well aware that he could convince anyone of anything required to further his own self-interests. He was bold, inflated, ambitious, entitled, and unencumbered by conscience. In short, he was a scoundrel. He broke our hearts without a second thought, and in the end, those of us who knew him best were just waiting for him to die.

CHAPTER 1: FOUNDATIONS

"In all human interaction there are what are called 'social microcosms.' A social microcosm is a pattern of human behavior found in society that can be reduced and repeated within a small group of people. In other words, we all have patterns of interaction—like the steps of a metaphorical dance—that can be seen repeating regardless of the size of the social setting. Interestingly, these behaviors are learned and established very early in life and are reinforced by an individual's experience insomuch that by adulthood, they become incredibly difficult to change. Again, like a dance, the steps become second nature to us. Only through considerable disruption to one's family, community or primary support system will an individual break free from the social system that helped to create them. The existing social system will often foment a homeostatic force in order to prevent that individual from breaking free. If that individual should choose to remove themselves, he or she will require not only an unconquerable desire to do so, but also a formidable personal identity, a clear personal code of standards and conduct, enduring support from emotionally healthy friends and decades of learning how to do it all differently. Each person would benefit from evaluating their own behavior in their various relationships and decide for themselves if a change would be better for them than to continue to repeat the same dance."

Parenting the EZ Way with Jessie Duque

My name is Jessie Duque. I am the youngest and only living daughter of Georgeanne and Conway Duque. I came back to Tarford Flats just a few months ago after my husband and greatest friend, Thomas, passed away.

Thomas and I were married when we were 24 years old. He had just finished his bachelor's degree at Northwestern and I was about to embark on my psychotherapy internship at a Mental Health clinic in Peoria, Illinois. During our 51 years together we had two rambunctious boys who grew into adventurous young men, and finally strong and doting husbands and fathers. After Thomas died following a short but fierce battle with cancer, my life seemed to stand still. My children are grown with families and lives of their own, and with Thomas gone, I felt swallowed up by that large family home- swallowed up and spit out without a purpose. After a few months of aimlessness and a steady accumulation of mail and dust, I decided it was time for a change. It was then that I chose to return here to Eastern Nebraska, the place I was born.

Years ago my dear older sister, Vernie, renovated a well-worn family cabin by the Platte river. It is rustic, quiet, and tucked away from the meddlesome world. I can't think of a better place to finish out my days and finally put to rest a secret my family has kept since the summer of 1975.

It's late autumn and the Canada geese started their migration a week or so ago. Their numbers can be awe striking. Their calls can sound as loud as an oncoming summer hailstorm as it batters the trees and rooftops in its approach. I love to watch their landings, their wings silently cupping and gracefully setting the bulk of their massive bodies down on the cold lake water. Occasionally a muskrat will venture out to brave a swim in the chilly water, but I am more likely to witness a chase between a coyote and a rabbit as the temperature continues to fall. The skies are a beautiful steel blue-gray and carry the scents of wood fires and cold prairie wind. This is a blessed place to live.

I have not always thought so. I spent many decades away from this place, in the fast-paced city of Chicago with my husband and our boys, but now that I am facing the end of my time on Earth, I find that quiet, simple, and separate are the words with which I want to define my final days. I am so grateful to Vernie who, in her own efforts to find sanctuary, had the wisdom to bring back to life this beautiful place by the water.

I have always had a penchant for history. In my youth I learned all I could about the American Revolution and the establishment of a young nation with such significant diversity. I marveled at the physical expansion of the nation, the revolutionary ideas in manufacturing and transportation, in the wild successes of the cotton, tobacco, oil, steel, coal and railroad moguls, and the opportunity for anyone to try to seize their own land and fortune.

On my 20th birthday I received a package from my uncle, Buddy who lived in the Northeast. My mother always told me that he was the other history enthusiast in the family. It turned out; Uncle Buddy was a fastidious family historian. He had compiled copious notes, records and photos of our family members from the Civil War era to present day. Along with the package, Buddy had sent a note. Over 5 decades later, I still remember what it said:

"Dear Jessie, as you venture out into the world, remember, it is just as important to know from whence you come as it is to know where you are going."

I realize that if I were to tell this story sufficiently, I must also start where things began:

My maternal grandmother, Lucinda, was an Atchison. Lucinda Atchison's granddaddy was one of three men who settled the area with their young families just after the Civil War. The three men— Franklin Atchison, Oliver Turnbull, and David Roane—had made a bit of money during the war and wanted to expand west. The Transcontinental Railroad had just been completed, and towns and settlements had sprung up all along the routes of Western migration. Iowa had been admitted to the Union in the mid 1840's, but Nebraska was still only a territory.

Across the Missouri river from Iowa sat the city of Omaha, whose stockyard industry was growing, as was its population and collective wealth. Adventurous entrepreneurs saw Nebraska as a land of promise, where a man with a head for business could make a fortune while enjoying the freedom from hectic urban life.

The area they chose to settle in was just north of the Platte River, a meandering body of water that stretches the 430-mile-wide expanse from the Wyoming border to the Missouri River. The slow-moving, relatively shallow Platte carries all kinds of silt and sand from the Great American Desert into the more fertile Eastern Nebraska lands. The soil near the Missouri River becomes thick clay, sticking to a person's boots, encasing the legs of horses, and pulling at the wheels of a wagon like heavy glops of endless tar.

The men aptly named the place "Tarford Flats," and quickly established themselves as shrewd, very capable businessmen, eager to capitalize on the demand for grains and goods they anticipated from the growing Western population. Atchison had been in the livery and transportation business. He had several wagons and even more good horses and oxen. Turnbull was the product of several generations of politicians and was masterful in organizing and administrating county government and law enforcement. Roane was a well-connected timber dealer who had a vast business network that spanned from the forests of northern Minnesota to the Black Hills of South Dakota.

After setting up a charter, the three families of Turnbull, Atchison, and Roane established and then ran everything in town from the issuance of building and water permits to who could own and operate businesses. Before too long, Tarford Flats became a lucrative stop for travelers who needed a break from the mundane, barren trip west. Those who stopped in Tarford Flats would say the town was sleepy. For those of us who have generational history in small towns, we recognize the constant commotion of the gossip mills churning in our midst

The three founding families were considered to be quite something by Tarford Flats standards. I have often mused at what those standards must have been. It could have been as simple as having ample supplies of soap and toothbrushes, or several complete place settings, but to hear the lore of the older residents, these families were at the upper crust of our little society, "pillars" of our community. Each founding family continued to promote their own importance and the assumed exceptionalism of their offspring. The following generations of children were expected to be the very best at their endeavors and to have the very best opportunities that could be afforded them. This often involved sending the older children back east for their secondary education.

In line with Atchison family tradition, when Lucinda turned sixteen years old, she was sent to an elite finishing school in Virginia to learn necessary domestic skills and the refined etiquette befitting a lady, and most importantly, to find herself a suitable husband. As fate would have it, Lucinda became a frequent attendee at social functions hosted by the Virginia Military Institute. She joined the prestigious Activities Committee, where she met and won the arm of Stedford Beaumont, whom everyone called "Major." Major Beaumont came from old and dwindling money. His family had made their fortune in horse breeding, but since the devastation of the Civil war, the demand for expensive horses had waned. Major was not inclined to toil in a stagnant horse trade. He was ready to move on, to establish new markets and new innovations in the future of livestock.

By the time Lucinda came back to Tarford Flats, she had a thoroughly rounded education (limited, of course, for the "gentler" gender), a husband, and a plan. She would help Major establish a great and powerful name for himself and their family for generations to come.

Within a few years, Major Beaumont had become a considerable force within the Atchison family business. He did indeed increase the family fortune, and he not only established new markets for livestock and livery, but he created an unexpected demand for more sophisticated sundries. With his East Coast connections via the VMI, Major was able to import items that folks on the dusty plains might have been lucky to experience once in their lifetimes. Soon the proud and prim people of Tarford Flats began to receive friendly gifts of painted silken scarves and Meerschaum smoking pipes. Of course, Major was quite aware of the influence of such treasures. Accommodating college registrars for instance might enjoy richly scented cigars and sweet dried fruits from sunny isles. If he was working an especially important deal, Major might procure for a willing benefactor the most glorious books bound in embossed leather with delicate pages lined with real gold shimmer. Women's church leagues and coffee socials would be all abuzz in admiration of Major and Lucinda Beaumont's tasteful "generosity."

Lucinda benefitted immensely from Major's business ventures and the growing Atchison-Beaumont empire. They were on the fast track to financial success and social influence. The Beaumonts lived a wonderful life with wonderful things and had a wonderful home with wonderfully little that went awry.

Life was all going perfectly according to plan when Stedford Jr. was born. The couple was ecstatic when Lucinda became pregnant. Both she and Major had begun to make great plans for their firstborn child. As often happens with children, however, we can hardly predict, much less control the challenges they will face.

Lucinda took to bed rest after the first trimester and spent most of the summer under a wonderful new electric fan, a gift from her husband. She was not seen for several months, but the women in town kept one another abreast of any news they might glean while dropping off casseroles or freshly baked bread. Much to their frustration, Stedford Jr. took his time and was born two weeks later than expected.

He was a chubby, happy baby, and he loved his mother. He stole her heart from the moment he arrived. They were inseparable. As he grew, he would watch Lucinda in awe as she played the piano, fixed her hair and makeup in the mirror, and put on her jewelry. To him, she was dreamlike, as if he could as easily be watching a mermaid dance among the waves. Lucinda's little boy felt safe with her and stuck by her side, enjoying the scent of her perfume and the sounds of her rustling skirts and her high heeled shoes on the hardwood floors. He was her constant companion. That's how he came to be known as "Buddy".

Buddy was a very sensitive, loving young man. He loved to care for the horses in the stables, to spend time under his favorite tree feeling the sweet breeze of summer and trying his hand at poetry. Of course, Lucinda insisted on the proper education of literature, music, and etiquette, while Major had his own requirements that Buddy learn about trade and economics. Buddy performed very well in all academics and established himself to be quite talented at predicting cultural trends. I remember my confusion at her strange affect when grandmother would say, with lingering sorrow, that Buddy had wonderful taste.

Four years after her brother, Mama was born. Even at birth, Mama had a beautiful, full head of espresso hair. Her eyes were the color of the sky before a storm, a muted cobalt rimmed by navy blue. Like her brother, she was a chubby, happy baby who seemed to stretch as she grew. By the time she was eleven years old, Mama had developed into a long, lithe wisp of a young woman with a refined jaw line, a long, graceful neck, and an air of confidence beyond her years.

Mama's full name was Georgeanne Belle Beaumont. Lucinda wanted to emphasize the French in Mama's heritage in the way she pronounced "Jzour-Jzahnn" and had learned enough of the French language during her finishing years to know that Belle means "beautiful."

Lucinda had always wanted a daughter to show off to the other women in her social circle. There was some serious competition at this time, with several beauties budding from the three family trees. Lucinda, however, felt she had several advantages, including access to the finest commodities and having married well. (Major was a head-turner, even in his older years.) Add to that Lucinda's fastidious attention to high class and etiquette, and there was no reason Georgeanne would be less than perfect. If she were to have her way, every moment of Lucinda's adult life would culminate in creating the prim princess, the pageant champion, the prize "show pony" in her beautiful Georgeanne.

Georgeanne was a natural superstar. She seemed to know the very moment she caught the gaze of a curious onlooker. She would transport herself through a room on graceful feet that made no sound. Her steps were unperceivable as she would glide—never bounce—across the sun-streaked, gleaming floors. She would let every smile reach her eyes and her dark lashes flutter just enough to set off sparks of infatuation in boys, girls, men and women alike. Georgeanne's pale skin was flawless—almost iridescent—and even in the hottest weather, she seemed to barely glisten, never looking too moist or soggy, but rather looking like a perfectly ripe, juicy, intoxicating peach. Lucinda knew she would be a smashing success.

Training Mama for pageantry seemed as silly as training a fish to swim. She was a natural. She was quite talented musically, and she also created the most beautiful cakes and flower arrangements—anything she could do to express her artistic nature. And she was kind. Mama had a generous spirit and shared what she had with those around her. She seemed to have everything she could want within reach.

Everything, that is, except her liberation from the pressure she felt from her mother, the sidelong glances of her envious peers and ready criticisms of their competitive mothers. Having never participated, I can only imagine that pageantry was frustrating with all of its social rules and confines.

Mama was at her core a very self-assured, intelligent woman. Unfortunately, many in her sphere felt those qualities were unbecoming to young women of esteem. Of course, Mama rebelled in her own subtle ways like paying backhanded compliments to her mother's peers, or snubbing invitations in favor of spending time alone. Lucinda was quick to correct Mama whenever she could catch her alone, which often meant that Mama made herself scarce once the crowds dispersed.

She did find great comfort in her big brother. Mama used to tell me stories of their elaborate tea parties in which Buddy would often play butler to Georgeanne and her dolls for what seemed like an entire afternoon. The two would sneak out from under their mother's influence to embark upon their secret adventures climbing trees and stealing apples. Many summer days were spent walking in the soggy grass pools that arrived near the river following a heavy rain. Buddy would capture toads and crawdads, laughing as Georgeanne would shriek with surprise.

Buddy loved my mother in all forms, whether she was a pageant queen or a messy, adventuresome kid. And Mama knew it. When their mother began her tirades of criticism or scolding, Buddy would often step in and act as a buffer. With his affable nature and his cheerful wit, he could soften his mother's scorn. Mama often told me how Uncle Buddy made her childhood more bearable, and how he had a way of bringing out Grandmother's kinder side.

I am surprised I hadn't considered before how frustrating that must have felt for Lucinda. She had a sweet boy who doted on her from the moment of his birth, and a daughter who grew more rebellious, headstrong and distant.

I have thought often about how parents raise their children. In my work as a therapist, I have frequently witnessed the strange dynamics at play within parent-child relationships. During my decades-long professional life, I penned several books and gave countless lectures. Their topics were varied, from living with anxiety, depression and grief, to improving relationships and communication. The most poignant of the topics, however, was parenting. I have found that those who experience the greatest heartache are parents. As a collective group of people, well-meaning parents suffer staggering guilt, doubt, worry, fear, regret, frustration, and helplessness. Add to that the circumstances of our own childhoods and the desire to avoid hardship and to exceed already unrealistic expectations, and I am sure anyone could be convinced that parenthood is akin to torture. I marvel at the strength, determination, and variety of sacrifices shown by strong parents— especially those parents whose strength is manifest in their ability to let go.

My grandmother, Lucinda, was such a parent. I am sure she meant to do well by her children, and I have no doubt she was quite influenced by her own parents and her own experiences. I am also sure, as her days became lonely, she felt the pangs of grief and wished that she would have done some things differently.

Of course, children do tend to make their own decisions, despite the efforts and intentions of their parents. Sometimes they may find that they are just not made to suit their environment. They have to escape for their sanity. I believe this is what happened with my uncle Buddy.

When Buddy returned from his first year of college, he seemed as though he had experienced a world of wonderful things—things our small town could not afford him. There was something a bit different about him, though. He was restless, impatient, and sought for a purpose. Lucinda sensed his restlessness, his angst, and wanted to keep him close to her, as though she could protect him from whatever it was that was awaiting him. Lucinda suggested to her husband that it might be the perfect time to expand the family business. They had been discussing entering the retail market and finally offering all of the wonderful sundries Major had been importing for years to repeat customers and tourists alike. They offered the project to Buddy, who loved the idea. They provided Buddy with a list of available imported items and enough money to buy or build the perfect shop, and within six months the Beaumont Boutique was born.

It was a two-story building with a grand entrance and curved staircases hugging either side of the huge main floor. The second floor was visible from the foyer and had a beautiful white iron railing that looked like lace from below. The effect was dramatic, and the combined floors looked almost like the tiers of a wedding cake from the table's point of view.

Buddy was a retail genius. Over the next six years, he transformed that block on Main Street into a shopping delight, the complete Eurasian experience. Coming from the North, the first stop was a luxurious salon complete with manicures, pedicures, and a beauty parlor brimming with the newest hair and makeup styles and products from Paris. As the door would swing open to the street, the scent of freshly cut lilacs would waft among the passers-by, arousing their senses to awaiting luxuries.

Just one doorstop south was the actual Beaumont Boutique which offered fine dresses, dress shoes, wraps, scarves, stockings, handbags, hats, perfumes, and lingerie- everything a refined lady could desire. With the Boutique, Buddy intended to create a shopping experience for women that was very much like the tea parties he remembered with Georgeanne, wherein a lady might be able to see herself beyond her current situation, perhaps incorporating some glamour and luxury into her life, feeling as though she were among friends.

Buddy brought in a stylish pair of soft pink tufted chairs and a wonderfully contrasting mint green and cream striped rolled-arm sofa. He found some white end tables with hand-painted wild roses whose stems encircled each table leg. Guests were offered cups of tea or, in the warmer months, lemonade. A tray of small cookies would always be within reach while they socialized and perused high-end magazines from Milan and New York.

The last stop on the block was a favorite in our little culture hub. It was the refined yet masculine wonderland which sat just through the beautifully tiled entrance to the Gentleman's Wear and Tailor. Upon opening the heavy lead-glass door, patrons would be met with cool air smelling of oiled leather, cognac, and lavender. The place was tastefully dimmed and lit from within by expensive lamps on mahogany tables next to hand-stitched club chairs. In a back corner of the store was a well-supplied reading area, complete with a complimentary wet bar and coffee station where men could await his adjustments or take a moment away from the demands of the world.

As business grew, Buddy invited Michael, a former college classmate to join him in the management of the businesses. This young man was much like Buddy in that he was soft spoken, refined, cultured, and very handsome. Buddy and Michael were a fantastic team. They were both terribly enthusiastic about their business, and about being reunited.

It was this young man who was caught passionately entangled with Buddy in a fitting room a few months later. According to Mama, Buddy and Michael developed a "romantic interest" in one another. She said that one day at the end of business, they became so overcome with desire for one another, they forgot to lock the door. They had also forgotten that Eunice Spanks from the Lutheran Ladies League was dropping by to pick up fabric remnants for the upcoming Spring Fling charity sewing bee.

Apparently, Eunice came into the shop and heard what she thought was an older man having trouble in the fitting room. Eunice was filled with concern. Recently, her own Harold had a fit of angina and lost consciousness for about 30 minutes in the bathroom, so Eunice assumed that might be what happened to this poor soul in the fitting room. She knocked on the fitting room door, alarming Buddy and Michael, who apparently had undone several of their clothes in the tiny room.

They rushed to get dressed without paying necessary attention to their suspenders. Buddy had his foot on his friend's suspenders, and when the Michael tugged, Buddy moved his foot. The clasp at the end of the suspender was sent hurling toward Michael's eye, where it hit hard and fast. Temporarily blinded and with one arm stuck awkwardly in a shirtsleeve, Michael fell backward through the fitting room door. As he fell, he grabbed for Buddy, who was still only half dressed, his pants strangling his ankles. The two of them fell with Buddy landing bare butt atop the heap at the feet of poor, charitable Eunice.

Eunice, to her credit, tried not to speak too much of the incident. She seemed to share in a strange sorrow with Lucinda (and as time went on, she was the same toward Mama). For a while, Mama said, the family thought the whole thing would pass like bad weather. It was unfortunate for sweet Buddy when the whispering began around town.

It may have been even more painful for Lucinda, truth be told. She was in an untenable situation between a strong and successful husband, the decades of family influence and position within the community, and her heart-wrenching desire to be near her oldest (and dearest) child. Buddy, however, could not stay in Tarford Flats and be the person he wanted to be. Maybe she showed her love for him best by letting him go to find his true self.

About eight years before I was born, Buddy left Tarford Flats. Michael had found him a job in New York City. He wrote to Mama every month, and we loved to listen as she read his stories about the big city. Mama would cry sometimes and exclaim how she missed him, yet I know she was relieved that he was out from under the strange pressure that exists in small towns.

The dynamics within small towns can be brutal. The families whose history is longest in the community develop deep roots. Like plants, those with strong roots multiply, gain strength, and overtake smaller, newer plants with ease.

When Tarford Flats was in its infancy, the Roane family created a supply for much needed products like lumber, hardware, building materials, and the like. As Tarford Flats and the Roane clan both continued to grow, the Roane monopoly expanded to concrete and steel. Any competition was successfully starved by the Good Old' Boy network. Nowadays the Roane family tree has many limbs. They, along with the smaller founding families of Turnbull and Atchison (Beaumont) make up the upper crust of our little community. With marriages, name changes, and more and more children, it would seem that our little town would be more practiced at assimilating, but the members of the old families fight hard against giving up their status.

My dear husband once said that he could categorize the folks in a small town into three groups. The first group consists of the elitists. They are the folks who stand on pedestals and let everyone else know that they are standing there. In the second group are the socially desperate folks—the ones who are trying to either create their own pedestals or climb on the footings of the elitists' pedestals. In the third group are the people who don't see the value in pedestals.

His pedestal theory is a wonderful concept when one sees it applied to the sociology of Tarford Flats and similar towns. The elitists spend a considerable amount of time and energy maintaining and defending their roosts. They will take extraordinary measures to crush new or emerging pedestals. They will eliminate, cover, or deny any structural flaws in their own pedestals, and they will tirelessly mock those whose pedestals are not as high.

My husband was one of the third group. Early in our marriage, he came with me on a few visits to Tarford Flats. During those visits, Thomas became familiar with the rigid social hierarchy in my hometown. He always found such fascination with the deference given to the great, great grandchildren of the founders.

When someone is in the elite class of a small town, he or she is always accompanied by the phrase (spoken or not), "Don't you know who I am?" In business, the elites receive special deals on merchandise, property, and even medical treatment, because those in the community want to have an "in." It is understood that they will not do business with ordinary salespeople but owners and management alone, who seem to be as aware of their presence as a police dog is aware of marijuana.

In my experience, it's the women in the elite group who are most afflicted by their circumstances. The pressures to maintain themselves and their families in their "perfection" are overwhelming. These women hold unreachable standards and perceive that everyone is waiting for them to fail. By default, they become terribly competitive and self-absorbed. Their every move is calculated to reap the most admiration from others. They may subject themselves to sleeplessness, starvation, emotional neglect, bitterness, obsessions, dark secrets, considerable debt, strained marriages, unfaithful husbands, and a lifelong sense of shame—all the price for maintaining the perceived status as a very important fish in an insignificant, tiny pond.

The pageant circuit in the Midwest is the vortex of such thought. Each summer, the crop of small-town debutantes would get all gussied up and trot themselves across manure-smeared scaffolds, reciting their deeply-held beliefs on topics ranging from the best way to start the day to the importance of setting a proper table. The well-practiced smiles pasted on their golden, sweaty faces did little to mask their cunning estimations of fellow contestants.

The true sport seemed more to be in finding the unforgivable flaw in one's peer and exposing it, the objective being to claw ones way to the top of the beauty tower regardless of the excoriation of those underfoot. Each step was worth the price of soul.

I suppose I should not have been surprised that the drive for validation ran so deeply in our family. I look back and see the evidence of incredible insecurity in Lucinda and the generations before. My grandmother had her share of secret sorrow. There was, of course, the absence of her sweet Buddy in her life, followed by a string of affairs

Major tried unsuccessfully to hide from her. Like most of the women in our family, however, she was unfailingly resourceful, determined, and ambitious. Like them, Lucinda had the gift of calculation and a slow burn in her stomach fueling her quest for vindication. And like those before her, she also had the ability to hide it all with a demure little smile. And then there was Mama, Lucinda's beacon of hope, a poised, brilliant beauty—everything Lucinda needed her to be.

But Mama was also a cynic. Mama saw firsthand the way women were treated and treated themselves. She was disgusted with the society in which she was raised, disgusted with the way women had been so willing to bankrupt their self-respect. And then there were the pageants, where all the girls could pretend to be held in the highest of esteem.

Mama knew she was being held up as evidence to disprove a fraudulent existence. Her mother was miserable. Major was an unfaithful snob. Buddy was …painful. Mama knew she was the one thing Lucinda could point to in her effort to convince everyone that her life was wonderful. If Mama was the best young woman in the county, maybe that would be proof enough that Lucinda was truly worthwhile, that her life was not a farce. Maybe Major's long hours and weekend trips with pretty young horse trainers were as innocent as he claimed. Maybe she was a wonderful wife and mother. Maybe what happened with Buddy was only a phase, or at least it was not her fault.

CHAPTER 2: GEORGEANNE

*"Most parents tend to live through their children to some degree,
although few would actually admit it. We project onto them our
goals, our values, our aspirations, and also our fears, anxieties, and
frustrations. We try to prevent them from making mistakes like the
ones we made or carrying on our less desirable traits or behaviors.
In some cases, parents will take extreme measures to protect their
children from consequences, all the while renaming our meddling as
being "invested" or "helpful," when really it is because we are
afraid. And maybe we should be. If we have failed to raise our
children with strict standards and high expectations, have we not
taught them to accept inadequacy? Have we allowed them to learn
by experience how to endure hardship and solve problems, or have
we taught them that someone else will always come along to fix
things and save them from responsibility? Unfortunately, we parents
often forget that more is taught through practice than is ever taught
through words."*
<u>Parenting the EZ Way with Jessie Duque</u>

When she was fifteen years old, Mama was crowned Miss Cass
County. This was back in the days when the contestants had to
change in makeshift tents behind the stage. The pageant rules stated
clearly that only the contestants were allowed in that area.

As the story goes, long before the winner had been decided, the
pageant judges had requested a break during the very tedious
"personal interview" event. Mama had been in the changing area
attempting to air out her stifling pageant attire.

It was as she was leaving the tent that she was met by one of the esteemed judges—a man Mama described as a coffee and tobacco-soaked, blubbery man with an overgrown dust-colored mustache. "The Walrus," as she referred to him, caught her alone, and in a bumbling lunge, he tried to fumble his way under her dress. As she pushed his moist, doughy arms away, he lost a cufflink from his sleeve. Then he coughed and sputtered and pulled out a dingy handkerchief. He clumsily wiped his sweaty face and dropped the handkerchief on the floor. Mama stepped on it and pulled it with her shoe under the hem of her skirt. The Walrus knew better than to try to go after it.

Seconds after the Walrus's retreat back to the judges' table, Mama found the custom-made cufflink on the ground. She wrapped it carefully in the handkerchief, which she noticed was monogrammed, and tucked the small bundle in her handbag. She knew her opportunity had come.

Rather than report the incident, Mama sent a message to the smelly old Walrus: first, listing and describing the items she now possessed which might reveal his repugnant attempt, and second, notifying him of her desire to compete for the title of Miss Nebraska at the State Fair, which would be held in Lincoln, the state's capital city. To this point, no one younger than sixteen years old had been allowed to compete. Mama knew that if the Walrus were to ask for special permission, however, it would certainly be granted. By the end of the pageant, Mama walked away with the county title and an invitation to compete in Lincoln later that year.

Mama came in as First Runner Up that year at the Nebraska State Fair. It was quite an achievement, and the best finish in pageant history for anyone from Tarford Flats. What was more important was the ultimate victory for Mama. She had succeeded in reaching the pinnacle of bragging rights for her dear mother. She could retire from pageantry with honor. Mama had negotiated her freedom with a disgusting memory and blackmail.

Mama said, "You deserve the life you accept." She may have said, "You deserve the relationships you accept," or any number of things. I swear she said this phrase a thousand times. Maybe that is the number of times I have said it to myself. What I do know is that Mama never did allow herself to be a victim of circumstance.

My father is a perfect example. He showed up at the Atchison stables when Mama was almost seventeen years old. Lucinda and Major had been discussing various finishing schools for their Georgeanne to attend in order to secure a suitable husband. Mama had no interest in more social engineering by her parents. She was certainly not going to let herself be corralled into some antiquated form of human husbandry. It was during this conflict that she caught sight of him, a tall, bronzed, muscular vision of adventure and passion personified. Georgeanne saw the figure of Adonis, wrapped in freedom and smelling wild, exciting.

Conway was certainly in favor of her affection. She was rich and beautiful, of course, and she was looking for a way out from under her parents' crushing control. He saw the arrangement as mutually beneficial. He had no money, no family of any importance, no real history. He was unattached and looking to attach himself well.

As the story goes, Conway's parents, my grandparents, were divorced when divorce was hardly an option. His mother, Doris, was reportedly quite a beauty, if a bit unruly. She lived in St. Joseph, Missouri, where she ran a popular boarding house for railroaders and folks making their way west. She had the kind of reputation that made married women nervous. Eventually Doris married one of her tenants, who by all appearances was a fairly decent man, even if he was not interested in being a parent. Doris was a woman who put her needs and the needs of her husband first. This was her second marriage, after all, and although divorce was scandalous, two failed marriages would make her a pariah. Doris concerned herself with making sure she was getting what she needed. She was not terribly nurturing. Conway understood early in his adolescence that she was not the type of woman to do much for her child, especially once her child showed the slightest ability to fend for himself.

Conway's father was a smart man who made terrible decisions. He tried his hand at several get-rich-quick schemes, always losing more than he made. He even owned a few businesses, none of which turned a profit. He had several casual relationships with women, often simultaneously. One less-reputable woman even convinced him to give his last name to her adolescent son, which he did without a fuss. Earl Duke thought that loyalty only applied to the person in front of him at any given moment. Conway was furious at this and at the rumors that Earl Duke was supporting this fraudulent heir without ever supporting Conway. Conway explained that he left town when his father began asking him for money. It was on the train ride west that Conway decided to change his name from Duke to a fancier "Duque." He wanted to change everything about himself that tied him to the family he was leaving behind.

And so he arrived at the Atchison stables seeking a job and a future. Georgeanne assumed he had arrived to save her from an impending sentence of co-ed dances and homemaking classes. She was beautiful, dynamic, and irresistibly confident. He was an equal reflection. Major and Lucinda were incensed. They clearly disapproved of Conway, whom they considered a gold-digger at best. Though Conway worked long and hard for Major and his industry, he was forbidden to step foot in the family home. They were deliberately kept apart. He was kept busy when Georgeanne wanted to visit the stables. She was sent on errands in town when he was finishing his workday. In the opinion of the Atchison ruling class, Conway Duque would never sully their princess.

The princess, however, had much different plans. The more her parents rejected Conway, the more she cajoled him. The more they criticized him, the more she defended him. It became such a struggle for power that when all was said and done, the only way Georgeanne could triumph over her parents was to marry Conway and get it over with.

Unfortunately, Lucinda and Major were prepared for a drawn-out fight, so she had to do something drastic to bring this battle with her parents to an end. Georgeanne told her mother she was pregnant.

Lucinda was not surprised by the revelation. She had already suspected that Conway had seduced Georgeanne into his bed. As far as Lucinda was concerned, the moment she started losing control over Georgeanne, her only daughter's future became hopeless.

Georgeanne was counting on Lucinda's reaction. She was well aware that Lucinda had little confidence in anything her daughter did outside of Lucinda's direction. It must have been with some bittersweet satisfaction that Georgeanne was so easily able to convince her mother she was pregnant. Mama was again faced with the reality that her parents had no faith in her.

Of course, Mama was not pregnant. She could not be. Mama had not compromised her virtue regardless of Conway's efforts to take her to his bed. With a familiar sense of disappointment toward her mother, Georgeanne knew that a pregnancy scare would result in a headlong rush to the altar.

Georgeanne and Conway were married when she was seventeen and he was twenty-three. Soon after the wedding, after the marriage license had been filed away at the county courthouse, Georgeanne feigned a miscarriage. She was not all too eager to become a mother. She fully enjoyed applying her attentions to her strapping husband.

Conway seemed to enjoy her attentions as well. He was the kind of man who had come to expect such. Conway continued to work for the Atchison stables and soon became familiar with the more profitable modes of transportation in the Atchison Enterprises. He gained experience driving delivery vans and over-the-road haulers. Conway had a knack for organizing shipments and freight haulers throughout the Midwest. Under Conway's orchestration, Atchison Freight came to life. And though Lucinda would never thaw toward the man who defiled her prize daughter, Major Beaumont could not ignore the considerable profits made through Conway's talents.

Much to her relief, Lucinda did find that Conway's roguish influence did not impact the pedigree of her grandchildren. The first grandchild was a beautiful girl. She had our mother's looks and Lucinda was certain she could recognize poise and grace in the child's movements. Lucinda went on and on about the little one—how her skin was like fine china and her eyes the color of sapphires. She insisted the baby have a cultured moniker. Eventually, Georgeanne relented and named her daughter Toile. Mama always loved the French artwork with the birds, the scenery, and the lovely women on canvas. She remembered seeing it when she went to the Nebraska State Fair. She thought its name, "Toile," was incredibly graceful when spoken in French. And because our mother was well versed in conversational French, she pronounced it correctly, and when she called for our sister, the name was enchanting. And it was! "Toile" had an ethereal sound. Of course, in Tarford Flats, Nebraska, everyone else called her "Toowhylah."

Our sister, Fern, was born in the winter. It was most likely the blizzards that season that kept visitors away, but Fern did not seem to generate or receive the attention of folks the way Toile did. Fern was not a joyful baby. She was restless, impatient, and her little brows were furrowed more often than not.

Even as a tiny tot, Fern delighted in defiance. She was always finding her way into mischief, always scheming her next venture to drive Mama crazy with worry. While Toile maintained a kind, gentle spirit and a measured temperament, Fern was mercurial and quite unpredictable.

Just under a year later, our sister JoVernadene was born. She was very small and instantly Fern's best pal. The two would experience life in tandem, with "Fernie" always in the lead and "Vernie" always following dutifully behind. Fern loved to play with little Vernie. She would cut her hair, cover her in mud, and on at least one occasion, she painted Vernie's entire body orange after getting into an opened bottle of iodine Mama kept with the first aid items.

Whatever purpose Fern had for her, Vernie would fulfill. Remarkably, Vernie never complained. She was an unusually faithful child and she loved her sister Fern, sometimes at her own risk. True to her character, Fern proved to be an impatient child and was quick to anger. Vernie was small, quiet, and accommodating, a combination of traits which often left her in the wake of Fern's frequent fury.

The orderly dynamic that had been established within the household when Toile was born was soon overridden by the ongoing effort to keep Fern, and by association, Vernie, out of trouble.

I came along a few years later, when Vernie had just started school. I remember the days spent with Mama at home. I can still feel the scratchiness of the braided wool rug on which I would play with wooden blocks and read my favorite stories. Mama would set out my lunch in the cheerful little breakfast nook—usually apple slices, a sandwich, and a glass of milk. I would munch away and watch her as she folded laundry or ironed my father's handkerchiefs. After lunch and maybe a few cookies, Mama would have me lie down in my room for a nap. She would gracefully pull the curtains closed and cover me with my favorite blanket, and there I would stay while she skillfully played the piano out in the front room. I so enjoyed those peaceful hours with my mother in the quiet of her mid-day routine.

All of that would change when my sisters came home from school. They would tumble through the door, noisily dropping their books and bags in the entryway. Fern would be the first to investigate the kitchen for snacks, quickly claiming them for herself and trying to resist Mama's commands that she share. She would then concoct all sorts of plans to lead Vernie into mischief.

Among my family members, it seemed that Toile struggled the most with Fern and her bossiness. As the oldest, Toile felt compelled to help our mother parent, to protect Vernie and to restore order to our home. Fern was unrelenting, however, and was not about to let Toile have control. The more Toile tried to intervene; the more Fern tightened her grip on Vernie. The stressful sibling conflict often resulted in tears of frustration. Mama recognized that Toile's efforts were inadvertently making the situation worse. When Toile was eight years old, Mama thought it might be better for her to spend some time away from Fern. She encouraged Toile to visit Grandmother Lucinda.

Lucinda was overjoyed to have her. With Mama's acquiescence, Lucinda started planning for pageants again, this time with Toile in mind. Lucinda would happily cart Toile all over town, introducing her to her bridge partners and the like. After, she'd take Toile to the beauty parlor to have her pretty brown curls smoothed out and her nails painted. Toile, of course, loved the primping and the fuss, and she loved the way she felt when the lady at the beauty parlor finally turned her chair so she could see her finished work. Toile would gasp and smile at her reflection, carefully watching our grandmother's expression in the mirror, calculating her approval.

Little Toile would then be treated with an ice cream, and the two would return to Grandmother's house to pour over the pages of the latest Sears fashion catalogue. The lure of fashion and beauty seemed to whisper to Toile in a way it never had to her mother. Little Toile wanted nothing more than to be the next Duque to grace the podium.

————————————

Several seasons of pageantry came and went. Toile had just become a teenager, and my other sisters would soon follow after her. Our grandfather had introduced us to horse riding, and Fern and Vernie spent hours at the Atchison stables, washing and brushing their favorite horses. Toile was kept busy with pageantry things, and I spent most of my time at home, with Mama. Life in our little world was peaceful and isolated. Days meandered along pleasantly like a shallow river on a summer Sunday.

At that time, over-the-road trucking was quickly becoming a much-demanded and well-rewarded industry. Conway always seemed to be ahead of the curve where business was concerned. He already had an impressive fleet of transport trucks and was doing very well for himself. He had drivers from California to the Mississippi River.

It was a cold and blustery day in Eastern Nebraska when, in December of 1941, the bombing of our dear Naval servicemen and women in Hawaii shook the nation. I was only five years old and hardly knew what was happening, but I've heard Toile recall her experiences at that time. She said that women and men alike were sobbing, angry, enraged. Many of the folks in town seemed like empty vessels, like the cicada shells that are left on the sidewalks when they have been shed. Everyone talked about the tragedy, ruminating as if talking could turn back time and erase the entire affair from reality.

Men and boys hurried to sign up for the service, ready to exact revenge on the other-worldly perpetrators who hailed from the likes of Hell. Everyone wanted to be a hero. Everyone wanted justice for our boys. Everyone felt afraid and wanted life to be predictable again. Everyone from the ages of four to ninety-four wanted to know that they would make it safely through the night because our troops would level Japan.

Well, not everyone was ready to enlist. Conway had another idea. He had been aware of the "managed wartime supply" of food and other items during WWI. Usually, the faithful citizens would voluntarily participate in creative cooking and mending, eating and using less, so our soldiers and allies would have more to eat, more to use. Most everyone was excited to contribute. Average Americans had been team players.

There was a section of society, however, that practiced more "independent" trade. If there was access to a product and they had the money to buy it, they believed that commerce should go on. It was their presumption that the trading of black-market commodities was beneficial to the nation as it would help to maintain the economic heartbeat.

Conway understood this and quickly arranged to add bootlegging to his repertoire. And why not? He already had the system in place with his extensive shipping business.

Over the next several months, Conway created a vast network of suppliers of hard-to-find items, like ladies nylons, silk fabrics, Venetian glass and fashion, fine watches and shoes, soaps and perfumes, Italian leather goods, rubber tires, aluminum, Belgian beer and French wine, vodka, cane sugar, tea, Egyptian cotton and tobacco, Moroccan leather, and spices.

Normal trade routes were shut down, and those who dared to transport goods overseas were at risk of losing everything to U-Boat attacks. Europe, Africa, and Asia were in chaos, and everyone needed money and was willing to trade whenever possible. Conway's supply network and his pool of ridiculously wealthy clients culminated in making Conway an incredibly rich man.

As is too often the case with men who amass wealth, they begin to venture into a lifestyle outside the confines of common morality. For instance, I knew a man once who had two wives when such a thing was not legal. His summer wife lived in their home in a mountain resort town and enjoyed the trappings that came with it. He was her husband from April until October, however, she lived a pleasant life year-round, complete with art, music, theater, friends, charities, functions, and the like. Similarly, his winter wife lived in a Southwestern metropolis. He lived with her from October to April. She also accepted and enjoyed her situation, even at the expense of knowing her husband was bedding his other wife for six months of the year. Stranger still, it seemed that the entire entourage of this man's friends and associates were happy to look past his indiscretions, to abandon the values they proclaimed to hold dear, rather than risk being excluded from his circle.

Conway was treated similarly by many of the folks in Tarford Flats as his business and influence grew. He loved the feeling of people seeking him out for business ventures, financial help, donations and sponsorships, endorsements, and for companionships. Conway had grown more self-confident, and at some point, allowed himself to become more important than anyone else. He felt he deserved more than a spot in line waiting alongside his children for Mama's time and affections. He wanted it all. Since Mama was still tending to her girls, Conway developed "friendships" with other women in town who would give him their complete attention. Over time, he had extramarital relationships with innumerable women in several states. These women as much as lined up, it seemed, for his attention. For their time and physical involvement, Conway rewarded them with money, gifts, clothing, and special trips.

I was raised to understand that women who trade their virtue for money, gifts, and so on—especially to a man who is already married—are disdainful at best, and yet there appeared to be no shame in having an affair with Conway Duque. He certainly felt none. I sometimes wonder if he felt his behavior was justified, as if he was rightfully punishing Mama for putting her children before him.

Our family is no stranger to scandal. Mama had seen her own mother go through the madness of family secrets and an unfaithful husband. Lucinda weathered her difficulties by focusing first on Buddy, then Georgeanne, then Toile, and later, by adding whiskey to her morning coffee. At the end, Lucinda vacillated between bitterness and denial, all while holding a drink in her hand. And, like a glass of champagne, her long-lived practice of pretending that everything was perfect slowly lost its fizz.

Of course, when Mama discovered Conway's infidelity, she was devastated. And, like her own mother had been, mama was overcome with the initial shock and denial, the self-doubt and extraordinary shame that descend like a wall cloud in a fast-moving storm.

At first, she believed his promises to end the affairs, and at first, Conway continued to hide his indiscretions. Georgeanne had tried all of the usual schemes to win back her husband. She paid him more attention, she planned romantic evenings, she kept everything to his liking… and he didn't seem to notice, or care. My heart ached as I saw my mother lose herself in her desperation to win back his interest

Faced with the reality that her future could look much like her mother's, much like that of many women of the day, Georgeanne Duque felt the panic rise in her chest. It was an overwhelming sense of failure and doom, the loss of security not only in her marriage and her family, but even her security in her own ability to function.

Eventually, on what she always referred to as her "last day of chaos," Georgeanne had an epiphany. She had been standing in her front sitting room, looking around at her beautiful, orderly home, trying to find one more thing to set straight, one more thing on which to focus her frustration, when she stopped cold. It was as if her brain lost the ability to think. Georgeanne looked down and noticed a bright patch of sunlight stretching across a thick new rug she had recently purchased. As if in a trance, Georgeanne found herself lying on that thick rug, awash in the sunlight that reached in at her through the window. For several minutes she remained in that place, lying on her back with sunlight warming her body. Her hands were clasped and resting on her belly, which rose and fell as she took deep, silent breaths.

It was likely because her mind was finally at rest that Georgeanne was inspired by a new thought. "I am no different than an iris," she thought. The irises in her garden grew strong and vibrant, and they were beautiful. One year, a boy she had hired to do some yardwork mistook the emerging iris blades for weeds and cut them off. The irises made a sad attempt to bloom that year, but it seemed they just could not reach their usual glory. The following winter was terribly harsh. The temperatures lingered below zero for weeks at a time. Many shrubs and bushes perished in the cold.

Many folks were doubtful that any of the perennials would have survived, but that spring, we watched the flower gardens closely to see if Mama's irises would return. To our joyful surprise, not only did the leaves appear, but they seemed heartier and more plentiful than they ever had before.

This was how my mother would again reclaim her happiness. She would find a way to transcend the pain, the betrayal, the anger, and the sorrow that had filled her life as of late. She would gather her strength and her wits, and ready herself again to take charge of her own future. Mama would bloom again, stronger and more powerfully than ever.

And so, Georgeanne began the task of gathering evidence. Over the next several months, she took advantage of Conway's late-night meetings and "business trips" to amass piles of evidence of his illegal dealings in bootlegging. She found the names of several women, who, while having their turn at Conway, were also married to influential men in the community. She even found out that Mr. Duque was actually born to an Earl and Doris Duke and had not been assigned a social security number, and more importantly, he had not been located by the Draft Board. Conway Duque, nee Duke, was the perfect candidate for a treacherous, bloody, brutal tour in the Pacific theater of WWII. And Georgeanne had all she needed to prove it.

When Conway returned from a trip to Colorado, Georgeanne prepared a beautiful homecoming dinner for her husband, complete with cold beer, prime rib roast, creamed asparagus, and his favorite, strawberry rhubarb pie. She sent us to our grandparents' house for the night. Conway arrived about an hour later than promised, but she wasn't even upset. She sat and listened with great patience to his lies about business dealings and made-up conversations with prospective partners. After the pie and coffee were served, Georgeanne made a proposal to her husband.

Georgeanne suggested that Conway give her a divorce and a settlement which would include half of his earnings to date with Atchison Freight (which amounted to about two million dollars in cash and stocks), all the bootlegged perfumes, furs, clothing, accessories, and fabrics he had in storage, as well as the option to purchase future items at cost. She also wanted the family home and the deeds to any property she brought to the marriage. In return, Georgeanne promised not to reveal any of Conway's misdeeds to her father or to the general public.

Conway balked at first, so Georgeanne sweetened the deal. She promised not to send already prepared letters to each of the men whose wives Conway had corrupted. She also agreed to let Conway walk away from his marriage and family without further financial obligations after the deal was done. Finally, Georgeanne informed her husband what she had discovered about his "draft-dodging" status. She told Conway that she had been encouraged by the local draft board to report any known draft dodgers, because by this time in the Pacific, with heavy losses and the war still being hard fought, strong and resourceful men were desperately needed.

Conway finally understood that his smart, beautiful, and underestimated wife held his life, his fate, in her hands. He took the deal and moved out of the house shortly thereafter. Conway let it be known publicly that he was ready to "move on" from Georgeanne. He tried to sully her name among those in the community, claiming that she was impossible, and he had been a victim of her moods, but it was clear to anyone who knew him that she had been the one who had finally had enough.

Conway remained in Tarford Flats where he maintained his position at Atchison Freight, but he did not attempt to hide his resentment of Mama. For the rest of his life, Conway would not allow anyone to mention Georgeanne's name in his presence.

As I watched my father excuse his behavior or find a way to blame his family for his infidelity, I became intent on protecting myself from the pain he caused. I sought emotional distance from him and his destructive personality. However misguided, I concluded that he could hurt me less if I regarded him as some distant character rather than my dad. When he left us, I began to refer to him only as "Conway."

My mother, on the other hand, began a wonderful adventure. She reopened the refreshed Beaumont Boutique and stocked the shelves with rare indulgences. She invited local musicians, who had to audition first of course, to play in the lobby for special occasions. My favorites were the stringed quartets, the Methodist bell choir, and the St. Francis Catholic School children's choir that came to perform at Christmastime.

Mama loved to decorate for the holidays. Little Vernie stood up high on the ladder as brave as could be as Mama would hand her the most beautiful ornaments for the freshly cut tree. There were always lit candles placed to fill the boutique with the scents of the seasons: bayberry and mulling spices for Yuletide, tulips for spring, coconut or lemon for summer, pumpkin and apple for autumn. Some of my clearest memories of Mama are intertwined with these scents.

There is something spellbinding about witnessing someone operate within their perfect element. Such was my experience as I grew up alongside Mama orchestrating her uncanny talents with style and ambiance.

Mama had wonderful taste, and she also had Buddy, who happily made her introduction with several New York distributers and fashion experts. He was as well connected as ever, and he was quite successful in his own right. With his help, Buddy's baby sister became a fashion and lifestyle magnate of the Plains.

Mama also began networking with pageant organizers throughout the state and into South Dakota and Iowa. She even hired a few seamstresses and began a mail-order service for pageant hopefuls with the perfect outfits and accessories based on their individual tastes and personalities. Fate had prepared her to harness her knowledge, money, and business acumen to create a rural fashion empire, and it all started in the Beaumont Boutique.

CHAPTER 3: TOILE

"There are several common roles children in a dysfunctional family may adopt. First, there is a Golden Child whose role is to demonstrate the (fictional) family functioning. The Golden Child will be very successful, orderly, driven, and self-sacrificing in order to maintain appearances. The Golden Child will take upon themselves the public persona of the family and then try to prove through their success that the family unit is without significant dysfunction or shame."

Parenting the EZ Way with Jessie Duque

It must have been a precarious thing to navigate such a close relationship with Lucinda without falling completely under her control. I don't know how Toile did it. I have marveled at her navigational skills my entire life. I have concluded that it was through very skillful diplomacy mixed with a deep compassion for others that she established her place in people's hearts. To the end, Toile was one who gave more than she received and who reveled in doing kind works.

I am sure Toile had her own insecurities, but we never saw them. To me, she was radiant. What's more, everyone loved her. She was genuine, thoughtful, creative, smart... and so pretty. She never made any trouble, even with her sisters. Toile took care of us when Mama needed help and she seemed to like being regarded as mature and responsible. The more she was able to do, to manage and direct, the more she enjoyed the sense of safety and security that comes with being able to do everything herself.

It stands to reason that Toile was a perfect and most favored granddaughter for Lucinda, whose life seemed to have had more loss than gain. Toile was swept up in all that was the debutante lifestyle. She learned at the feet of our grandmother all the tricks to presentation, poise, class, and charisma. She loved the idea of transcending the mundane and believed that life really could be enchanted.

Toile completed her run as a young beauty queen. She also attended the Miss Nebraska pageant. Her talent had been "trends in modern fashion," and she modeled her glamorous forward-thinking outfits throughout the pageant. Toile finished a bit lower in the finals than our mother had. She did, however, come away with many more friends and contacts for networking. She had big plans for the pageant business in her future.

The summer following high school graduation, Toile married her longtime sweetheart, Ken Cash (K.C.) Turnbull. Thankfully, our mother disposed of the family tradition of finishing schools and let her daughters come into their own lives of their own accord. Toile, who had been meticulous in so many areas of her adolescent life, seemed to have her future all figured out. Without doubt, she was intent on avoiding the disasters that her mother encountered by marrying an untamed man. She wanted a husband she could count on to be loyal, faithful, and financially comfortable.

Ken Cash Turnbull, the great-great-grandson of Oliver Turnbull, fell in love with Toile when he was in the 5th grade and she was in the 4th. He began his courtship walking her home from school to protect her from the ornery boys who also wanted her attention. He was as loyal as a Labrador Retriever and as protective as a German Shepherd. He was not arrogant or proud, but wanted nothing more than a comfortable life with my sister. He was crazy for Toile and she knew it.

K.C. was one of three boys born to Butch and Leona Turnbull. Rudy, their oldest boy, was killed as a youth when he and some friends decided to race their cars on the dirt road north of town, forgetting that during harvest those roads are shared by tractors, tillers, and trailers. He had been driving a Chevy 210, which normally was as strong as a tank, but it was no match for the trailer loaded down with corn that had just pulled onto the road from the field. Rudy was two years older than Ken Cash. K.C. and his older brother butted heads, as brothers do, but K.C. said the loss of Rudy always reminded him to cherish those he loved because they can be gone in an instant. I have often wondered how much Rudy's accident affected K.C. It may have also been Toile's influence that caused K.C. to be so different than his brothers as time went on.

Darren, the youngest of the boys, grew up under his mother's protective eye. Darren could do no wrong according to Leona, and he had her and many other women in town wrapped around his finger. Darren loved women almost as much as he loved himself. He was quite good-looking and had great success in athletics and in overall high-school popularity. He also had a penchant for drinking, womanizing, and elbow rubbing, often doing all three simultaneously.

As is often the case in small towns, individuals who experience local notoriety expect that the rest of the world will also recognize their greatness and reward them for it. Under this illusion, Darren was convinced he was destined for more. Darren spent a few years in Tarford Flats after finishing high school and then decided to go to California to seek after his own fame and fortune.

K.C. remained in Tarford Flats to help his father, who owned the only Ford and farm implement dealership in the four surrounding counties. Butch had been elected mayor a few years earlier, at which time he outfitted the entire law enforcement community with new Ford vehicles, for a commission of course. With Butch's attention being split between business and politics, K.C. soon became the Vice President of the Sales department, which he thoroughly enjoyed. K.C. loved to travel around town and the neighboring farms, talking to anyone who had a minute or two, and he was as smooth as any Turnbull, capable of selling anything to anyone if he could talk long enough.

And so it was that Toile and K.C. made their home in Tarford Flats, where they planned to stay forever. They bought a two-story plantation-style house on the west edge of town with plenty of shade trees and a beautiful front yard which Toile filled with perennial flowers and colorful shrubs. The home's large, wrap-around porch was so perfectly decorated that it looked like it had come straight out of *Southern Living* magazine. Toile came to life while she learned the business alongside Mama at the Beaumont Boutique, where she loved to be. Her blossoming artistic talents filled the front windows and grew into wonderful indoor seasonal displays.

When their son, Texas, was born, Toile spent less time at the store but could not stay away from fashion entirely. She began to solidify professional relationships with pageant coaches and directors, and authored a monthly newsletter informing interested local girls about all things that were pageant related.

Even more than she loved pageantry, Toile loved little Texas. He was as precious as the rising sun to Toile and K.C. They doted on him endlessly and he wanted for nothing. He was a sweet, happy, handsome little boy. Toile and K.C. wanted more children—enough to fill a trolley if they had their druthers—but that was not to be. Texas was their one and only.

After ten years or so, K.C. began to tire of the family business. He didn't like to feel strapped to a schedule, trapped in an office, and he wanted to spend more time with his son before he grew up and moved on.

Darren Turnbull had returned from California, a bit more worn for wear. He had lots of stories about spending time with celebrities, traveling in their entourages, invitations to galas and weekends in Las Vegas, but they were only stories. In reality, Darren, who was as handsome as any man who had ever lived in Tarford Flats, was average in Los Angeles. He worked as a chauffeur to the rich and famous. He drove them to their galas, but was only allowed in through the service entrance, and that was only to use the toilet or get a cup of water. So, Darren returned, like the Prodigal Son, to our sleepy town and exclaimed that he was ready to take up the role of "businessman."

K.C. was more than happy to afford him that opportunity. On Darren's behalf, Butch Turnbull bought out K.C.'s share of the family business. The sum was more than enough for K.C. to purchase a few hundred acres to try his hand at farming. Because he was more predisposed to be a "gentleman farmer," Ken Cash had enough spare time to become a city councilman. For K.C., it was the perfect marriage of the romantic, respectable, liberating, masculine occupation and the enviable social influence and esteem that comes with politics. He loved hob-knobbing with the locals and attending events around town. K.C. really did love the community and loved county politics. K.C. was present for every ribbon cutting and award presentation, and his picture always seemed to be in the paper. If K.C. were to confess the greatest benefit of civic networking, he would surely say that it was that he never had to pay for a meal while he was in office.

It was around the time Texas was about to start school that Mama decided that she wanted to retire. With Texas now busy during the day, Toile had more time with which to manage the shop, and she had been well groomed to take over the business. Over the past several years, Mama had made plenty of money and had created a beautiful boutique to give to her oldest daughter.

Major and Lucinda had each required Mama's attention in their old age. They had since passed on, and with me away at college, Mama found herself with idle time on her hands. Mama had raised her family well despite her parents and despite Conway. She was almost fifty years old and she was feeling restless. Mama wanted to experience life outside of the Midwest while she still had the verve to experience it well.

A handsome gentleman had been trying to woo our mother away from Tarford Flats. He was a dynamic floral wholesaler named Xavier who for years had begun supplying the Beaumont Boutique with exotic blooms and indoor succulents. "Xavi," as she had called him, was a few years younger that Mama, but he was foreign, cultured, and intriguing, and he was crazy about Mama. He offered to take her along on his trips around the globe where he would be seeking and purchasing the more rare and elegant plants.

At first Mama thought he was sick with infatuation, but he persisted. Eventually, as she began to consider his offer, Mama made him promise that he wouldn't try to marry her, as she had no interest in letting another man have a say over her choices. He finally agreed, and Mama began her new adventure with the swarthy, passionate Xavi to the flower rich lands of Holland, Columbia, India, and more. My heart rejoiced for her as she peaked in her happiness toward the end of her beautiful life, much like the grand finale of a magical fireworks display.

Toile was an incredible conductor of all business related to fashion and style. She had accrued a following of pageant hopefuls and had even asked me to begin writing a weekly column for the Tarford Flats Sunday newspaper. (Strangely enough—for anyone who knows me—it was indeed a fashion and etiquette column that was my first published work.)

After years of hard work, Toile became a sought-after consultant in five neighboring states. Her life was an orchestration of systems and delegations. It was in her constitution that Toile exacted her duties as daughter, granddaughter, sister, wife, and mother. She was far too busy to think about her feelings. She had too much on her plate to consider the heartbreak our father had caused, for instance. She had kept her focus, accepted her role as Mrs. Ken Cash Turnbull and did a fine job of keeping appearances and raising their son. Toile was forty-five years old, and she was confident, smart, and magnetic.

Her sweet boy, Texas, had grown up well. He was smart, athletic, and adventurous. Toile and K.C. spent their time chasing after him— as a little boy at play, as an adolescent in sports and activities, and as a young man looking to find his place in the world. Toile and K.C. loved to watch him grow. They were consumed with Texas. It wasn't until Texas was in his senior year of high school that Toile really had time to look around at the life she had been living. It was then she discovered that she was utterly unfulfilled. In fact, Toile was bored to tears and feeling dreadfully stagnant.

Decades earlier, when we first learned about how our father had stepped out on Mama, Toile was shocked to the core. She could not understand how anyone could be unfaithful to a woman of such caliber. As far as she could tell, Georgeanne had been a wonderful wife. In fact, she had studied and mimicked everything her mother had done in trying to navigate her own way to adulthood.

Toile felt her mother's pain at his betrayal. Even more, Toile felt personally betrayed—by her daddy, by the community, by the implied promise that if she were perfect enough, she would have a perfect life, free from heartache. Conway's deceit was a deep and lasting blow from which Toile never completely recovered. The pain that our father left behind as he walked away from his girls hardened like a bitter nut in her heart. She could not shake the thought that love can breed lies, that true love should not be trusted, and that even the most wonderful woman can be tossed aside.

Toile vowed never to be hurt by a man again. So she married Ken Cash, who had been chasing her since elementary school. He was a man she could allow to love and adore her and keep her very comfortable. Oh, but how comfort can become suffocating to a woman who yearns for more! Toile soon found herself dreaming of adventure beyond city council issues, beyond a new shop opening on Main Street; she wanted intrigue far beyond wondering who fed her husband lunch that day.

Then she met Eric. Toile had driven to Denver one winter to help advise the Jefferson County Fair Board on pageant issues. The weather was turning nasty and the skies were almost violet, heavy with looming snowstorms. Toile had booked a few extra nights at the hotel when she realized travel back to Tarford Flats would be risky at best. In the hotel ballroom, Toile attended a style expo for pageant coordinators and the like. As Toile meandered through the booths and visited with various venders, she passed by the catering area.

The scent of sweet butter and flaky golden pastries overcame her. These were not the pastries one would find in a country market. These were divine. She could detect delicate wafts of fresh cream, Swiss chocolate, and rich, sweetened soufflés. Toile stood amidst the bustling attendees, the venders, the tables, and the mannequins, and she closed her eyes. She was transfixed. Her bosom was filled with excitement, yet dread: excitement at this unknown, as yet unexplored sensation, and dread that if she were to open her eyes, she might again be disappointed by the banality that surrounded her, maybe finding that the scents promised more than they could deliver.

Toile let herself stay there with her eyes closed, unaffected by those around her who may be staring or concerned. She had denied herself for so long of so many things. She had always thought of consequences before she acted. She didn't eat sweets, she didn't gain unnecessary weight, she put on makeup and fixed her hair before leaving the house, she attended every parent-teacher conference, she was on the City Commerce welcoming committee, she joined the right clubs, she always sent Thank You notes and Christmas cards, she regularly flossed her teeth, she didn't gossip, she never dated "bad boys"....

Something in Toile awakened in that moment. She opened her eyes, looked toward the pastry tables, and beheld a tall, masculine figure in white chef's attire. He had dark, thick hair that curled around his ears and his strong neck. His skin, in contrast, was the ivory shade of sweet cream. He moved like an artist, delicate and careful, yet confident in his craft. His hands were beautiful. Toile caught herself imagining how his cool, gentle hands might feel on her skin. She imagined his scent, like vanilla and nutmeg. Toile drew a quick breath and came back to herself. He had noticed her and flashed her a smile that felt like a shock of heat from her chest to her toes. His eyes were warm brown, the color of melted milk chocolate. Toile found herself suddenly craving that chocolate and anything else he had to offer.

It had been two full days of bliss when Toile finally prepared to return to Tarford Flats. She had spent every possible moment with Eric, in the most sensual, gratifying encounter of her life. He had come to the Colorado mountains from Quebec to pursue his dream of baking. As he spoke, his deep, accented voice caused Toile's thoughts to drift to charming candlelit cafés and grass-covered hills where freshly washed linens danced in the breeze.

They had not slept together. She had remained faithful to K.C. in the way he could appreciate. Toile had reasoned, how could he understand this uncharted plane of her being? If he doesn't even recognize its existence, could he be angry at not possessing it?

For Toile, what she and Eric shared was something much more intense—at almost a cellular level. They shared a passion that existed beyond their bodies. Eric had devoted his life to pastries. He dreamed for them, guided their development, celebrated their potential, and felt pain in their failure as much as any parent would for their children. He was so careful, thoughtful, and tender toward—and regarding—his creations. And as Eric revealed to her his recipes, his processes, and the pastries' magical coming to fruition, he did so with such description, such intensity, that Toile felt more alive than she had in a very long time. She was part of something she had not known she had been desperately lacking. And now she faced going back home.

Eric was also grieving her departure. For years he had longed for someone with whom he could share his passion. His longtime girlfriend, a poetry professor at the University of Colorado in Boulder, seemed at first to understand him, seemed interested as he told her about his pastries, how they were made, how he dreamed they could be. Now she busied herself with students, lectures, poetry, and had no time nor desire for his culinary creations. What he shared with Toile had rekindled his own sense of connection to another passionate being.

He found her before she made her way out of the hotel. She had been weeping, resigned to returning to life as she had known it before: a life without passion—predictable, ordinary. At that moment, Eric vowed to remain connected to her heart as she would be connected to his. He gave her a beautifully decorated paper box about the size of a small clutch. It was so light that at first Toile thought it was empty. He asked her not to open it until she began her journey home.

Toile waited an hour before she gave in to temptation and pulled over the car. The box had been sitting on the passenger seat in the afternoon sunlight. It felt warm when she lifted it. As she opened the lid, she was met with the intoxicating scent of confectioner's sugar and toasted almonds. She beheld two small, flaky éclairs along with a note. One éclair was covered in thinly sliced copper-colored almonds and filled with a caramel, nutty crème, interlaced with a ribbon of burnt-sugar syrup. The other was filled with a darker chocolate, and between the flaky pastry layers there appeared to be delicate yet brilliant green leaves. With her fingers trembling in happy anticipation, Toile carefully lifted the handwritten note, which I now have among my keepsakes.

It reads:
My beautiful muse, I have been on a quest. I must find the way to express to you my love, my desire, my need to keep you within my soul. It is because of you that I have come alive. I dare say without you, life may be droll, so much that it might not constitute a life at all. I know that you understand me best as I understand myself—through pastries.

I have sent with you two éclairs. The beauty in éclairs is not only in the filling, though I have chosen to fill them as you have filled me. The dark chocolate invades my senses as have you. In your essence I can find such richness, such depth, that it overwhelms my consciousness. I can focus on nothing else but what it must be to have a taste. The hazelnut crème is soft, inviting, safe, yet cultured—all of which I experience in you.

The mint and almonds within the layers of the pastries might inform you of my feelings of refreshment, yearning, and new life, the experience of a cool breeze and a crackling fire. I will think of you in this way whenever I catch the scent of toasted nuts or fresh mint.

Finally, the ribbon of burnt sugar syrup weaves through the pastry as I know my experience of you will weave itself into my dreams—the intense heat changing the innocence of the sugar into something so much more...lasting.

The best part of these beautiful creations is that they require a gentle touch, not too much interference or one might spoil their potential and make them tougher than they need to be. I do hope the world understands that you must be treated this way. For you are a delicate masterpiece.

Boundlessly yours, E.

And so it was in this way Toile found her balance between a life she had made and loved and a life she would love to make. Eric sent her pastries and notes monthly, like the "jam of the month club," we would tease. We knew, however, that Eric's letters kept her together, helped her to feel intimately valued and understood. The pastries transported her to her own version of paradise in a way that felt safe, contained and insulated.

CHAPTER 4: JO VERNADINE

"Other roles in dysfunctional families might include the 'fixer'...
When a child is given too much information about family issues, or
when he or she is too often involved in adult conversation, that child
may take it upon his or herself to try to fix the dysfunction. The role
of 'fixer' is most often self-assigned, as most adults realize that a
child is incapable of effectively impacting adult interactions or
issues. It is usually the case, then, that the fixer is frustrated with
repeated failed attempts at trying to fix the family. This child may
tend to recreate the fixer relationship with others throughout his or
her life. The thought behind this is that if he or she cannot fix the
family, at least he/she should be able to fix others in need. Thus, the
fixer may seek out others who may have significantly difficult social
or emotional issues with which to have a relationship in order to
satisfy the ongoing compulsion to 'fix.'"   <u>Parenting the EZ</u>
<u>Way with Jessie Duque</u>

We used to tease Vernie that she was supposed to be born a boy.
According to Mama, Conway was convinced she would be. He had
suffered through the births of two daughters, and frankly, he felt he
was due a son, an "heir apparent" to which he could pass along his
empire. He had planned to name his son after one of his
grandfathers, Vernon Joseph, who had been kind to Conway. When
Vernie emerged from the womb a girl, Conway bitterly refused to
change his mind about the name. Mama finally came up with the
name "JoVernadine," which he sourly accepted.

Vernie was always so eager to please our father. I have wondered if she was aware of his disappointment that she had been born a girl. Looking back, it seems that she lived her childhood under the assumption that she had done something wrong or shameful. It was almost cruel for her to have to carry the name JoVernadine, which carried with it the weight of her father's bitter compromise. She was teased mercilessly in grammar school, at least until everyone began calling her "Vernie." That name fit her perfectly. It still brings to my mind images of her quick, spunky smile and her endearing, often goofy expressions.

Vernie was a sweet, thoughtful girl who, for the longest time, was bullied by our older sister, Fern. As soon as Vernie could sit up by herself, Fern began to dictate what she could touch, eat, drink, watch... in fact, most of her childhood experiences were the result of Fern's bossing, pushing, and prodding. Vernie was smaller than the rest of us. Although her size difference may have been attributed to her young age, Vernie was also smaller than all of her classmates. As a child, she tended to stand behind others when she was in a group, as if she was trying to disappear. It could have been that she was trying to sneak her way out from under Fern's control without making any waves.

Vernie would have been content to play by herself in the quiet of her closet. Vernie's closet was a child's wonderland. It led from her room, which was on the top floor of the house, into an unfinished garret above our parent's room. Vernie kept her most cherished treasures in that space where she could disappear from the rest of the world. It was there that Vernie played for hours with Mama's old but beautiful handmade dollhouse. Vernie loved to examine the curve of the tiny chairs and table, the ornate carving on the headboard of the tiny sleigh bed, and the wonderful cabinetry of the miniature library.

Our father had brought back some scraps of silk fabric from one of his suppliers, and with Mama's help, Vernie upholstered the worn little sofa and chairs and made tiny curtains, sheers, and bedding for her tiny masterpiece. Vernie loved the thought of being able to change her world by changing décor. When all else failed, she could at least feel some control in fixing a drab room or sofa. Besides, being the younger sister of a mercurial tyrant like Fern, this musty sanctuary was often the only place in the house where Vernie could find peace.

Up in her closet, Vernie was the first child to become aware of the strife between Conway and Georgeanne. As she would consider the dollhouse, the placement of furniture, and the creation of different themed rooms, various words from below would waft up through the rafters. She heard phrases like, "How could you?" and "Who is she?" and "Where were you?" and "Which number is this one?" A good tongue-lashing was not uncommon in the Duque home with four very different, very headstrong girls, but there was something different about these phrases. They were laden with pain.

As she explained to me much later in life, Vernie spent much of her childhood in her own imaginary world, a coping strategy born of necessity. Vernie was afraid of the intense feelings coming from her parents' room, yet she dreaded going out into the house to face Fern's unpredictable whims. So, she stayed in her closet with her fabrics and miniature décor, trying to make her own miniature world beautiful: trying to create a fantasy in a dusty attic.

From the day of her birth, it seemed that Vernie felt compelled to earn her father's love and acceptance. She was desperate for his acknowledgment and positive attention. She sought to please him in nearly everything she did. As a result, Conway loved Vernie the most out of all his girls. He loved how small she was, loved how she tried so hard to be good, loved how hard she worked for his approval, and loved how she idolized him. I don't know if it was because of his special treatment of her that she chose not to see what kind of man he was or if Vernie wanted so badly to believe he was the father she wanted him to be that she succeeded in fooling herself, but in many ways, his betrayal hurt her most of all.

As things deteriorated between Conway and Mama, her daddy would tell Vernie that his love for her was the reason he would never leave, no matter how miserable things were with Mama. Vernie felt torn in her loyalties to her parents. She loved and admired her mother, but also felt sorry for her father. She wanted to forgive whatever he had done to Mama and bring him back to the family. She wanted Mama to be nicer and try to get along. Finally, Vernie thought if she alone tried hard enough, she could make up for what he resented about his life with his family, whatever might be driving him away. And yet, regardless of her efforts to be sweet, nice, thoughtful, and perfect, Conway turned his back and walked out.

Vernie felt his abandonment in everything that was "home." She would catch a whiff of his cologne or the scent of shoe polish or his gun-polishing chamois and her heart would ache for him to come home. His spot at the table became the dumping area for the kids' lunchboxes as they returned from their school day, and yet Vernie would wish to see him there reading the paper or inviting one of the girls to play gin. She would feel overwhelmed with a sense of failure and guilt for not having been enough. Vernie soon realized that staying around the house had become painful for her.

As soon as she could, Vernie embraced any available activities that might keep her busy and away from home. As her activities increased, so did her happiness. She joined a children's choir and then the community theater group. She participated in horse riding and 4-H and even entered some of her interior designs in the county fair. Vernie excelled in performance arts and had a lead role in the high school musical production of "Oklahoma!" She graced the halls of school, home, and even Mama's shop with lively renditions of "I went to Kansas City on a Friday..." and any other numbers she could remember.

Vernie was naturally lovely, happy, and a little naïve. Although she was smaller, Vernie carried more than her share of compassion in that body of hers. She went out of her way to make others feel better, less anxious, less intimidated—probably because she had lots of experience with those feelings. And so it was that most people were drawn to Vernie because of her kindness. Boys, especially those who were sensitive, insecure, thoughtful, and somewhat troubled, would seek Vernie out for companionship. She felt drawn to them, too, because she sensed they really needed her. Even better, these particular young men seemed to need her friendship and acceptance much more than a physical relationship. This was just fine with my sister. Vernie didn't really know how to trust a young man. Sex, it seemed, would cause her to feel vulnerable, which, to Vernie, was terrifying. Therefore, she dated young men who had as little interest in sex as she did.

It was after a series of these sweet young men who had dated Vernie were discovered to be more interested in dating other men that Vernie received the nickname "Turny Vernie." Confused, she had to ask K.C. what "turny" was supposed to mean. He explained that she was being accused of "turning" those young men homosexual.

Vernie was heartbroken. Could it be true that it was because of her those boys were now homosexual? God knows Vernie had been blamed for stranger things in her life. Was she doing something wrong or behaving in a way that was repulsive? What if it was true that she was responsible? What's worse, what if the absolute truth was that Vernie was not a fixer, but a virus, an antigen that corrupts all men to repel women they would otherwise desire? In her mind, the evidence quickly accumulated. She began thinking of all the men in her life, the childhood friends who had moved away, her father who had left her at home… who knew their true motivations?

It was at that moment that Vernie decided to save any more young men from her "turning" powers. She resolved to live as a single woman, an old maid, a spinster hermit for the rest of her life. She made big plans to design her own cavern in a place far from any single men in the area. Sure, isolation would be a challenge, but it must be far better than living with the guilt of the end of human procreation.

And so, after she graduated high school, Vernie convinced Toile to let her start a small decorating business as an extension of the Beaumont Boutique. Eventually Vernie took over the second floor of the Boutique and officially named the section "Beaumont Décor." Vernie loved her business even more than the expected she would. She was energized to create wonderful spaces, to have a chance to control the impact of a person's environment.

When she wasn't working at the shop, Vernie went about refurbishing an old family cabin tucked in the trees by a small lake. It is the cabin in which I have chosen to live now.

From the outside, Vernie's cabin looks like a typical log cabin surrounded on three sides by aspen and birch trees. On the stone front porch sit two rickety but working rocking chairs and some fishing supplies. Coming down from the porch are ten steps made of old railroad ties that lead down to a nice yet rustic dock. There are four pillars that hold up the extended roof covering the porch. Through the front door you can see a quaint sitting room with a fireplace that is nestled in a stone dividing wall. On the other side of the wall is the kitchen. The fireplace is open to the kitchen for baking, and there is also an old stove, beautiful wood cabinetry, a deep enameled iron sink, and a breakfast nook with a window that looks out onto a vast alfalfa field.

The cabin has indoor plumbing with a functioning toilet and a footed bathtub, and in the bedroom, Vernie installed a huge skylight so she could see the stars as she drifted to sleep. Off the back of the cabin, Vernie built a large pantry and mudroom where she could wash and can food, do her laundry, and keep her tools out of the weather. When they were young, my boys loved to visit the cabin and play with the "old-fashioned" implements, like the hand-operated clothes wringer and the metal sieve and wooden pestle Vernie used when she made her famous wild grape jam. The cabin functions year-round with the help of the stove and fireplace for heat in the winter and wonderful drafts through the open windows in the summer.

At night, the faint smell of kerosene wafts across the room as the fuel-lit lamps flicker and crackle. Owls and coyotes can be heard throughout the night, and Cardinals, cowbirds, and Robins welcome the dawn. Twice a year, the Canada Geese make their migration through the area. The Platte River, which feeds Vernie's lake, runs from west to east just about two hundred yards away. During migration season, the river is peppered with the large cacophonous birds.

The geese are not the only regular aviary visitors to the area, however. Occasionally, a group of wild turkey walk through the brush toward the water. Their numbers are huge, sometimes over forty birds including hens and poults. Wild turkeys are not quiet, and they are sometimes intimidating. Male "Tom" turkeys look almost as big as a full-grown boar when they are on full display. They will crow and rush at whatever they might perceive as a threat.

I sit eating my yogurt and look out at the alfalfa field in the morning light. Mornings in Nebraska are wonderful. The field has recently been plowed and prepared for planting. I can see the sun-streaked plot of land through the trees near the cabin where the Toms are already at work trying to woo their much smaller mates. The scene reminds me of Jeffrey Buck.

Jeffrey Buck was a military man who spent the past decade as an army drill sergeant. He spent the decade before that as an army medic stationed in Northern Asia. He was a large, powerful man who knew how to become quite intimidating when needed. He was also very private, patient, and fiercely loyal.

Jeffrey came to Tarford Flats after taking early retirement from the Army. His aunt, a widow who had lived in a bungalow on the edge of town for decades, was quite old, frail and in need of his help. She had no children of her own, but Jeffrey had captured her heart as a young boy, and she loved him dearly. As her time became scarcer, she asked Jeffrey to help with managing her affairs and to take care of her home after she passed away. Jeffrey was wonderful with his dear aunt and he made her last months as comfortable as they could be. He stuck by her side, cooked for her, fed her, brushed her hair, tended to her aches and pains, and read to her from Reader's Digest magazines.

A few weeks after his aunt passed away, Jeffrey ventured into the Beaumont Boutique seeking some advice on updating some of the décor in the bungalow. His aunt had not done much with the place for the past several years, and Jeffrey was not too fond of the old lady knickknacks and crocheted wall hangings. Although he was still considering whether to stay in Tarford Flats, he wanted a space he could enjoy and to update the decor to make it more appealing to potential buyers. Jeffrey approached Toile, and after a quick introduction, he asked if she had any design referrals. Of course, she told him she would send someone over the next morning to see the property and suggest changes that should be made.

Not surprisingly, Toile had already been made of aware of the strapping Jeffrey Buck and his circumstances. Hardly anything happened in Tarford Flats that was not tittle-tattled by everyone on Main Street. Toile did not mention any of this to Vernie, however. She also did not mention that the man Vernie was to meet for a design consultation was handsome, chivalrous, and single. She knew Vernie would beg off the assignment if she were to detect a set-up.

So, Vernie packed her sling bag with pads of sketch paper, pens, and measuring tools, hopped on her bicycle, and made the four-mile ride to town expecting to meet anyone but a man like Jeffrey. When he opened the door, there she stood, five foot two inches tall in her flats and clam diggers, blonde, blue-eyed, bronzed from her outdoor living, and glistening with sweat that comes after a minute of exercise in the humid Midwest morning. He adored her instantly but was sure she was much too young for a man in his forties.

Vernie, who was thirty-eight, was also taken aback when the door opened. She felt simultaneously excited, intrigued, nervous, and furious with her older sister, who she knew had set this plan in motion. Vernie gathered her wits about her and proceeded to go throughout the home measuring and planning. Jeffrey, meanwhile, continued to talk to her about anything they may have in common. He knew she loved the rustic way of life, so he shared his own stories about the Asian wilderness, the forests, and the wildlife. He told stories about scouting big game with his buddies during R&R. They saw tigers, leopards, and all kinds of exotic creatures. He asked Vernie if she might be able to help him create a space in the bungalow to harness that wild Asian ambiance. Vernie was intrigued both by Jeffrey and the decorating challenge, but she remained aloof, professional.

When Vernie packed her things and left the bungalow, Jeffrey was disheartened at her apparent lack of interest. It was all Vernie could do, however, to pedal her way to the Beaumont Boutique and not ride straight back to that strong man.

A few days later, Jeffrey had been taking a walk to the market when he noticed a passenger bus pull off to the side on the road. As the wheels finished sliding over the gravel shoulder, the bus driver opened the door and frantically called for help. Apparently, there was a woman on board who was minutes away from having a baby. Jeffrey's medical training had become second nature, and he rushed to offer assistance. The woman was clearly panicked and struggling. She was beginning to seize up in terror. Everyone around was quickly becoming hysterical.

This was the moment that Jeffrey's experiences all fused into a spectacularly unexpected miracle. Channeling his drill sergeant persona, Jeffrey quickly took charge. He was magnificent. He commanded immediate obedience from all those at the scene. He directed those who could help to do so in various activities. He sent some to the café for hot water and towels, and the others he directed to watch over the queasy folks who had been sent to sit in the shade.

He then focused on the young woman in labor. Jeffrey recognized she was beyond mild coaching. He had seen this before when the soldiers under his command would find themselves frozen in fear. Jeffrey became the fierce, fearless, confident drill sergeant this young woman desperately needed him to be. He commanded her attention and demanded that she respond according to every directive. This manner of yelling at the laboring woman was incredibly productive. She was able to recognize his control of the situation and her anxiety subsided. She found Jeffrey to be trustworthy and safe. The baby boy was born just a few minutes later, and Jeffrey was a hero.

Such an event takes about three minutes to reach from one end of Main Street to the other in a town like Tarford Flats. It took two minutes to reach the Beaumont Boutique and Vernie Duque.

Vernie considered what she knew about Jeffrey Buck. Like the woman on the bus, Vernie also felt that he was trustworthy and safe. He had been wonderful to his dying aunt and loyal to her even after her death. But he was strong, unafraid of jumping into life—even the parts of life with chaos or risk.

As Vernie rode her bike from the boutique to the edge of town and past Jeffrey's bungalow, she did not speed up as she had in the past few weeks. Vernie stopped her bicycle under the shade of an old elm tree on the other side of the street and gazed upon the quaint setting. She watched for Jeffrey to appear as she waited patiently under the huge tree.

Eventually, Jeffrey appeared from around the side of the house. He was dressed in an old t-shirt and jeans, which were faded and dirt smeared. He grabbed a wheelbarrow and approached a large stack of flagstone that had been unloaded near the front drive. As he began to fill the wheelbarrow with various sizes of stone, he spied Vernie across the street. He was obviously happy to see her as he smiled and waved her over. Vernie was hesitant and suddenly a bit anxious. She felt drawn to learn more about this man, however, and finally decided to acquiesce.

Jeffrey led Vernie to the back yard as he pushed the heavily laden wheelbarrow. As Vernie rounded the corner into the back yard, she gasped. Jeffrey had transformed the space into a beautiful replica of an Oriental garden, complete with a small fishpond and modest fountain. The yard was heavily shaded and smelled of Midnight Jasmine, which had been recently planted around the flagstone sitting area.

As Vernie stood in awe of the wonderful garden, Jeffrey came near enough to her that she could smell the salt on his skin that comes from long, strenuous labor. She could feel the heat that radiated from his strong body behind her and she was overwhelmed with the sense that he desired her. This was such a new feeling for Vernie. For so long she had believed that she was undesirable, even dangerous, to men. The feelings were so strong, so completely overwhelming, that Vernie could think of nothing but running away.

Without a word, she turned, ran to her bicycle, climbed on, and rode as quickly as she could to her cabin, to her refuge, to the grown-up version of her closet in the attic. And yet, she could not escape the desire that began to grow within her. She would find herself imagining Jeffrey fixing the sink while wearing only those dirty jeans, or out on the dock tying up the small rowboat, or again, clad only in those jeans, swinging an axe at the firewood, his muscles rippling and the brisk air around him smelling of pine and salt.

Vernie had never before experienced raw lust, and she loved it. The intensity inside her continued to grow, and as it did, Vernie felt she had to make a decision. It would be so like her to retreat and wait for the feeling to fade away. She could busy herself with her work around the cabin or with projects at the boutique. She and Toile had been working on renovating and reopening the former Men's Wear and Tailor retail space so that she could expand her home décor business… but her thoughts kept going back to Jeffrey, that garden, his arms, his chest, and those jeans.

Then Vernie had an epiphany. The animal instincts that had been invading her thoughts had inspired her. The wild Asian theme that Jeffrey was looking for in his bungalow could be brought to completion through animal prints. Vernie imagined Jeffrey's masculine form among various fabrics with tiger stripes, leopard spots, lush plants, faux ivory and jade carvings, and bamboo curtains. Even more exciting to her was the idea of sharing that experience with him.

When Vernie finally made her decorating proposal to Jeffrey, he was amazed. Vernie understood him more than any woman in his life had before this. Jeffrey embraced Vernie and she didn't refuse him. He flooded her with his desires to know her thoughts, her ideas, her passions for décor and for life.

Vernie fought the fear that rose inside her in the face of such passion. Her only experience with such strong feelings to this point was in the face of Fern's wrath. She was so tired of being afraid of things. She was tired of the fear of disappointing Toile, of angering Fern, of growing close to men who may reject her, of her own feelings of disappointment, anger, love, desire. She was thirty-eight years old and had been too afraid to fully live her dream. She knew that Jeffrey was a virile, strong man who was willing to help her with that dream.

Their courtship was exciting yet comfortable, as if they had known each other forever. Jeffrey loved that he could provide for Vernie whatever she may need, but as independent and capable as she was, she did not need for much. As Vernie continued to perfect her home décor store, Jeffrey worked on things at home in the garden or the kitchen. She would come home to a myriad of marinated and grilled masterpieces. His specialty was Korean cuisine. It was the food he had fallen for while on his many travels in the Far East. The crisp, fresh crunch of fresh vegetables dressed with sweet, tangy vinegar paired magically with his braised beef bulgogi, tender sweet-skewered chicken, and spicy barbecued pork.

They would spend their evenings at the bungalow, and in the summer, in the beautiful water garden Jeffrey had made. Most weekends, they would retreat to the cabin, enjoying one another without any interference from the rest of the world.

I once asked Vernie if she had ever wanted to have children with Jeffrey. Her response helped me to understand and appreciate their relationship in a completely new light. Apparently, Jeffrey had given considerable thought to having a family when he and Vernie were to be married. He was in his early forties when they met and he knew that if they wanted children, they would have to start a family soon. He adored my sister and honored the independent life she had made for herself. Jeffrey also knew that Vernie's own childhood had been hard on her, and she still carried some of that pain with her. After some honest discussion, Jeffrey and Vernie concluded that if they were to have children, it would be for the wrong reason- to fall in line with society and fulfill the expectations of others. Neither Jeffrey nor Vernie could reconcile the feeling that this would somehow seem fraudulent. Instead, they committed to spend what remained of their lives having their own adventure, one in which he would stand guard for her, give her strength and encouragement and freedom to discover herself. Vernie would learn to trust Jeffrey and would allow herself to be vulnerable with him, and in doing so would discover a love she had never known was possible.

Over time, Vernie's Beaumont Décor became quite popular. In fact, in 1969 a reporter from a monthly style edition from a large Omaha newspaper did a story about Beaumont Décor. The young man had spent considerable time learning about various retail gems to be found in smaller communities within an hour of Omaha. The economy in Omaha at that time allowed for many folks to travel in search of treasures for their homes and wardrobes.

One of the reporter's colleagues suggested that the he visit the Beaumont Boutique in Tarford Flats. When he arrived, the urbane reporter was charmed by the quaint, orderly rows of storefronts, the flowerpots set out on the sidewalks by storeowners, and the small café tables brought outside so patrons could enjoy the shade as they ate their lunch.

As he stepped into the Beaumont Boutique, the young man's enchantment was complete. He marveled at the attention to detail, the sense of comfort and personal service that were increasingly hard to find in the bigger retail stores like Sears and Montgomery Ward. Toile accommodated his requests for the history and the typical clientele of the boutique. She knew, however, that his attention would be rewarded most when he met Vernie. Vernie's energy and creativity were contagious and truly inspiring. Toile was right, as she often was, and she beamed with pride for her little sister when Beaumont Décor appeared on the cover of the next month's style edition of that large Omaha newspaper.

Vernie really had created a masterpiece. In her shop she had a variety of displays she called "stages," as if they were the scenes of some glorious theatrical production. The fabrics and décor varied from whimsical to classical, and all of them very tasteful. To stay true to her inspiration, Vernie had a huge section she called the Wild Side devoted to animal prints and exotic artifacts that she brought in from all over the world. She was an "Artist in Residence" in her store, and she loved the idea of sharing her gift with all who ventured through the doors.

Vernie's store also became a frequent destination for children and adolescents who enjoyed her junior decorator activities. She brought in Mama's antique Victorian dollhouse and even had more modern models of ranch-style homes and condominiums built for kids to decorate however they liked. The young folks who showed real talent were even afforded the opportunity to design a stage in the most frequented area of the store. There were even a few adolescents whose decorating prowess led them to qualify and compete in the national 4-H competition. It was such a source of pride for Vernie that she could help the youth of Tarford Flats create a beautiful world for themselves.

Vernie's husband Jeffrey, meanwhile, felt an increasing call to study midwifery. Of course, as a retired soldier he was well aware that such a career move would raise eyebrows, especially in the 1960s and 1970's of rural Nebraska. He knew that such an unconventional vocation for a sturdy man such as himself could be a great challenge, but he could not shake the feeling during that fated bus-birth that this was what he was now meant to do. Jeffrey decided to take some classes at a nearby college to subsidize the education he had already received as a medic. He received his Midwife's license a year or two later and was wonderful at it. He had a depth of compassion that he had not been able to demonstrate as a drill sergeant that he could now express toward his clients.

Women came from far and wide to received Jeffrey's treatment. While at first, each woman had some level of fear and uncertainty, Jeffrey made each of them feel safe and confident in his fearless hands. Many women through the years developed crushes on their masculine caregiver, but he never broke rank. His only interest was to succeed in his mission to deliver those children. And he was forever faithful to Vernie, his sweetheart for over thirty years.

CHAPTER 5: FERN

*"Another key role in a dysfunctional family is that of the 'scapegoat.'
When a dysfunctional family experiences tension or frustration, the
family scapegoat becomes the identified problem. This person may
be completely blameless, but because the family requires someone to
take the blame, their behavior, personality, or even their existence is
understood to be the cause of the unhappiness. The scapegoat will
often grow up feeling that they are flawed and unworthy, or if they
have enough fortitude, they will be angry and rebellious at the
injustice of it all. Unfortunately, even in adulthood, the anger or self-
loathing will cause the scapegoat to continue to put themselves in
emotionally harmful situations. They might continue through a series
of relationships that are doomed to fail because that is what is
familiar to them and they have learned to expect it. Sometimes, the
scapegoat also serves as the chaotic distracter: one who is always
on-call to create distraction when the tension begins."*
                    Parenting the EZ Way with Jessie Duque

I remember watching Mama in the kitchen on the days she would
bake pies for the summer street dances. It seemed like the whole
county turned out on those sticky evenings for the live music,
dancing, socializing, and food that lined the sidewalk on makeshift
tables. Mama's pies always seemed to be a crowd favorite. Mama
used old family recipes she had inherited from her favorite aunt. The
recipes always called for the best ingredients, and Mama knew how
to get them. She would cut and roll the dough and expertly fill the
pies. She even had a special dough-cutter that made zig-zag edges on
each long strip of dough that she would then weave together atop the
filling to make a beautiful lattice.

Mama had a ceramic blackbird that she would place in the middle of her pie before putting in the oven. That silly bird would be embedded to its neck in pie crust and fruit filling, and its silly little head would jut out, beak wide open as if it were indignantly squawking its opposition to its predicament. Mama said that bird's beak allowed a way for the heat to escape the pie so the whole thing wouldn't boil over and be ruined. Now, as a child, I fully understood that the bird was a lifeless kitchen tool, yet I felt so sad for the bird, which sacrificed itself to save the pie. This is how I often consider my sister, Fern.

It was in the dead of winter that Fern was born. In fact, it had been stormy for weeks preceding her arrival. Tarford Flats was under three feet of snow, and the winds were fierce. Inside the Duque home, however, everything was cozy. Conway had been snowed in at Cheyenne, roughly five hundred miles to the west, because the roads were covered in ice and drifts. Toile was tucked snugly in her bed when Mama's labor started. Contractions came on fast and Fern was born within the hour. Mama, headstrong as she could be, knew no one would be there to help with the delivery, so she birthed Fern in the bathtub while Toile slept peacefully.

Fern was strong, healthy, and feisty—even as a newborn. She was the opposite in temperament from Toile, who had been considerate, reserved, and refined. She was moody, unpredictable, and prone to storms, much like the Nebraska weather. Fern learned early how to command attention from a room full of people, even if it meant making them uncomfortable. Everything she did was just a bit too loud, too showy, too intense.

Even as a little girl, Fern was wild. When Mama went out for groceries or other errands, she would try to keep little Fern nearby only to find that she had found yet another way to sneak away to explore and run free. Fern was not a classic beauty like her mother and sister, but she was striking. She took after her Grandmother Doris, with her thick mane of blond-streaked hair, blazing green eyes, and her freckled skin. Fern lived her life outside riding horses bareback through the country, climbing trees, and swimming in the lake by the cabin. Her skin was almost brown by the end of the summer, which made her already stunning white smile look like a flash of lightening. Unfortunately, Fern's natural beauty could change in an instant to something much more terrifying.

On the plains, tornadoes are actually pretty common during the spring and summer months. They usually develop as evening approaches following clear, hot days. The sky quickly begins to fill with huge, indigo clouds, which move swiftly to the east. We who have lived through the awesome storms know to watch the skies for certain signs that they are developing. We look for wisps that trail along the bottoms of the huge wall clouds, or the swirl in the skies above our heads as the fronts collide. One of the most telltale signs that we are in trouble is the phenomenon in which the air all around us takes on an eerie green hue.

In the same way, we learned to watch Fern for signs of an impending rage. She might walk just a little differently, or have a clip to her words, but it was the forward set of her jaw that made us want to run for cover.

Fern did not like rules or restrictions. In fact, whenever she was told she couldn't do something, she heard that she just couldn't do it in front of anyone. She would not allow anyone to tell her where to go, what to do, or who to be. Fern was unmanageable, impatient, passionate, stubborn, and cunning.

She was so much like her father in this way, and it led to clashes of an epic proportion. Similar to an earthquake that is large enough to cause a tsunami, Conway's anger would grow so quickly that it would shake the earth and any of us who were near the epicenter were jolted by his wrath. Our father reacted poorly whenever he was bored, hungry, tired, stressed, or when he felt he was not given the proper deference. The air about him would grow thick with tension.

We watched his movements and expressions grow increasingly more aggressive until he was ready to yell. Then, our father would delve into personal attacks and criticisms of any of us who were caught near him at the time. He would bruise the rest of us with insults, but Fern he would hit.

Fern, who was so much like him, knew nothing but to fight back. Where others may have acquired the instinct to flee, Fern never did. She clenched her fists and set herself for battle whenever Conway started in. She rarely got out of those encounters without a bruise, a bump, a bloodied lip or a twisted wrist- wounds that would usually heal within a week. Her rage, however, did not heal. Fern's anger festered within her, a toxic brew which, when it finally came coursing out, would be directed toward the rest of us- hurling insults and accusations, pulling our hair, pinching, slapping and threatening.... just like him.

Part of Fern's diatribe always included a comparison between herself and her sisters. She would bemoan that she was always the one everybody hated, she was always the one who got in trouble. She made no secret of her resentment of Toile. It might have been that Fern sensed from a very early age that Toile was Grandmother's favorite that she chose to behave the way she did, knowing that her outlandish behaviors would get her equal amounts of attention. It could be that Fern believed she would never measure up to Toile, so she did not even try. I believe, however, that she was just so much like our father that she didn't even realize there was another way to live. Fern was acting solely on instinct.

I believe that is why Fern felt so confused about her place in the world. She wanted to be loved and accepted, but refused to see how her behavior hurt those around her. She wanted to believe she was good and moral, while at the same time, she wanted to feed her cravings for excitement, risk, and attention. Whatever gene it is that causes a person to consider consequences to their behavior was not present in Fern, and because of that, she assumed that she didn't do anything wrong. She was blameless in her eyes, and therefore she could do nothing to improve. She truly believed that it was for some cosmic reason she kept getting into trouble.

When Mama got after her for misbehaving, Fern cast blame on others, made excuses for whatever she could not justify, or lied outright. Sometimes Fern would lie even when presented all kinds of proof to the contrary. She found that often she could use her denials to outlast anyone who was trying to punish her for her actions. Mama found her to be exhausting- and I know she also felt guilty for the way our father had treated Fern.

When Conway left, Fern struggled to reconcile his absence. On one hand she enjoyed the freedom from his temper and the fear of the inevitable next fight. According to Fern, she had finally been set free to do what she wanted. Still, she missed our father's attention. Fern came to believe that the relationship she shared with Conway had more depth than his relationships with the rest of us.

It was a year or so after Conway's departure when Fern started fooling around with boys. She had just turned 14, and her body suddenly became very interesting to the boys with whom she had spent previous summers swimming and riding horses. She loved the excitement that came with this new form of attention. It started with incidents of mutual curiosity with boys her age under the football bleachers or behind some bushes near the community swimming pool. As she grew and matured, Fern realized she could attract the attention of older boys—boys who were more experienced, had more freedom… boys who had cars.

Many of the folks in town spent their time talking about Fern. She certainly provided them the fodder for gossip. They assumed that her behavior was because our parents were divorced, or that she was a hellion because she was jealous of Toile or Vernie. There were even suspicious whispers that maybe Conway had done something unspeakable to Fern, that maybe that was the real cause of the divorce. I believe it was much less sinister and complicated than that. Fern loved the way she felt when boys wanted to touch her, she loved being told that she was pretty, and she craved adventure. It was just part of who she was.

It was the summer of 1948 and Fern had just finished high school. Tarford Flats by this time was a town of about twelve thousand people, including surrounding farms. This made it one of the larger towns in the state, one that would draw folks in from smaller communities.

There were, around this time, several traveling carnivals that would come to a town our size for a week during the summer. Of course, there were the usual carnival rides—the tilt-a-whirl, merry-go-round, and Ferris wheels, as well as the games of chance or skill, like dart-balloons, bottle ring-toss, and shooting games. Local venders would also set up booths for various edible offerings with such a variety that a person could stay three full days and never eat the same thing twice.

We would all be ready to celebrate our freedom from lessons and nagging teachers. We would sprint to the fence around the carnival site where we would gather and watch with noisy anticipation when the "carnies" began to set up shop. Usually, the carnival workers were strong, unattached young men who went about their task with relative urgency.

Fern loved to watch the young men at work. Their lean, tan, muscular forms rippled under their shirts as they wrestled with ropes and steel. After a while, as the heat and humidity rose, their shirts would come off, which, to Fern, was like the unwrapping of a gift. Following careful preparation and consideration, Fern would put on her most flattering sundress and sweep her long, golden hair up into a messy ponytail, leaving her long, freckled neck exposed, and she would walk her long, pretty legs through the Carnival grounds. Even if the carnival grounds were not yet open and were off-limits to the locals, Fern never seemed to get in trouble for striding past the barricades. Truth be told, it was yet another thing she found thrilling about the carnival.

That particular year of 1948, Fern found her favorite ride. It was called the Loop-o-Plane, and it was unlike anything she had ridden before. There were two sixteen-foot arms that were designed like hammers. One end of the arm had a passenger car that held four to eight people. On the other end of that arm was a counterweight. Each arm was connected to an axel in the middle. Once the ride started, the hammers would begin to move, one on either side of the axel, so that one would swing clockwise, and the other counterclockwise. As the ride came to full speed, the hammers would come full circle, pausing at the top so the passengers would be suspended upside-down in the cars.

Fern loved the feeling of the centrifugal force driving her upward until her orientation was completely reversed. She loved the way it felt to have the weight of her body upended, a complete escape from the pressures she usually shouldered. It was a consummate physical experience with the overwhelming force, the exhilarating build-up, and the final release of all the rage and sadness she allowed to pull her down.

Fern began to understand herself that day. The experience of extremes that would be unsettling to anyone else actually helped her to relax. She thrived on adrenaline and excitement that was far beyond that which had been afforded her in Tarford Flats. This regular world into which she had been born could not accommodate her needs. Fern needed to run wild.

Fern stayed at the carnival day and night that week, completely ignoring the curfew Mama set for all of us. She met up with a handsome Native man a few years older than her who seemed quite confident, if a bit aloof. His name was Slade Horsefeather, and he came from a long line of proud Lakota. His family lived on the Pine Ridge Indian Reservation in South Dakota. Slade was a man of very few words, but he came across as the kind of man who was eerily calm in the face of a raging storm. I believe he may have been the first man near Fern's age who wasn't terrified of her.

The morning after the carnival packed up to move to the next town, Fern left our home. She took a few things in a duffle bag and hitchhiked her way to Grand Island, which was where she would find Slade. Mama was furious at first, and then felt guilty, as if she could have prevented Fern from being Fern. Finally, after a few weeks passed, Mama seemed to come to terms with her daughter's actions.

We all had to, and we all felt differently about her absence. Although the gossip was at full speed for a while, it eventually dropped to a quiet hum, which Toile appreciated greatly. She had become beleaguered by the murmuring about her family throughout the town. Vernie loved the silence and the strange peace that came to rest in our home.

I was intrigued. Fern, to me, was something of a riddle, a puzzling one-person performer who could mesmerize the crowd with charisma and a dazzling smile while setting the theater on fire. I found myself waiting to see what she would do next—careful not to get too close in case things exploded.

None of us were worried about Fern, however. She was, after all, the smart, scheming and fearless opportunist her father was. In our experience with Fern, no news was good news.

About a year after Fern left Tarford Flats, Mama had received word from a fellow pageantry retailer she had met a few years before in Cheyenne, Wyoming. This woman, whose name was Marti, had a very successful dress and gown shop and was very involved in the Cheyenne Frontier Days pageant each year.

According to her story, Marti was doing some pre-pageant coaching with some young women at the fairgrounds when she came upon a stunning young woman with golden hair, bronzed freckled skin, and the most dazzling smile she can remember seeing in ages. Fern was setting up a small booth in the art show area from which she planned to sell some of her craft work.

During their conversation, Fern began to tell stories of her upbringing in the hot, muggy, rolling green plains of Tarford Flats. Fern, who is no stranger to storytelling went on to describe the various kinds of trouble she and her younger sister Vernie would get into. Marti's interest was piqued with the mention of Tarford Flats, the locale of her friend's Boutique. When Fern mentioned Vernie's name, Marti was sure she was talking to one of Georgeanne's beautiful daughters.

Marti went home, sorted through a pile or two of pageant paperwork to find Mama's number, and gave her a call. It was during this phone call that Mama learned she was a grandmother.

Apparently, Fern and Slade Horsefeather found out she was pregnant a month or so after she left home. Slade used his carnival earnings to buy a renovated school bus in which they made their home. When the carnival season came to an end, Slade contacted family members in Cheyenne who set him up with seasonal work.

This was relatively common with Slade and his family. The tribal culture ran strong within their group, and their nomadic ways were deeply ingrained. Family members often travelled between different settlements from South Dakota through Nebraska, Wyoming, and Colorado.

Fern, always restless, thought this nomadic lifestyle would be ideal. She and Slade drove the old bus to Wyoming and found a spot of public land where they hid their home near a riverbed in a thick grove of trees.

Fern gave birth to her eight pound daughter, Mina, in late winter. Fern stayed with Mina in the cozy bus and made crafts and jewelry with hemp, stone beads, and shells. It was these same wares she was selling at the fairgrounds when Marti happened upon her. To her credit, Marti reported, Fern looked happy and healthy and seemed to be enjoying her life with Slade and their daughter.

Like the weather on the plains, however, Fern was unpredictable and tended to defy reason. None of us expected any sort of serious commitment when it came to Fern. She was just not the type to stay put.

It was early spring, 1955, when Fern showed up again in Tarford Flats. She brought with her a man she referred to as her husband, although we were never sure that was official.

Things had been moving along as usual in Tarford Flats. Mama's business was very successful, I was close to graduating high school, Vernie was fixing up her cabin, Toile was chasing Texas who had just learned to run, and life was fine. The two of them showed up on a Saturday morning just as Mama was leaving to open her Shoppe.

I had been lazing in bed that morning, so when I heard the knocker, I could only peek around the top of the stairs to see who might be visiting. I watched Mama from behind as she opened the door, and she just froze like a lizard in the face of a snake.

At first, I didn't recognize the pair because the man was so boisterous and the woman was a step behind him. Then, as Fern stepped forward to hug Mama, I realized it was her, and pajamas or no, I bounded down the stairs.

Of course, Mama invited them in to rest in our front room and then put a call in to Toile, asking her to post a note on the boutique window that the place would be opening late today.

The man who had come in with my sister was the first to walk into the house and again into the front room. He had an air of self-importance that seemed to contradict his appearance. He appeared, for lack of a better word, filmy. He smelled of stale cigarette smoke and also the sweet, acrid smell of gasoline or motor oil. He moved around the room, eying Mama's tasteful décor, fine furniture, and precious collectibles. Finally, at Fern's gentle prodding, he came around to stand nearer to her and join the group.

Fern looked lovely, if a bit worn for wear. She was just as willowy as ever, so it took me but a second to notice she was pregnant. I was in the middle of a happy exclamation of congratulations when Mama came into the front room. I realized that Mama probably noticed the bump long before I did, and she was reserving her excitement pending an explanation. Fern, knowing Mama well enough, rushed into her story of the past seven years.

Apparently in the Lakota culture, child-rearing is shared by many women in the household. The children are taught social skills, how to work, household and communal chores, traditions and morality, tribal history, and many other things. Fern, who was innately defensive and insecure, took their efforts as a statement of her inadequacy at raising her daughter. She grew evermore frustrated with Slade Horsefeather's family interfering with her life.

According to Fern, she thought what they were trying to teach her daughter was stupid and outdated, and she knew how to be a parent without their help, and inevitably, with Fern being Fern, she chose to get ornery. She would load up a horse and take Mina off camping for a week or two, not letting anyone know where they were, or if and when they would be back. She would make efforts to turn Mina away from her Aunties and Grandmother by telling her stories of their "cruelty."

Slade, who had been back on the carnival circuit, would get frantic messages from his family, and he became furious with Fern. When Fern went on a solo camping trip up by Medicine Bow, Slade's mother and sister took Mina to the reservation in South Dakota and enrolled her in school. Fern came back to find that her daughter and several of Slade's family members were gone.

As she told her story, Fern started to behave more like the fourteen-year-old version of herself, blaming Slade and his family for ruining her relationship with her daughter. She created a scenario of bullying, manipulation, false accusations, and abuse all at the hands of the Horsefeather family.

What's more likely is that Fern and her intense and impulsive behaviors were at the center of all the chaos, and the Horsefeather family wanted a stable upbringing for Mina. She had been going off on her own, leaving her child in the care of others for who knows how long, and when she was around, she had been manipulative and quick to lash out at everyone. To have been grateful for the help and support never occurred to Fern. She had to be the victim of the situation.

In either case, Mina was taken by family members to the Pine Ridge Reservation where she was to be raised. According to Fern, because of the "stupid" rules regarding tribal membership, Fern was not allowed to live on the reservation without consent, which came as a complete shock to her. It was the Horsefeathers who stole her daughter away and left her with nothing. She was all alone, drowning in the unfairness of it all. At least, that is how she intended to tell her story.

Fern still had the renovated bus, which she relocated to a trailer park in Pine Bluffs, Wyoming. She found a job in a diner that provided her with two free meals a day and enough money to pay her meager bills. This diner was how she came to know Dewey, who was now the best thing that has ever happened to her.

Dewey Rue Wayne was now parked beside Fern on the settee in Mama's front room. Even as he sat—tall, thin, and slightly slanted—he held himself in a way that seemed overly confident. He took up more space than was necessary for his body, and even more with his presence. Fern sat beside him, demurely glancing at him as if he were quite a prize. Behind the settee was a large picture window through which Mama and I could see an old Pick-up truck loaded up with all of their belongings. We surmised that they were looking for a place to land. Mama listened cautiously as Fern told us all about Mr. Wayne.

According to Fern, Dewey Rue Wayne worked in an auto repair garage across the street from the diner. She exclaimed that he was probably the best mechanic in three states. Dewey could fix any car or truck he came across. Customers came from all around to have Dewey Rue Wayne fix their cars. He was a genius in many ways, actually. He had come up with some brilliant ideas for inventions, which, of course, were then stolen by lawyers or the government. He also had a line on some investment opportunities that were going to pay off big.

Fern saw Mama glancing toward the rusty truck parked in front of her beautiful picture window and nervously began a hasty explanation. Apparently, Dewey had privately shared with Fern that he was a man of significant wealth. He had come from an important family and recently received a large inheritance. Fern went on to explain, as Dewey sat smugly beside her, that he had been raised with such privilege that when he turned twenty, Dewey determined that he should spend the next ten years of his life as a poor man so that he could get a sense of how the less fortunate live. Dewey smiled confidently at this point, and I noticed immediately that he was missing his front teeth. I tried not to stare, and yet the more I looked at Dewey, the more I felt uneasy. Mama also remained cool. Fern, sensing that we were not yet convinced of Dewey's good breeding, shoved her hand before our faces. "Look!" she said. "He even bought me a ruby!"

On Fern's left hand was an ornate silver ring encrusted with several small bits of colorful glass that surrounded a larger, pea-sized red gem. It looked quite like the pageant jewelry Mama had in her boutique—the kind that was designed to sparkle under stage lights but would not cost a lot to replace if lost.

Mama gave Fern a smile and the perfunctory nod toward Mr. Wayne. He then took the occasion to tell Mama about his extensive research into rare gems and the best places to buy them. Dewey Rue was certainly eager to impress a couple of women from a little place like Tarford Flats.

The conversation finally arrived at the reason the two were here in our home. Dewey sat looking uncomfortable as Fern tried to explain their predicament. She said that the garage in which Dewey worked was crooked, and that the owner employed mostly family members. Money and tools began to disappear, and of course, rather than blame the real culprits, everyone turned on Dewey. He was fired on the spot with the agreement that no charges would be filed against him if he went away quickly and quietly.

Fern said that the timing of his dismissal was actually a blessing, because she was having trouble with her own boss. Fern said that she was being forced to pool her tips with other workers who were nowhere near as efficient and less friendly to the customers. She let it slip that she also got in trouble for giving away food to some of the guys in town, but quickly followed that revelation with "but, everybody was doing it, and I was the only one who got a reprimand."

Fern and Dewey were unemployed in a small town, both having been fired from their jobs, which made getting another job in Pine Bluffs close to impossible. Fern explained that the baby was due to come within a few months, and that this was as good of a time to move as any, and she knew that since Dewey was so good with engines, there must be something for him in Tarford Flats.

Fern tried her hardest to arrange the facts of her situation into something that looked much better than it was. Fern had burned her bridges and not taken any responsibility, and she had hooked up with a likely thief and liar. Now she wanted to bring this scoundrel into Mama's home and her good graces.

Just as Fern began to explain that they would be needing a place to stay for a while, Mama cleared her throat. She was pleasant enough as she stood and offered Fern and Dewey a glass of iced tea. Dewey accepted, and as Mama disappeared to the kitchen, he gave a self-satisfied nod to Fern, who was not smiling.

Mama's good breeding and perfectly honed social grace may have appeared to be encouraging to a man such as he, but Fern was not fooled. Fern was beginning the slow burn I had seen so many times before. She shifted in her seat and clenched her jaw, and I quickly found a serious matter that most certainly needed my immediate attention.

I found refuge on the back porch, but I could hear Fern's rant through the open kitchen window. A fury of words hurled through the air, buffeted only by Dewey Rue's efforts to get her to quiet down, to relax, to think of the baby. Phrases like "stuck-up," "high and mighty," and "Who do you think you are?" hung in the air as thick as the dust during harvest until they were whooshed away by the slamming of the front door.

Mama appeared on the back porch, barely ruffled by the recent storm in our front room. As we heard the truck start and drive away from our home, Mama smiled, smoothed her hair, and said, "And now I am off to work."
Oh, how I loved Mama. She was truly unflappable. I suppose much of it was born of necessity, what with her pageant upbringing and then having to hold herself and her family together through the scandals Conway had brought upon us. I am sure it was painful for her to see Fern, who was so naturally beautiful and charismatic, fall into such a state, and yet Mama kept herself together. She was not about to be conned again.

Mama could spot a manipulator coming from miles away. She knew that even with Fern, if she were to give in just a little bit, Fern would embed herself so deeply into Mama's pockets she would never leave. I admired Mama's resolve. And I readied myself for whatever Fern might do next. To my surprise, over the next several weeks, nothing happened at all.

I tried to keep track of Fern's activities through the usual gossip channels in town. From what I had heard, she and Dewey began attending the Presbyterian Church after receiving some charitable donations to help them furnish a small house they found to rent. The house was on the other side of town, closer to the railroad tracks.

Dewey began working for Conway's freight business and proved to know a lot less about trucks than he had advertised. Our father chose to prove his generosity on occasion, and in this case, he paid for Dewey to take a few classes to learn enough to be a passable employee. I believe, knowing Conway as I did, that his desire to help Fern and Dewey was because he did not want the folks in town to see him embarrassed by their destitution.

Toile was the first to hear the news of Fern's son. Some Presbyterian women who had come into the boutique had told her. Apparently, he was a healthy baby boy who had been welcomed heartily by the congregation. Toile learned that the church ladies had even hosted a baby shower for Fern and Dewey to which none of us had been invited. The ladies, according to Toile, seemed to be sensitive to the awkwardness of our situation with Fern, and patted Toile's hand gently as they tried to explain that they were just trying to look out for that sweet little boy.

Mama and Toile were aware of Fern's predicament. She had made a few quick visits to the boutique to try to explain that Dewey was pressuring her to align herself with Conway instead of her mother and sisters. Dewey thought it would be more advantageous for her to reconcile with her father so that she and Dewey would be in his favor. I suspect the pressure was even greater now that Dewey was the father of Conway's grandchild.

The boy, Danny Wayne, was Dewey's pride and joy. Dewey planned on giving his son anything he desired, including every moment of his spare time. When Danny was born, Fern seemed to fade to the background. Even with the arrival of their daughter, Freshie Lynn, a few years later, Dewey would not share his affections with anyone but his son. I supposed he had some drive to be the opposite man his father had been, yet as is too often the case, people who behave in such extremes tend to get exactly what they are trying to avoid.

There was something about Dewey that I couldn't figure out for the longest time, something that gnawed at me whenever I saw him— and made me want to get away as quickly as I could. It was like I was too close to a hungry, stray dog, not knowing if it was tame or deadly. I picked up bits of information about him from some of Fern's church friends and acquaintances around town, and I was able to assemble a picture of Dewey Rue Wayne that was anything but flattering.

Dewey was born to an alcoholic father and a mother who fancied herself a "spiritual guide." When he was very young, Dewey and his mother left their home (and everything in it) in Louisiana and headed to New Mexico so she could be closer to like-minded spiritual folks. They lived off the donations of her clients and parishioners, so sometimes money was very tight. More often than not, Dewey and his mother stayed in the homes of charitable old widows, promising to help them in whatever tasks they had to complete. Dewey spent a few turns in an orphanage and home for wayward boys, either because his mother could not afford to keep him, or because he was too hard for her to control.

As an adult, Dewey had become a smarmy, lying opportunist who would play on the sympathies of others. When the tents went up in the summer and the revival meetings began to fill the fields around Tarford Flats, Dewey was sure to share his "testimonial," in which he detailed his acts of lawlessness, selfishness, and misery as a prelude to his newfound joy in religion. He told tales about having to spend time in jail for burglary and abusing the charge accounts of his widowed hostesses. He did paint quite a picture of a despicable cad. Then Dewey would wax strong in the words of the Lord and did so with enough inflection and contrition to bring the crowd to tears and hearty applause. He was mighty fond of himself and loved the attention he got from the more gullible folks in town.

More than anything, though, Dewey valued his newfound connection to money and influence. It was the rare conversation in which Dewey would not let it be known that he was the son-in-law of Conway and Georgeanne Duque, brother-in-law to Toile and K.C. Turnbull.

It is a strange thing how often rural Midwestern folks are misunderstood as simpletons. Some of the most brilliant businessmen, scientists, and entrepreneurs make their lives in these parts. There are sparsely populated counties in Nebraska in which good old ranchers are worth millions. There is a family in a rural town on the other end of the state whose massive crop operation is traded in the worldwide market. Some of our neighbors hold patents for hybrid crops that have brought their families enough money to retire and travel the world over for decades to come. Yet, because they are not consorting with artists and academics, rural folks are considered dolts. It doesn't seem to occur to anyone on either coast of this nation that Midwesterners have made a conscious choice to live this way, that this way of life speaks to their sense of liberty, honesty, and strength. A life on the plains leaves little time for nonsense, drivel, and pretense.

This is where a man is only as good as his word, where truth doesn't change, and where swindlers are hated. Folks on the plains have had decades of experience running off snake-oil salesmen and crooked rainmakers. They can pick up the scent of a "weasel" in less than five minutes.

Dewey Rue Wayne may have momentarily piqued the sympathies of the sweet-natured Presbyterian women, but their husbands were another matter. Dewey was earning a reputation as a dishonest man. Local men who gathered for coffee each morning stopped making room for him at the café tables. What's worse is that Dewey's behavior started to reflect poorly on Conway. He had quickly earned the reputation as a lazy mechanic who talked himself up but didn't deliver.

It wasn't long before complaints about his work made their way back to Atchison Freight and landed on Conway's desk. In an effort not to lose face, Conway brought Dewey in from the garage and set him up in the parts department where he would be responsible for making orders to the various distributors. Even though Dewey was aware that customer complaints had resulted in his job change, he took on the attitude that this was a big promotion. He dressed in a shirt and tie when he went to work, and his boasting was louder than ever.

Things at home were not going well for Dewey and Fern. In fact, their fights were also louder than ever. Dewey began to realize that although there was plenty of money in the Duque family, he was not going to see any of it. Conway was a selfish man who had been raised to believe that money is not to be shared with one's children, and Fern's mother felt nothing but contempt for him. As Dewey felt more humiliated at Conway's business and among the folks in Tarford Flats, the more he became angry and resentful of Fern. He was incensed with her inability to ingratiate herself to Mama and that he had not been given the same respect in the family that K.C. had. He blamed Fern for all of it, berating her for being the daughter no one cared about, who was nothing compared to her sisters. He shamed her for being with an Indian and for losing her daughter to his tribe. He called her a worthless, dirty whore.

To further humiliate my sister, Dewey started flirting openly with Bunny, an unmarried bookkeeper at Atchison Freight. Bunny was not terribly lovely. In fact, her eyes were noticeably offset, and she had an unfortunate overbite, but Bunny's other attributes more than compensated where most men were concerned. She was buxom in every way. Bunny dressed for work with care. She enjoyed crisp cotton dresses with wide patent-leather belts that cinched her waist, and matching pumps that brought out the shape of her ankles and shapely calves. Her bottom was quite rounded, and she sat as if it were an overstuffed tuffet, with her back straight and her chest lifted. Bunny's top barely reached across her considerable bosom. The desperate little buttons that closed the top at her cleavage struggled all day to stay put.

Her expression was usually one of confusion, although that was mostly due to her eye placement. Bunny was nothing if not naïve… and gullible. Men had come and gone, and each one had made just the right promises to keep Bunny hanging on to the hope that he would finally be the man to offer her a future.

The cruelest irony was that, as Dewey set his sights on possibly the most gullible woman in town, and as Fern finally began to recognize his lies and destruction, Fern was the one left feeling most responsible for the disastrous relationship in which she had found herself.

I don't know exactly when Dewey started hitting Fern. I saw her around town, maybe at the grocery store or with little Danny and Freshie Lynn at the ice cream stand. I remember seeing the occasional bruise on her arm or leg, but she always said it came from a hiking accident or slipping on the rocks by the lake. We didn't really understand how awful things had become until the day Dewey was fired.

According to Fern, Dewey had been embezzling from Atchison Freight since he started with the parts department. He would submit orders for unneeded parts and make payment, only to return the parts later and pocket the refund. When Bunny, the buxom bookkeeper, caught on to his scheme, Dewey reportedly broke down in tears. He confessed to her that he was miserable with Fern, that she had made his life unlivable. Dewey begged Bunny to look the other way, promising to repay every penny once he could get himself and his poor son a place to live where Fern couldn't get to them. Dewey then focused his efforts of persuasion on naïve Bunny. She was easier to convince than even Fern had been and was totally converted to Dewey by the time Conway realized that they had stolen thousands of dollars.

On the day Conway called Dewey into his office to fire him, Dewey and Bunny promptly left the business. She was to go home and pack her things and then pick Dewey up near his house. On his way home, Dewey stopped by the bank. He casually strolled to the counter and told the teller to close out all of his accounts. He told her that he and his family were moving away because he had been offered a great job, but he needed all of his cash now to set up his new home elsewhere.

With his pockets full, Dewey walked into his house and got his suitcases. Fern, Danny, and Freshie Lynn were still at the park, so Dewey was able to pack up his things without a fight. He also packed up Danny's essentials and a few toys and loaded his haul into Bunny's waiting car. Fern and the kids came up the sidewalk to see Bunny's car loaded up with stuff. Without a word, Dewey grabbed his son from Fern and shoved him into the front seat next to Bunny. Fern began to scream, and Dewey quickly and fiercely picked her up and carried her into the house. Bunny nervously buckled the little boy in and resettled herself behind the wheel of her idling car.

Neighbors heard the familiar yelling from the direction of Dewey's house, but when Fern began to scream, they came around to see if they could help. Someone said that during the fight, it sounded like a wild horse was loose and kicking at the walls of the small house. A few seconds later, Dewey exploded past the front door, angrily wiping blood from his cheek and spitting in the grass as he strode past the small, terrified crowd of onlookers. Bunny's car sped away as Danny, stuck between Dewey and his new woman, cried for his mother. The dust settled in front of the little house and the place was eerily quiet. Someone was told to call the police. Plump little Freshie Lynn, now two years old, sat in the grass looking at a ladybug while the panic-stricken neighbors went in the house to find Fern.

CHAPTER 6: LINNY SPITT

"In my years of working with parents and their children, I still find it remarkable how much importance a child places on the father's opinion. Most children of compassionate mothers understand and have experienced that their mothers will always find them to be smart, interesting, and somehow worthwhile. The opinions of the fathers, however, are not guaranteed to be so adoring. It seems that fathers hold the power to build up or tear down a child's confidence and self-worth, and the criticisms of the fathers are regarded as truth. Rejection, replacement, or abandonment signify to the child that their father no longer finds them worthwhile or important. I have yet to find in family dynamics anything quite as destructive to a young person as rejection by their father."
Understanding Boundaries the EZ Way with Jessie Duque

Conway lived in a massive house that had five unoccupied bedrooms. It was a multilevel stone beast in the older, more established part of town, and it had an enormous, beautifully shaded back yard complete with a marble statue of a centaur surrounded by giant azaleas. The mature trees that stood around the perimeter of the yard were home to hundreds of birds that were fed in abundance by the mulberries that grew freely. In the morning hours, cardinals and kingbirds would enthusiastically greet the day. They were soon joined by orioles, brown thrashers, robins, and warblers, and the serene yard would burst with the cacophony.

Long before my father bought that house, a retired district judge and his wife lived there. They were wonderful people. My sisters and I would ride our horses through town and one of our favorite stops was the judge's front yard. They had a wild plum tree on the north corner and an apple tree on the south. We would gingerly stand upon the backs of our horses to reach the fruit. I am sure that when the judge's wife saw us, she was fraught with nerves at our daring quest. Oh, but it was worth the risk to life and limb! The plums were so juicy we would stain our clothes, and those green apples! They were so crispy and tart our mouths would start to water as we rode near the trees. On occasion, if either of them was outside at the time, the judge or his wife would allow us to explore.

We would look for garter snakes and salamanders, snails and toads in the stone window-wells of the old place. Moss and ferns took over the shade and made a beautiful hiding place for slimy creatures. My sisters and I would climb along the giant rocks and trees that framed the back yard. We were all proficient climbers, but none of us were as skilled and daring as Fern.

Once Fern convinced Vernie to climb way too high in the judge's massive elm tree. Vernie was amidst the wavering top branches, begging to come down, when she realized that taking any step could throw off her balance enough that she could snap a branch and plummet to the ground. Fern, in an effort to steady her, put her hand like a bicycle seat under Vernie. The awkwardness of the moment struck them, and they began to laugh. Vernie, now relying on Fern for her safety, laughed nervously for fear that her sister, also laughing, might lose her grip. As the laughing continued, Vernie quickly realized that she had to pee. She tried with all her might, but could not stop herself from wetting her pants, and much to Fern's credit, as the warm pee ran down her extended arm toward her shoulder, she never did drop Vernie. Oh, we loved that beautiful wonderland. We all had great memories of that yard and the sweet couple who invited us in.

When our father bought that big stone house, he had the fruit trees removed because he didn't want the mess in his yard. Shortly after that, Linny Spitt moved in.

Conway met her at a filling station in Fort Collins, Colorado, in the summer of 1952. She was just a few years older than Vernie, and was just as small. Her given name was Lynette Spitt, but she went by Linny. She had pretty eyes, but they were small and deeply set, which, along with her pointed features, made her look like a rodent. Her wardrobe consisted of dungarees, sleeveless tops, and espadrilles until Conway bought her some classier "threads".

When Conway brought Linny back to Tarford Flats, he told everyone that she was a wonderful young woman who just needed a little help to get set up on her own. He said she was a really hard worker, a smart and personable kid who just had a bit of bad luck. I don't know if any of the story they told was true, but according to Conway and Linny, she had been living in Northern New Mexico where her family had a large melon farm. She loved working in the farming industry and had become quite an expert in melons when the man she had been married to was sent to prison. According to Linny, after her husband's conviction and incarceration, he then became insanely jealous of a friendship she started with another man. Because her husband was a man with outside connections and a tendency toward violence, Linny was afraid that he would try to kill her or her new friend, even from behind bars.

Linny and her friend, whose name I have never known, decided to move to Denver, where he got a job at a meat packing plant. At this point in the story, things are even less clear. Linny said that her relationship with this man got "complicated" and that she had to find another place to live, which led her to that filling station in Fort Collins.

I don't know how long she was in Fort Collins, or what kind of work she did at the filling station, but when Conway found her, the station owner had set up a cot for Linny in the back. She didn't have many personal items, maybe a few changes of clothes, some toiletries in a small suitcase, and some trinkets and photos in a box that she used to hold a lamp next to her cot. When Conway saw the tragic condition of her life and how pretty and sweet, she seemed to be, he decided that he would save her from her circumstances.

Conway had his run with several women in town, and as much as he wanted to deny it, his reputation gave him away. When he brought Linny into his home, no one was fooled by the claims that their relationship was more the platonic, mentoring type. Linny didn't help the situation by claiming some ownership over Conway's property. It had been just a month or so before Linny started to refer to everything that had been Conway's as theirs or even hers, inviting folks over to their house for drinks, or charging a new set of dishes to their credit account at the mercantile store.

Conway didn't mind at all. In fact, he seemed to enjoy it immensely. He had a little tart of his own, a young woman who would clean his house and run his errands, organize his personal life, wait on him hand and foot, and be on call for any physical needs he might have. And, she was the most junior mistress he had ever obtained.

At twenty-two, Linny was one year younger than Toile. Conway was still quite handsome at forty-eight and now felt that he was the envy of every warm-blooded man in town. He also loved the way Linny looked at him, like he was the man who saved her from the brink of despair, like she had been his damsel in distress and now she was all his to groom to his liking.

Conway never was a man to take criticism from a woman. In fact, that had been the reason he jumped around to so many women, even when married to Mama. He was a man who craved admiration and was above reproach, simply because he was Conway Duque. He was, I know now, a textbook narcissist.

Conway spent a considerable amount of time erecting his reputation- and protecting it. His choice of protection was most often to attack his critics. Conway had information on everyone in Tarford Flats. He would use anything necessary to obliterate their reputation and expose their weaknesses. Conway was ruthless when it came to protecting his persona.

In short, Conway protected Conway. So, when Dewey nearly beat the life out of Fern, Conway went into action protecting himself. He certainly did not want to be associated with any kind of domestic abuse. In fact, he placed the blame squarely on Fern, her moods and her eagerness to pick a fight. Conway found a way to appear the long-suffering, benevolent father to what he hoped everyone would see as a wayward, troubled daughter.

When Fern was left bloodied and broken by Dewey that dark day, concerned neighbors entered her home afraid of what they might discover. Fern was found in the kitchen of her small home, crumpled in a heap near the back door. A father and son who witnessed Dewey's departure loaded Fern carefully into a car and brought her to the small hospital on the north end of town. Fern had suffered two broken ribs and a broken wrist, and she was covered in bruises and dried blood that had clumped in her hair. Her beautiful green eyes were swollen nearly shut, and what could be seen of them was fiery red.

Another of Fern's neighbors scooped up Freshie Lynn and brought her to the Beaumont Boutique, where the woman then broke the news of the assault to Mama, Toile and Vernie. With little Freshie in tow, my mother and sisters immediately rushed to the hospital where they remained, not wanting to leave Fern. Vernie found a blanket and wrapped Freshie snugly in it and placed her in a molded plastic chair where she napped peacefully.

Fern had been given a dose of morphine for pain and was quite sedated. The scene had calmed down considerably by the time Conway finally came to the hospital.

Conway didn't go in to check on Fern, but made his way to the nurse's desk. After some quiet conversation, the nurse rose and found the doctor, who walked with Conway into an alcove for a more private conversation. The two emerged, appearing to have reached an agreement, and the doctor asked the nurse to collect Fern's belongings because she would be going home with Mr. Duque.

Fern, still in and out of consciousness, was discharged from the hospital. She was loaded into a wheelchair packed on either side with pillows to help her to sit upright. At Conway's insistence she was taken to his house, where he set her and Freshie Lynn up with their own rooms under the auspices that this would be a much better place for Fern to recuperate.

Knowing him as we did, Mama, my sisters, and I knew that Conway Duque would do anything to avoid public embarrassment, especially the scandalous kind. Conway would not let folks say that he left his bloodied and broken daughter to languish in some hospital bed while her two-year-old daughter stayed with his ex-wife. He wanted the whole matter of Fern's situation to disappear.

Over the next few months, Conway exerted constant pressure on Fern to wipe her hands of Dewey Rue Wayne. He told her that Freshie Lynn didn't need the stress, and that it was likely going to cause her and her daughter significant embarrassment as her relationship disasters would be on public display. Fern's stomach churned at the idea of cutting all ties with Dewey. She desperately wanted to see her little boy again and hoped that eventually Dewey would try to contact her to work something out.

Toile and Vernie encouraged Fern to seek justice for herself and her babies by pressing charges against Dewey for felony assault. They wanted Fern to fight for herself the way she had in her youth. In the end, though, Conway prevailed, and Fern not only gave up on seeing her son again, but on finding any kind of justice for herself. For the longest time afterward, Fern seemed to believe she deserved every bit of heartbreak she endured.

Conway also let Dewey slip away without having to face charges. He did not want the good people of Tarford Flats to think that Atchison Freight was anything less than the highest quality operation, so Conway sent one of his men to find Dewey and strike an agreement. Dewey was to never to speak of Atchison Freight or set foot again in Cass County, knowing that if he did, the sheriff would be on his heels with an arrest warrant.

Conway was not a compassionate, sympathetic, or generous man to his children. That was something he had never considered. He was very concerned about his reputation, however, which was often manifest in his great generosity to those outside of his family. His rescue of Bunny was just such a case. Bunny had quickly grown tired of Dewey Rue Wayne and his unhappy child. Danny whined constantly for his mother, and Bunny was little consolation. Eventually Dewey grew impatient with Bunny's failed attempts to comfort the child. He began to bark at her and call her names, just as he had with Fern. In her misery, Bunny reached out to Conway for help.

Therefore, the final bargain struck with Dewey included the condition that Bunny would return with her car to Tarford Flats. Bunny, according to Conway, was not to be used and abused anymore by Dewey. These events informed me that Bunny was another special woman to Conway.

Bunny had been working for Conway since she was 18 years old and had been quick to catch his eye. Like so many women had, Bunny believed that Conway was offering her a real future with real commitment. She felt honored when he made it known that he wanted a physical relationship. Their affair lasted for several years, up until he made that trip out to Denver and found Linny in the filling station. Bunny was especially heartbroken when Linny showed up and Conway was too busy for Bunny's affections.

Conway must have felt some measure of responsibility for Bunny's anger and subsequent betrayal because he refused to acknowledge her part in the theft. In fact, when she returned to Tarford Flats, Conway gave Bunny a beautiful player piano he had imported from St. Louis, Missouri, and several rolls of her favorite songs. Bunny was invited to work again at Atchison Freight, although this time, there was usually someone checking her work.

Linny wasn't told about Bunny and her previous relationship with Conway. In fact, Linny wasn't told about most of the women with whom Conway had "special" friendships. Linny was not a pleasant woman by nature. She was bossy, ill-mannered, rude, and whiny. Most people in town tended to avoid conversations with Miss Spitt. Her usual interaction with folks consisted of her barking orders and expectations and their mumbled acquiescence. As far as Linny was concerned, she was an extension of Conway Duque and all of his entitlements.

The bigger offense, though, to anyone who knew Mama and my sisters, was that Linny thought she was on the same level as the Duque women. The differences, however, could not be clearer. Mama had taught us to value learning, diplomacy, compassion, generosity, and kindness. As a result, we were beloved by the community. Many soft-spoken men and women were fiercely loyal to Mama and by extension, Toile and Vernie. Even I felt the effects of their positive regard when I came to town. Those same people felt deeply sorry for Fern who had to live with the likes of Conway and Linny.

Although she and Freshie were dependent on Conway for their survival, Fern also tried to keep her distance from Linny. Living in the same house had been easier at first because Linny left Fern on her own to recuperate. Because Conway didn't want Fern to be an inconvenience, he had wisely put her in the room furthest from the one he shared with Linny.

Linny, who had been living with Conway for eight years before Fern moved in, had redecorated most of the rooms in the house with a more contemporary flair. The strong plaster walls were papered with dizzying geometric designs or velvet and metallic embossed medallions. Some rooms had been completely redone in bleached wood paneling.

Freshie Lynn's room was an explosion of purple and pink floral wallpaper, with matching curtains, pillows, and a bedspread. Freshie's room had its own bathroom, with its own toilet, sink, and footed bathtub. The floor was covered in dusty rose tile, and the walls were again overwhelmed with massive flowers. Freshie loved her room. Toile had just given her a book about a beautiful princess who had fallen asleep in a bed of flowers, and Freshie was convinced that if she were to sleep in this room, she too would awaken as a princess. From that point forward, Freshie began to shed the worry that had wrapped itself around her young life. She began to believe that she was a princess, just like the ones in her storybooks, the ones who escaped the ogre to live happily ever after in their beautiful floral bedrooms in a giant stone castle.

The room Fern now occupied had been used for storage during Linny's decorating rampage and remained blissfully untouched. After she recovered from her injuries, Fern removed most of the boxes and furniture to the basement and washed the years of dust and dirt off of the walls, which were revealed to be a soft shade of Robin's egg blue. The floor was dark-stained hardwood with a subtle sheen. Fern found a rag-braided rug to lay aside her spindled bed frame. She had a fluffy white feather bed with a light floral quilt, a modest nightstand with an old hurricane lamp, and a walnut chest of drawers. Fern's favorite spot in her peaceful room was the cushioned cotton window seat that faced the beautiful garden in the back yard. She cracked the window in the evenings, and she could hear the toads, crickets, and the occasional hoot of an owl as the cool breezes entered her room. In the mornings, Fern would wake to the sounds of birds she loved so dearly.

As Fern grew stronger, she would take Freshie out into the backyard garden to play and explore. Freshie would imagine that they were characters in fantastic stories, usually involving princes and dragons and hideouts high in the trees. They would investigate various animal tracks they found in the soft morning mud and smell every flower they found. In the evening, Fern and Freshie were often found sitting quietly in the moonlight amidst scores of fireflies. As she held Freshie's warm little body on her lap and watched her daughter's eyes flicker with amazement, Fern felt overwhelmed with love and gratitude for these moments. Fern was remembering herself again as she sat and watched her little girl find all the wonders of that beautiful garden.

Conway had been given an earful about Fern and Freshie playing in the mud. Linny had mounting complaints that a pretty and engaging little girl like Freshie should not be raised as a Tomboy, climbing trees and playing with bugs. Linny lamented that if she had daughters of her own, they would be proper young ladies and not encouraged to run wild like Fern. Linny did not find any limits to her criticisms of Fern. She scoffed at Fern's minimalist existence; she was embarrassed by Fern's lack of effort with her long hair and loose-fitting shift dresses. Even Freshie Lynn caught on to Linny's disapproval of her mother. Little Freshie tried hard to do up her own hair and clothes. She only wanted to wear pretty dresses and wanted to walk like a fancy princess. After considerable murmuring from both Freshie and Linny, Fern finally agreed to let Linny take her daughter to the beauty parlor. When Freshie returned, she not only had a haircut, wash, and style, but also manicured nails with new orange polish, an orange headband, a pretty new orange and yellow plaid dress, and a new tiny handbag. She also had a new appreciation for Miss Linny Spitt.

The next few years saw Freshie Lynn turn slowly away from her mother toward the enticing world Miss Linny continued to flaunt. When Freshie turned six, she got her first pair of heeled pumps. She would wear them as often as possible when in the house to avoid getting them the least bit dirty. She had seen fancy women in magazines wear beautiful chiffon robes with their heels as they brushed their hair in the evenings.

Freshie begged her grandfather to find a robe in her size just like the fancy ladies wore. Conway found three robes and had them packaged in stunning foil-wrapped boxes with huge satin bows. He presented them as gifts to Freshie, Linny, and Fern for Mother's Day. Linny and Freshie were overjoyed with their gifts and squealed as they stood up to put them on. The card that had been attached to Linny's box fell on the floor at Fern's feet, and as Fern picked it up, she could not ignore the note inside: "Thank you for being a wonderful mother to my granddaughter…."

Fern's box also had a note. It said: "Happy Mother's Day. Love, Dad"

Shocked and dismayed, Fern rose and excused herself to her bedroom, explaining that she had a terrible headache. She stepped over the box that contained a fuchsia chiffon robe with artificial feather cuffs and silently made her way upstairs while her daughter giggled and twirled in her little fancy robe.

Linny continued to work her way into the center of Conway's life. She was careful to caress Conway's ego enough that he did not grow weary of her and was always willing to travel with him and serve as his social planner. She took great care of her appearance. She learned to cook the meals that he liked, and most importantly, she never, ever criticized him.

In return, Conway would continue to surprise her with favors and gifts—sometimes so over-the-top that folks in town would whisper for weeks. One such gift was the procurement of a vibrant yellow 1963 convertible Lincoln Continental for Linny's thirty-fifth birthday.

Of course, Linny was overjoyed with her new car. She found countless reasons to drive around town and park her massive car in the most conspicuous spots. Then she would exclaim to anyone who would listen that driving that car was as smooth as riding a pat of butter across a warm skillet. When the community swimming pool opened for the summer, Linny would dress in her bikini top, short shorts, and heels, grab Freshie Lynn, almost seven years old, and her inflatable toys, and drive her car to the parking lot where there was always a crowd of young men eager to help the flirtatious Linny and little Freshie make their way into the fenced area with all of their totes.

It was really quite a spectacle, with Linny leading the way to a poolside table, followed by Freshie being carried on the shoulders of a strong young man while a few of his friends stumbled after them, loaded with their ridiculous-looking haul. It was obvious to anyone present that Linny was enjoying every ounce of attention she was drawing from those around her. What should have been obvious to Linny, however, was that she was quickly becoming the most despised woman among women.

Conway Duque never did seem to understand the female undercurrents in small towns. Maybe his ignorance was a reflection of his upbringing, but Conway was completely unaware of the spreading resentment of Miss Spitt, her gaudy car, her ridiculous heels, and her tight bikini tops. Her incessant boasting and flaunting about their lifestyle made him feel enviable, successful. Conway hadn't considered that others might see it differently. And, of course, in true Conway form, he reasoned that they were just women—and women were not to be taken seriously.

Anyone with a bit of sense would recognize that Linny brought it on herself. She certainly did not give any thought to learning social norms, especially among the more respectable women in town. There are certain ways things are done in polite society, and Linny hadn't seen the need to learn them.

———————

They say that you can cook a live frog by putting it in a pot of cool water, then slowly increasing the water temperature over the stove. The frog is so oblivious to the rising temperature that it never seems to recognize it is being cooked. Over time, the frog just stops breathing, but it never fights to get out of the pot. No lid was ever needed, because the frog never had an inkling that it was being boiled to death.

The women in Tarford Flats considered Linny similar to a frog in a pot. Her social demise was clearly on the horizon. They just stayed out of the way and let her esteem die slowly. She continued to do herself in with bragging and showing off, becoming more entitled and demanding. She was even more intolerable than the Roane women. She was also becoming flanked by scandal. There were mounting incidents in which Linny made some terrible decisions and desperately needed Conway to save her from her own poor judgment.

There was an incident where she had been stopped for shoplifting from a high-end department store in Lincoln. She, of course, insisted that she had mistaken the very expensive designer bag on her arm for the one Conway had gotten for her the week before. Conway made arrangements to pay for the bag and the entire incident would have gone away quietly had a young woman from Tarford Flats not been the clerk working at the counter.

Then there was the incident at the pool with young Kevin Roane. Kevin had just finished a difficult junior year at UNL and had taken a job as a lifeguard, at which he could relax, sit in the sun all day, and have his nights free with his friends. The pool closed around 6:00 p.m., and everyone was supposed to be gone by 7:00.

One night, the pool manager had taken his family to the ice cream stand, and they walked back home by way of the swimming pool. They passed by the parking lot as the sun was setting, and the manager noticed a glint of sunlight reflecting off of a fancy yellow convertible tucked behind the bushes near the fence. With his three little girls in tow, the manager peered through the fence just in time to see a topless Linny Spitt run from the locker room and leap into the pool, giggling and squealing as she was soon joined by Kevin Roane. Had it not been for the shrieking of the little girls as they witnessed Linny's naked breasts flying through the air, Linny and Kevin would not have noticed their audience and more indiscretions might have taken place. As it was, however, Linny and Kevin immediately swam to the edge of the pool between themselves and the crowd and hid themselves as they explained that Kevin was just giving Miss Spitt some private lessons and that her swimming suit straps had snapped, so they were looking for the pieces of her top on the bottom of the pool.

Of course the pool manager knew this was not the case, but he found himself in a difficult position. Mr. Duque and Kevin Roane's parents would line up to destroy him if he were to ever to mention what he just witnessed. Wisely, he quietly turned and gathered his family and led them back on their route homeward and instructed his wife and children to forget everything they saw at the pool.

Linny was beside herself as she waited for weeks for any gossip of the swimming pool incident to reach Conway. She had not been to the pool again, and when Freshie asked to go, Linny either feigned a headache or made up some appointment she could not miss. Finally, Freshie's desire to go swimming was fulfilled when she was invited to a birthday pool party that was being held for another little girl her age. On the day of the party, Freshie loaded up all of her swimming gear and sat waiting for Linny to come out in her tiny top and short shorts. Instead, Linny emerged from the house wearing a tee and clam diggers, tennis shoes, a sun hat, and large sunglasses. Linny dropped Freshie off near the front gate without fanfare and sped off before anyone could whisper about her.

Later that evening while sitting at the table, little Freshie announced that she would like to have some private swimming lessons at the pool, except unlike Linny, she wants to do it with her clothes on. When Conway asked Freshie to what she was referring, Freshie went on to tell the story of Miss Linny as told to her by the daughters of the pool manager. According to Freshie, Linny was indeed topless, but was being helped by the lifeguard to find her missing top. The biggest revelation at the birthday party that day was that Miss Linny didn't even get in trouble for running at the pool.

I don't know how she did it exactly, but I imagine it was a combination of Linny's desperate efforts to convince Conway of what she called an obvious misunderstanding and Conway's need to save her from the judgmental women of Tarford Flats, but miraculously, Linny survived the Kevin Roane affair. She was much more contrite and attentive to Conway from that time forward. Conway also seemed more invested in knowing Linny's whereabouts. He was very clear that he would not have her visiting the public swimming pool again, but we weren't sure about his reasoning. Maybe he assumed other women were endeavoring to see her embarrassed again, or he didn't trust Linny to behave. In either case, Conway forbid it, and that was that.

Early summer mornings are beautiful here in Eastern Nebraska. While the sun begins to crest the horizon, the air is heavy with dew and gray clouds blanket the sky. I sit out on the porch in one of Vernie's rockers. I've wrapped myself in an old cotton quilt and have brought along a warm cup of blueberry tea and some granola I baked yesterday in Vernie's ancient gas oven. It is the strangest sensation, but when a slight breeze passes, I am sure I can smell lilacs and fresh linen.

It is in such moments that I miss my sister, Vernie. I am reminded of her every day. I feel her presence in the simple things, like this wonderful well-used quilt and the dried flower sachets she tucked in the dressers and closets. Vernie had a way of creating the most peaceful places. She brought an air of comfort with her into her homes and in her relationships. I often wonder if Vernie ever stopped feeling too much empathy for people like Fern, or if she just learned to cope with it through creating peace in her surroundings.

Poor Fern. I can't imagine the heartbreak she suffered at the hands of so many. She too was a victim of terrible judgment and even worse impulse control. Then, when she was at her weakest, she was taken in by the most selfish man she had known. The better part of me argues that Conway could not be so awful as to try to destroy his own daughter. To this day, I still find myself trying to believe he was just thoughtless.

It was a morning just like this—dewy and gray with just the slightest breeze—that Vernie got a call from Fern. She was not sure who it was at first. It could have been any one of her sisters sobbing on the other end of the phone. It came down to the process of elimination after she heard the phrase, "I can't believe he did it."

Vernie thought of all the possible men involved and who could hurt someone badly enough that they might break down so dramatically, and she thought it must either be Conway or Dewey, both of whom were directly involved with Fern.

Vernie pulled on her shoes, jumped on her bicycle, and raced to Conway's big stone house. She yelled a greeting as she opened the massive door, but there was no response. It appeared as though everyone had stepped outside, because Linny's purse was still on the table with Freshie Lynn's little handbag right next to it.

Vernie climbed the steps to the second floor and walked down the airy hallway to Fern's room. The door was cracked and the windows were open enough to let in the occasional breeze. Fern was crumpled in a heap on her bed, wrapped in her own cotton quilt. She had been crying so hard her eyes were swollen and looked painful as she tried to open them. Her entire affect seemed as though the most violent storm had passed through her and left a pile of wreckage where her will had been. Vernie was terrified at the sight of her once powerful sister in such a state. She went quietly to her side, not knowing what else to do, and as she leaned in, Fern was able to collect herself enough to whisper, "the trees...."

Vernie had a lurch in her stomach as she walked to the window to peer out into the vast back yard. It was then that she realized there was a constant humming sound she had overlooked in her worry about Fern. Vernie looked down and beheld a scene that broke her heart. There in the yard was Conway talking to some kind of foreman or contractor. The man had unrolled some sheets that looked like blueprints. On Conway's arm was a giddy Linny Spitt, with her hair all done up and with pants so tight they appeared to hamper her movement. Freshie Lynn was skipping about Conway and Linny in obvious excitement. About ten yards from the group was a small bulldozer being operated by a large man with a kind face. Vernie noted that his kind expression seemed out of place as he was digging out layer upon layer of dirt to create a massive pit in that section of the yard.

As Vernie tried to take in the scene, her eyes finally fell on the source of the humming sound, and she let out a gasp. The beautiful trees that surrounded the yard were now only jagged pillars sticking up from the dirt. Their beautiful limbs and low-hanging branches that held so many songbirds and so many memories had been severed and stripped and now lay bare, waiting to be sawed into pieces and sold as firewood. The yard had a post-apocalyptic feeling now, with ruin, destruction, and signs of despair in every direction. Conway was putting in a swimming pool. He didn't want the trees with all their leaves making a mess of things, and Linny wanted more sunshine in which to laze about and get a tan.

The man with the bulldozer spotted Vernie in the window, her expression so very despondent, and he looked upon her so kindly and compassionately it made Vernie turn away. How could a stranger recognize the pain Vernie and Fern felt at the destruction of their childhood wonderland, the place little Vernie wet her sister's arm, where little Freshie and her mom watched the fireflies late into the night? How could a man with a kind face see their heartache when their own father could not, would not consider them in the least?

Vernie and Fern wept together that day. They wept for all the pain caused by broken promises, caused by fear, shame, rejection, and abandonment, by raging tempers and cold hearts. They wept for the missed chances at happiness and the stupid choices made out of guilt, anger, or spite. They wept for the damaged relationships, the scars that remained from wounds so long ago. Fern and Vernie, once so inseparable, were bound together again in their heartache and their mourning for the father they would never have. What was even more profound was that through their shared sadness, both Fern and Vernie began to understand one-another. Vernie considered Fern, her life of mistakes and self-loathing, her attempts to be happy and loved, only to fail again and again. Fern finally understood Vernie, her desire to hide from conflict, from love, and from the world outside to avoid the same pain. They were not so different, after all. And now they wept as sisters until they collapsed on the soft feather bed in that beautiful, airy room and fell asleep to the distant chirps of crickets and toads.

CHAPTER 7: TEXAS

"Anxiety takes on many forms and shows itself in myriad ways. We tend to think of an anxious person as someone who frets and worries, bites their nails and needs constant comforting, when in fact it is more likely that a person with anxiety learns some rather complex ways to try to reduce his or her discomfort without drawing the attention of others. Often one with anxiety is mislabeled as bossy, controlling, impatient and "hung up." Upon further examination we can see that the attempts to control, dictate or organize things is a direct reaction to the real fear that things will fall apart otherwise. In extreme cases, we see the development of obsessions and compulsions that seem unreasonable to the observer, yet to the anxious person, have become absolutely necessary to maintain some sense of control and safety in their world. Unfortunately, anxiety becomes a family issue because everyone connected with the anxious person tries to modify their own behavior to decrease the likelihood of an anxiety attack. In doing this we actually allow the anxiety (or fear thereof) to metastasize until it dictates the behaviors of everyone involved."
   Living with Anxiety the EZ Way with Jessie Duque

When I was a young parent, I remember the fiasco that ensued when I tried to get my boys to clean their room. Things would start out okay, with basic directions and expectations, but then they would start to play and become distracted. In my effort to have the job completed I would literally pick up where they left off. They may have tried to help to some degree, but I am sure they spent more time playing than cleaning. Sometimes I would get so involved in the process I would refold the clothes in their drawers and reorganize their closet.

Before I realized my error, which I had repeated so many times it is embarrassing, I had taught my boys that first, if they play, I will do their job, and second, I would likely find fault with any job they did attempt and I would redo it anyway.

Even as a practicing therapist it took me a while to recognize that my behavior was anxiety driven. I suppose it was because I had no other working point of reference than my own brain. I finally recognized the problem, however, while chastising my oldest son, then 11 years old, about how he didn't seem to care about getting good grades or keeping up his room unless I harangued him about it.

"Why is it that you don't feel the need to clean your room or do your homework when you have been asked?" I inquired.

"Well, I guess I figure you worry about my room and my grades enough for both of us," He answered.

Despite all of my efforts, I had taught my boy the opposite of what I had intended all because my anxiety trumped his opportunity to learn from experience.

Ken Cash was a fastidious man. He had a certain way of doing things. Actually, he had a certain way of doing everything. It could easily have been said that he was obsessive-compulsive, although in those days, that diagnosis was not nearly as ubiquitous.

When KC left the dealership, he had every intention of throwing himself into farming. He had visions of his lush plots of land, dark and sweet with freshly plowed rich and fertile soil. Then as the crops began to grow, he envisioned beautifully uniform sprigs, growing in unison toward a beckoning sky. He imagined the satisfaction he would feel looking over his glorious fields, rows upon rows of beautiful plants, the setting sun inviting the cicadas to usher in the twilight. He had sold his share of the dealership to Darren, and had a nice bankroll with which he purchased his equipment (at cost, of course,) and everything he would need to begin his new vocation. Every purchase of gloves, coveralls, hats, boots, irrigation pipes, seed, and tools led him closer to what he expected to be his true calling.

The first two years went very well. He a hired man who was quite experienced in farming. The two of them turned out a bountiful crop and KC was ecstatic.

The next few years, however, were more difficult. In year three there was a late freeze that pushed back planting by two weeks. Then late spring rains flooded many of the tiny seedlings. K.C. became more anxious as he was forced to recognize his powerlessness against the weather. He became obsessed with almanacs, weather charts, measuring and predicting any abnormal conditions. He would read all of the reports and listen to the agricultural news in the evenings and retire to bed still planning and arranging things in his mind. He had to find a way to conquer his feeling of helplessness. K.C. would get up early, work the fields in the first morning light, then go into town and sit at the bakery with other farmers, listening to their complaints and opinions as if his life depended on it. And it did.

K.C. could not endure failure after making such a bold decision to leave the family business. He did not want to appear a failure or a fool. He knew that people were watching and waiting to see if K.C. Turnbull would fall on his face and prove himself unworthy of Toile Duque.

Over the next few years, his beautiful fields suffered the onslaught of grasshoppers, fungus, corn smut, grubs, drought, heat, hail, flooding, and frost. What K.C. imagined would be a peaceful and orderly job continued to present stressful, urgent concerns with few immediate interventions.

In his efforts to control so many anxiety-producing variables, Ken Cash Turnbull became irritable, impatient, frustrated and defensive. Even his son, Texas, who had been enthusiastic at the thought of farming became reticent to help when his father was around.

Texas would do small jobs for his dad here and there, but the actual farming was done by K.C. On the occasion that Texas was asked to plow, plant or irrigate, KC would watch him closely and jump in to fix any misstep. A times, his anxiety would overtake him and he would push Texas out of the way and do the work himself.

Texas became incredibly sensitive to his father's moods and intensity. He could predict what kind of day it would be by the way K.C. opened the refrigerator in the morning, how loudly the screen door slammed as K.C. walked out onto the porch, and the way the truck sounded as the tires crunched on the gravel driveway. Sometimes if things seemed too miserable, Texas would develop a stomach virus or a headache, anything to give him a few hours to wait for his dad to cool down. Other days, Texas would focus on completing individual jobs out of sight of his father, but jobs he could complete and report favorably to take the edge off of K.C.'s anxiety.

Because farming is a lifestyle as well as a job, it was difficult for K.C. to keep work stress from affecting his relationships with his wife and son. As K.C. continued to become increasingly tense and persnickety at home, Toile found reasons to avoid his company. She worked a lot more at the boutique, and continued to develop her consulting business. She had developed an interest in European chocolates and baking, and spent hours alone reading pastry books in her study. K.C. could sense that his wife was pulling away, and yet could not see that it was his own anxiety - his increased agitation-that was the cause. Instead, K.C. naturally assumed that as he had feared, Toile was becoming disappointed in him and was shunning him because he was a failure. It seemed with K.C. that everything other than perfection was an utter disaster.

K.C's mother certainly didn't do him any favors. Leona Turnbull was a difficult person to stomach. She was a vain, privileged woman from a moderately wealthy family in Omaha. Her father had been a military strategist enlisted to help with the Americanization of the Indian population, and his rank afforded the family access to the more esteemed social circles. When she was in her early teens, her father was elected to political office. As a result, Leona had grown up among other young debutants of the day. Leona learned early that life was about competition, and to compete with others in that social realm she would have to convince everyone that she was exceptional, which she did with limitless boasting.

It became absurd, really, the things she would boast about. She would boast about the social connections, expensive clothes, handbags, furniture, vacations that she may (or may not) have taken, restaurants she patronized, gifts she had given, charitable contributions she made, her husband's political standing, his influence and business success…. but most of all, Leona would boast about her boys. She would boast about when they learned to talk, walk, sing, read, and use the toilet. She would boast about their athletics, academics, physical attributes- some of which I am sure they would prefer not to be known. If any of these things seemed the least bit ordinary, Leona would change the dates or details to make sure her boys were again in the lead.

And, she would keep records. Leona had lists that spanned for decades detailing the gifts she had given and received, Christmas cards sent and received, invitations she had received, and especially ones she discovered she hadn't. She even had a list of who sent flowers or condolences when young Rudy passed away. Leona kept records of everything, and she would refer to them often.

I am sure it was daunting to grow up in a home where every mistake or oversight was noted, recorded and shelved for future reference. I can't even imagine what it must have been like to live under the pressure of someone heralding your magnificence to any who could hear, and at the same time having to double check every action for flaws. I really believe K.C. did the best that he could while stressors and fears circled like vultures over his mind.

In my many years of working with anxious people, I have found that when we live in response to fear, we often end up with that situation we fear most. In our efforts to avoid a perceived fear, we create the exact environment for that fear to germinate and grow under our very noses. The same became the case with K.C. His fear of losing his wife and son because of his failures made him so difficult to be around that even those who loved him most looked for ways to avoid him. K.C. wanted nothing more than to share this life of farming with his boy, and yet, due to his own need to make it perfect, he began to push his son away.

It was 1970 when Texas graduated high school. Out of loyalty, he tried to work alongside his father and help with the farm, but found the situation exasperating, so when Texas finally turned nineteen, he announced he was joining the Peace Corps. A relatively young program at the time, the Peace Corps held an appeal of escape and adventure for a lot of young men who preferred not to go to war in Vietnam. Texas boarded a passenger train headed for Florida from whence he would travel the world.

When he arrived in Florida, Texas underwent a brief orientation and a concentrated course in Spanish. After a few weeks of training, Texas found himself near the region of Santa Marta, Columbia where the sandy beaches grew into the northern tip of the Andes mountain range. Texas had entered a completely different world.

Texas appreciated the distance from Tarford Flats more than he could have imagined. Of course he had never known anything different than life in that place. He had always been known as the son of K.C. and Toile, the grandson of the Deque's and Turnbull's. He was considered an eligible bachelor from the time he turned 15- not for marriage, but certainly for dating exclusively, which would likely lead to marriage. That was how things were done among the elite in Tarford Flats.

Texas loathed the idea of small-town elites. He saw what the pressures of that strange society had done to his father, his mother, their marriage, their parents… He experienced the doubt of sincerity of his friends, peers, teachers, girlfriends…. He hated that people presumed who he was and what he was about before even hearing him speak. People did not seem interested in Texas. They were interested in his breeding and what they could take from him.

It was in the jungles, mountains and sandy beaches of Columbia that Texas sloughed off the bitterness that had come to encase him. He was scrubbed clean by the simplicity and modesty he witnessed in the native Columbians. He grew to love them in a way he never before understood- love them in a way that felt fresh and free. It was because of this compassion that Texas found the drive to do everything he could to help the people for whom he felt such great responsibility.

Texas spent the next two years helping the poor people of the northern mountains to establish more effective irrigation and crop management techniques. He had learned quite a bit from his dad after all. In fact, as the memories of frustration and confusion Texas had regarding his father began to abate, he began to understand the blessings of being a bit neurotic and attentive to detail. Texas's fields were meticulous. His ability to visualize water flow and growth patterns led him to design plots of land that would yield superb crops. The villagers began to share stories of the young American man battling with the most difficult areas in which crops had struggled to grow only to come out victorious with generations of healthy plants.

As he began to expand his work within the Northern mountains of Columbia, Texas began a partnership with a young man named Daniel whose family was very poor. A few years earlier, Daniel's father became frustrated with the Columbian government because rich landowners had taken over local courts and banks and were squeezing out poorer farmers without redress. Daniel's father had lost his last attempt to reclaim the land that had been swindled from him. He was consumed with anger toward the corrupt system and along with friends and neighbors, joined the FARC or Revolutionary Armed Forces of Columbia. It had been eighteen months since Daniel and his family had received any word from his father, and they were afraid that he might be dead. The family was struggling more than ever to hold onto what little they had, which included nothing more than a small two-room hut with a dirt floor and thatched roof, forty acres of land on the side of a hill, and the clothes on their backs.

Daniel and his brothers tried to maintain the coffee crop their father had begun years before, but could not seem to turn much of a profit. Daniel was desperate to find a way to save his family from ruin. He had a thought, but did not know whom to approach. Many of his fellow villagers were also destitute, and may be tempted to steal Daniel's idea or worse, turn him in to the corrupt authorities in hopes of a pittance reward. Seeing it as his only option, Daniel set his mind to becoming acquainted with Texas Turnbull.

For a few months he worked alongside Texas, observing the way he treated the poor, the elderly, the children. He watched to see if Texas's word was true or if he was a liar seeking after his own interests. And, although Texas was certainly imperfect as a twenty-year-old man, he was not desperate as the Columbian young men had been. He could afford to live by more sophisticated standards and this, to Daniel, was reassuring enough that he decided to take the risk and approach Texas with his plan.

Within his rows of coffee beans, Daniel had set aside an area of about one acre for marijuana. Now, marijuana grew freely in Columbia, but much of it was of poor to fair quality.

There was, however, a type of marijuana plant in the region that was gaining great popularity among those in the illegal marijuana trade. "Columbian Gold" was in high demand because it had all of the sought-after attributes of quality marijuana without any negative side effects that come with the lesser strains. Daniel was hoping to create a hybrid strain of Columbian Gold marijuana with increased hallucinations that might achieved through the adding to the soil of a certain fungus.

He recognized that Texas had some experience with soil and crop manipulation. Texas, on the other hand, was intrigued to be sure but not entirely up to the task. Nor did he know if he could trust young Daniel with such a risky endeavor.

In an effort to further persuade him, Daniel invited Texas to his small hut to meet his mother and siblings. Texas and Daniel left the next morning on a six-mile hike that took the better part of the day.

When they finally arrived in the tiny village Texas was shocked at the beauty of the place. It was nestled expertly into the side of a steep hill. The huts were built to withstand great storms without sliding an inch. Everything the community did was arranged in such a way that they seemed unaffected by the huge cliffs and crags a few yards away. The view from this place was spectacular. Texas could see the entire face of the adjoining peak. Behind it he could see still more peaks, a bit taller, as if they were elders watching over the shoulder of the younger mountains. Between the peaks, low-hanging clouds slept on the tops of the trees. Texas found himself not wanted to move.

His reverence was broken by a boy he assumed was Daniel's little brother. He looked exactly like Daniel but was missing a few teeth in his goofy grin. In lisp-laden Spanish, the boy invited Texas to join the family for dinner. He took Texas by the hand and led him to the family's hut. Daniel's mother had two pots suspended over a low burning fire. In one pot she had soaked and slow-baked beans until they were so soft, they lost their shapes. In the other pot Texas saw what appeared to be chicken stew, which Daniel's brother called "Sudado de Pollo." There were succulent chunks of meat in a spicy, flavorful broth, with wild onions and other root vegetables.

Daniel and his three brothers were seated in a circle on a thick woven blanket and had left a space for Texas and the younger boy. When he sat down, they passed him a basket in which he found a dense corn loaf wrapped in a banana leaf. Texas picked up the tamale and took a bite. He expected the bundle to be dry but was surprised to find that it was moist and delicious, and filled with seasoned pork. It seemed to have been soaked in chicken broth because the flavor was surprisingly savory. All the men seated on the blanket watched Texas's face as he tried the tamale, waiting for his reaction. Texas began to understand that this meal had been prepared just for his arrival. It then occurred to him that Daniel's entire family was desperate for Texas to agree to help Daniel, and that they were each willing to risk arrest to undertake this venture and save their home.

He watched the brothers laugh together, trade jokes and make wry observations and Texas felt more at home than he had for years in Tarford Flats. These people who had nearly nothing had found a treasure in their love for one-another. There were no snide remarks, no criticisms, no scorekeeping or periods of icy silence. There was just an overwhelming sense of peace... and warmth that could even be tasted in the food.

When Texas realized that Daniel's mother was not among them, Daniel explained that she and his younger sister were eating outside because there was not enough room in the hut. Texas could not hide his confusion. Daniel had never talked about having a sister. He talked about his brothers all the time- their quirks, personalities, skills and talents... but nothing about a sister. Realizing his oversight, Daniel was quick to act. He called out to his mother and asked her to send his sister in to meet the American visitor. Texas could overhear the girl's protests as she maintained that she didn't have to do everything her brothers told her and that she was busy with her own dinner and would meet him later. Texas could also hear Daniel's mother, embarrassed by her daughter's outburst, quietly trying to set the girl straight.

Columbia in the 1970's was still a patriarchal culture, and Lucia was reminded that she needed to be agreeable. Soon after her mother stopped lecturing, Lucia growled and stomped into the hut clearly ready for a fight. She was fifteen years old and taller than Texas expected. She had long, dark hair that fell over her shoulders in unkempt waves. Her dark eyes seemed to hold a fire as she expressed her frustration with her older brother for summoning her. Lucia's voice was full and smooth and even when she was angry, that voice warmed him inside like spiced dark chocolate. Texas had to remind himself that she was only fifteen years old.

Lucia noticed Texas looking at her with what she assumed was amusement. Quick to strike back, Lucia readied herself for battle. In one movement, she swept her dark waves up from her shoulders and tied her hair in a knot at the nape of her neck. She shot a sharp glare at Texas who immediately shrank back in awe. This caused Lucia to giggle at which time she flashed Texas a smile that, for him, would become a craving. Texas found her stunning, mesmerizing and terrifying. He also knew he would do anything to spend his life with her.

The more time he spent with the members of Daniel's family, the more Texas adored them. The youngest boy, Felipe, was very smart and very observant. At ten years old, he had a lot to study in the midst of his older siblings. Lucia was the next oldest followed by Julian, seventeen; David, eighteen; and Paulo, nineteen. Daniel was smaller than his strapping younger brothers and at twenty-one had likely stopped growing. He was different in other ways, too. Like Felipe, he was keenly observant and very smart, but he was also very wary. It became obvious to Texas that Daniel had been more affected by his father's difficulties, his absence, and also by the incredible responsibility he felt as he assumed the role of patriarch of the family.

For Texas, it was as if a layer of film was slowly being pulled back from his eyes. What Texas understood to be true- his family, his upbringing, his place in the world- suddenly seemed so insignificant. His father's anxieties, his mother's loneliness, the pressures of a small town in Nebraska slowly receded from his thoughts. Texas began to feel awash in the fresh mists of his new and present reality. Texas had experienced a seismic shift. He was reborn, in a sense, and he could now choose what to value, what to take with him in this new existence. For all that he thought was big was now little, all that he thought was important was now meaningless. He was in the poorest part of the world, with the simplest of people, and yet he was in the midst of greatness. To Texas Turnbull, the epitome of a life well lived would be one measured in connection to those he loved and served.

Texas spent a week in the mountains with Daniel's family discussing ideas and making plans to help them with their financial dilemma. Daniel knew that Texas was taking his time, that he could have concluded the planning within a few days, but he was happy to oblige. He watched as his friend drank in the culture of Daniel's village and enjoyed time with his brothers. The visit was not only good for Texas, however. Daniel had never seen his sister this happy.

After the first awkward day or two, Texas and Lucia became friends. Texas made her laugh like she hadn't in years. They would sit together, talking quietly when Lucia would suddenly laugh out loud, throwing back her beautiful head and startling whatever critters might be near. Texas would then flash a self-satisfied grin as he witnessed his beautiful companion slowly falling in love with him.

During this period in the Columbian drug trade, individual farmers who chose to participate in this enterprise did so on a very small scale. It was culturally understood that one could enter into the trade without much interference from law enforcement provided they were given incentive to look the other way. Texas and Daniel needed to assess what they did not yet know about the business. Certainly there were other modest farmers who knew how to begin this sort of venture. The two decided they needed to begin a very quiet, careful business network.

Several shipments left the ports of Santa Marta every month and often farmers would meet one another near the ports to discuss business. They were all very sensitive to the situation regarding his father, and the farmers welcomed Daniel in without hesitation. Meanwhile, Texas and some of his colleagues in the Peace Corps also began to share ideas and information about the various marijuana operations they had seen. In order to avoid suspicion, Texas left Daniel and his brothers to their work and he resumed his work with the Corps.

It was nearing the end of his two-year commitment when Texas received a letter from his father. Ken Cash was not a man to sit still long enough to compose a letter and Texas was troubled when it arrived. He had been so enthralled with the new project for Daniel that Texas had not given much thought to things occurring at home in Tarford Flats.

In the past several months, he had received some packages from Vernie- usually candies, granola and dried fruits she had made. She had stuffed short notes in the packages which were lighthearted, and light on information. There were a few that mentioned his mother, Toile, and her travels to various pageants to consult. Vernie told him about Jeffrey's midwifery and how busy he had been. There was no word about Fern. Texas knew as we all did that with Fern, no news was good news.

This letter, however, was the first he had received from his father. Texas had gone down to Santa Marta on the coast for supplies and to check in with local Peace Corps leadership when he was handed envelope from Tarford Flats. Texas arranged for the supplies to be delivered, then made his way to the base of the mountain again before slowing down to read his father's message. Texas arrived at the edge of a grassy area where he found a smooth boulder on which to sit. After he read and reread the letter from K.C., Texas remained on the boulder on which he had been sitting for more than an hour.

He noticed a line of several ants making their way along its base. He wondered, are other creatures ever tempted to fall out of line? Do they have a sense of selfishness or adventure that causes them to depart from their expected path? As much as he dreaded and despised the thought, he knew he had to return home to fulfill a duty to help his father.

The homecoming party for Texas was anticipated but somewhat disappointing. As is often the case, when a person leaves his family to go and explore the world, that person grows and his perspective changes. A homecoming is often a shock in that those at home may not have changed much at all.

Ken Cash and Toile had arranged a huge potluck and barbeque and invited anyone they could think of to celebrate the return of their boy. The gathering began in mid-afternoon and lasted late into the evening with plenty of beer-drinking and loud laughter. How strange it was to see his father and his mother behaving as though they were the happiest, they had ever been, especially considering the letter Texas had received a few weeks before.

In his letter, K.C. explained the hardships the farm had endured with record numbers of grasshoppers and hailstorms. He could not seem to stop the outpouring of money and failed attempts to save the crops. K.C. admitted to spending hours each night drinking beer in the barn, trying to escape the impending disaster. Apparently, Toile had also begun to pull away from him and the more desperate he felt, the more distant she became. Texas could tell by the urgency of K.C.'s letter that he thought Toile was going to leave him, and if that were the case, he will have lost everything.

Texas knew his mother would not involve him in their marital conflict. She had very specific boundaries between herself and her family. As he was considering how to go about helping his parents, Texas spotted Vernie and Jeffrey across the yard. Vernie had always seemed to know the most private struggles within the family. She would be the perfect person to ask for help.

Texas approached his Aunt and Uncle and after scooping Vernie's little body up in a quick hug, he asked to speak to her about his parents. True to form, Vernie had carried Toile's secrets in confidence. She could see, however, the earnest efforts Texas made to understand. Vernie shared what she felt she could.

Apparently, Toile had become even more withdrawn than usual from K.C. She had made more recent trips to Colorado where she had a really good friend. She didn't tell K.C. about this friend because their relationship was not sexual, but K.C. became suspicious about her absences. Finally, during her last trip out of town, K.C. went through Toile's study looking for anything that might explain the distance he felt.

At first, he gave little thought to the stacks of letters he found tied with a string in the back of a drawer. They had a strange letterhead with a Boulder, Colorado address. The paper was soft, like linen and smelled like cookies. In a fancy script he could read the word "Patisserie" at the top. He assumed that they were from some company trying to network their way into the pageant circuit.

Then he found the box. It had been opened and appeared to have contained some kind of flaky pastry. K.C. felt a strange sense of childlike joy as he stood inhaling the simple, splendid aromas of almond, sweet cream, butter and cinnamon. On the box K.C. saw the same script and the same Boulder address. He knew then that he had to read the letters more carefully, if only to find out more about this amazing baker.

As he read, K.C. was overcome with shock which then lead to denial. As he pondered how his Toile could possibly be the same woman receiving these letters from Eric, K.C. became incensed at his wife, her duplicity, and then at himself for being a fool. He soon grew despondent at the concept of ending his marriage.

It was out of sheer desperation that K.C. had written to Texas in Columbia. Shortly after he sent the letter, he reached out to Vernie and Jeffrey with what he had learned about Eric. It was clear to him that this man, Eric, loved Toile, but it was a version of Toile that K.C. had never known. K.C. was utterly confused. He knew and loved his wife dearly, and at the same time felt completely betrayed, confounded, and concerned. "What kind of woman has two separate lives?" he asked Vernie.

Vernie could not answer. More accurately, she would not answer, because the truth is that most women have at least two separate lives. Most women live the life they have made- a life of work, hardship, troubles, laughter, joy, love, sorrow, and pain. And, most women have another life- a life of dreams, longings, wishes, release... but a life that rarely comes to fruition. How could she explain to K.C. that Toile needed Eric as much as she needed him and Texas without destroying the desperate man in front of her? Vernie chose in that moment to share a story with her brother-in-law:

When Toile was a little girl of about 8 years of age, she had a young friend named Joel whom she had met in school. Joel and his family lived on the outskirts of town in a rundown little house. They had an interesting yard, however, complete with goats, chickens, a cat and her kittens and two Shetland ponies which Toile and Fern loved to pamper with brushing and sugar cubes. Toile and Fern would walk to Joel's house, which was only about a mile away and play with Joel, his little brother, and their animals. Joel was a year older than Toile, and although 9 years is an age when many boys are ornery toward girls, Joel was very kind to Toile and Fern.

Over the course of the summer, Toile developed a crush on Joel. She would have dreams about him at night- dreams in which he was a knight, or a prince, or a strong jungle man who would save her from certain doom. Toile would share her dreams with Fern as they would walk to see the ponies- and Joel. Fern began to tease Toile about marrying Joel, and on one occasion, Joel overheard. With a sly grin, he exclaimed that he would be happy to marry Toile, and they could do so that very day.

Fern quickly picked a bouquet of wildflowers while Joel retrieved a flour sack from his mother's kitchen which Toile fashioned into a powdery veil. Joel's younger brother served as a minister and the two were married in the back yard while Joel's mother hung out laundry and smiled at the ceremony. Soon enough, my sisters made their way back home for dinner.

A few days later when Conway was at the Truck Wash belonging to Atchison Freight, he was chatting with the employees when a new hire approached him. He introduced himself with an air of camaraderie and explained that he was the father of Joel, Toile's schoolmate. Assuming that Conway had already heard about their play-wedding, Joel's father teased Conway a bit about their children's' nuptials. Conway, of course, had no idea to what the man was referring, and seemed irritated with the discussion, so Joel's father let it drop, playing it off as a misunderstanding.

Conway did not let it go so quickly, however. He had been embarrassed in front of his employees and made to look like a fool. When he got home, he gathered Fern and Toile, sat them at the table and interrogated them about Joel, their friendship, and the "wedding." Fern, who was only 6, told her father every detail she could think of. She made sure to inform him that she was the one who picked the bouquet.

Conway's eyes darkened and his cheeks became crimson. When he dismissed Fern from the table, she looked worriedly at her sister, then slid off the chair and scrambled to her room. Conway Duque proceeded to lecture Toile about the way things were to be in his home and with his children. He was so angry that droplets of spit flew from his mouth onto her face, yet Toile knew better that to wipe them off. His tirade began with an assault on her character. He said that she was reckless, foolish to be friends with a kid of that breeding, that obviously she enjoyed playing in filth. Conway said that she had no self-respect, and obviously no respect for him if she was going to make a joke out of her family and his standing in the community. He accused her of having no consideration for all he had done for his family by achieving the status he had. Finally, her father completed his diatribe by telling Toile that she had better learn the difference between a lady and a whore, and that he had no interest in being the father of a whore.

Conway stormed out of the kitchen, onto the back porch, down the steps and got into his car which he drove away in a huff. Little Toile was left alone at the table, confused, humiliated, crushed and afraid. She stayed there for several minutes with huge tears tumbling down her rosy cheeks, trying to understand what had just happened.

Toile changed that day. She was awash with shame, rejection and abandonment all because she had done something that had embarrassed her father. Conway didn't talk to her for a month so that she would understand the seriousness of her infraction. From that moment forward, he was distrustful of his oldest daughter and seemed to suspect her of underhandedness. Whatever pedestal Toile might have been on was now a hole out of which she could not climb.

It was shortly after that Toile began pageantry. Strangely, pageantry felt safe. In that world a person is only judged on what they choose to reveal. It was blissfully superficial. No one could reject her, shun her, or break her if they didn't know who she really was or what she really thought.

Toile never talked about the time her father turned on her. It was much too painful. Instead, she created a safe, predictable world that was above reproach. Ken Cash was from a good family and a safe choice because he fit the criteria of a suitable husband on whom she could depend. Eric symbolized the dreams and longings she may have had, but also may have caused her to be vulnerable, humiliated or disappointed if the dreams became too real. Her career and the Beaumont Boutique were necessary to showcase her accomplishments and make her feel worthwhile.

Toile navigated her life through manageable, organized compartments to reduce the chance of ever feeling completely crushed again. Toile was systematic as she parceled parts of herself to find what she needed without becoming vulnerable. She obviously hadn't seen the risk of doing so. It all seemed so much safer at the time. Now, however, Toile found herself disjointed, compartmentalized and paralyzed by fear. She didn't know how to open herself to risk, and she didn't know how to open herself to love-true, trusting, lasting, painful, beautiful, deep, passionate love.

As Vernie finished her explanation, a look of understanding settled on K.C.s face. He felt such sadness, such compassion for Toile, who had carried these feelings of shame for so long. He understood her desire to find passion and admiration from a safe distance. He sympathized with her fear of vulnerability. K.C. also realized that his own need for perfection may have caused her to feel even more afraid of his eventual rejection or disenchantment with her. He wouldn't have been the first man she loved to turn away from her.

K.C. knew then that Toile loved him in a way that suited both of them best at that time in their lives. She loved K.C. and she understood and forgave his shortcomings. Toile found a way to fulfill her needs in a way that K.C. could not because of his own struggles and insecurities. She sought out friendship with Eric as an act of kindness to her husband, knowing that any additional pressure on K.C. may have been more than he could manage.

At that moment, in an act of wisdom and selflessness, K.C. chose to accept Toile's relationship with Eric as something that was necessary for her happiness. He would not follow suit with Conway Duque. He would not lash at her or make her feel ashamed or unworthy. He would love his precious Toile, no matter what.

When Toile returned from her trip, K.C. helped her carry her things inside where he had prepared fresh-squeezed lemonade. As she took a cold, refreshing gulp he swept her up into his arms and held her close and still. There was no angst in his touch. She breathed in his scent- the scent that reminded her of home, and as the cool taste of sweet and sour lingered, strangely everything seemed to make perfect sense.

When he had heard all that Vernie had to say, Texas saw his father not as the tense, impatient perfectionist, but as a wise, enduring man who provided his family with unfailing, unconditional love. In his heart, Texas felt the welling up of love and appreciation for the father he was just beginning to see. In his stomach, Texas felt regret and shame at how harsh and shortsighted his youthful criticisms of his father had been.

Ever observant, Vernie caught his expression and set him straight with one statement:
"Life isn't much different than taming a wild mustang, you know. Sometimes you make a bad judgement and get thrown to the ground. Just get back up, Texas. Get up, dust yourself off and try again."

CHAPTER 8: FRESHIE LYNN

"Child-rearing is such a tricky thing. Often, we learn too late that with our actions we teach our children far more than we do with our words. Many well intentioned parents start out innocently enough, doting on and caring for their children, only to find their children expect that treatment to continue into adulthood, and resist assuming personal responsibility... Parents who feel the need to rescue their children from the consequences of behavior unintentionally teach their children that rules do not apply to them, that they are somehow the exception, or that they require rescuing because the world is too hard for them to manage... Parents who accommodate their children's every desire invariably teach that child that there are no limits to their desires, moral or material, and that the depth of a parent's love is manifest in fulfilling a Christmas list. In any case, the way we teach our children to recognize their place in the world is the way in which they will attempt to make their way into adulthood."
<u>Parenting the EZ Way with Jessie Duque</u>

Fern finally left Tarford Flats for good in the summer of 1965. Those of us who cared for her felt hopeful in her absence. For Fern, things only seemed to get worse after Conway put in the backyard pool. Linny became ever more intolerable with her sense of entitlement and endless opinions. Worse yet, Freshie Lynn followed her example in nearly every way. In a predictable progression, Freshie began to idolize Miss Linny and wanted to spend all of her time with the woman. Of course, Freshie was young and terribly impressionable. Her reality was limited to that which she could understand. Her mother seemed weak, quiet, and unremarkable while Miss Linny was exciting, interesting, and gave her nice things. Of course, Freshie felt love for her mother, but found greater tangible reward in spending time with Miss Linny from morning to night.

Fern would awaken on summer mornings to the sounds of little Freshie Lynn splashing and squealing in the chilly water as a satisfied Linny Spitt looked on. Then, like clockwork, Freshie would come up with a fantastic menu for breakfast and Linny would eagerly accommodate her. Fern knew that with Freshie and Linny, it wasn't just about breakfast. Whatever Freshie wanted, Linny would find a way to satisfy her. Linny took pride in how she was able to steer Freshie's attentions away from Fern and toward herself- as if the child was a prize to be won- and appeared to do so with Conway's blessing. Linny was convinced that little Freshie Lynn had a special place in Conway's heart, and through her, Linny could cement her own hold in his home and his future.

When Freshie was happy, she was a delight. She learned which looks and expressions could entice or entreat others to bend to her will. Freshie had inherited her mother's striking green eyes as well as her brilliant smile. With all of the swimming and time spent in the sun, her hair was bleached almost white like spun honey and her skin was the color of caramel.

Freshie had also inherited Fern's stubborn streak, and when Freshie sensed a challenge, she would widen those big, beautiful eyes and lower her forehead, which would cause her naturally spiraled locks to fall around her pleading face. It was a look that could charm almost anyone, including, of course, her grandfather. Nothing was too indulgent for his granddaughter, and Linny had become adept at finding ways to spend Conway's money on Freshie, and on herself. The two of them, Freshie and Linny, ruled the house. Soon enough, the enormous house grew cramped and contentious. Fern knew she had to plan for her escape.

For several months, Fern disappeared into her vast, sunless room. She slept often, ate little, and wrote in her books. She wrote for hours at a time and filled hundreds of pages. No one knew what Fern was writing about as she stayed in her peaceful cocoon. She didn't share it with anyone, and given her life experience, I am sure she was worried she might be considered a lunatic.

I was in graduate school when Fern sent her journals to me. It was shortly after she moved away from Tarford Flats for the last time that I received a note and a package containing several of her journals. The note read;

"Dear Jessie,
These are so precious to me. I know they will be
safe in your hands.
Maybe when I'm settled, I will send for them...
maybe not. We shall see what
life has in store.

Love, Fern"

The message was as cryptic as ever, and probably for good reason. Fern had been beaten down by almost everyone she allowed to get close to her. She could not afford any more vulnerability. I began to leaf through the pages that were filled with her handwriting. In the variations of her script I could recognize the times she felt tired or angry, hopeful or filled with despair. Occasionally I would come across a rough sketch Fern had drawn, sometimes of trees, clouds and birds, sometimes of items in her room, sometimes of herself, but mostly of her children.

I started to read the first page with a bit of confusion. I was not sure of the audience. It seemed to be an outpouring if desperation and grief and conflicting messages of victimhood and guilt. It took a few moments for me to finally understood what she had been doing. Fern had been corresponding with God.

She began her first journal with a series of questions that went on for at least forty pages. Fern had questions regarding every painful aspect of her life. She asked about her own nature as a young child and an adolescent. She asked about her relationships with her mother, her sisters, her father, and why they had all been so difficult. She asked about being drawn to men who would reject her. She listed various mistakes she had made and questioned her worthiness as a human being. Then, somewhere in the middle of her journal, Fern got a response:

"Dearest Fern, I grieve for you, not because of what you have lost, but what
   you have not yet found."

Her confusion was evident after the first response and was met with scribbled attempts to defend herself, to justify or excuse her behaviors. As I read on, however, Fern seemed to relax and focus her efforts not on defending herself, but earnestly seeking understanding.

Slowly, over time, Fern began to receive more answers, like long-awaited personal revelation, written in her own hand. She filled several more pages- sometimes pleading, sometimes whining and blaming, but more often earnestly seeking understanding about herself and her place in the world. It was in her most humble and broken moments that Fern seemed to get a response, and the responses were perfect. They were filled with kindness, love, patience and understanding for a woman who had been fighting herself for so long.

As I read through the pages of Fern's journals, I witnessed my sister coming to terms with her mistakes, her failures, and her regrets. Pages upon pages of lamentations and self-loathing were reconciled with gentle reminders that she had done the best she could in her given circumstances.

Fern began to see that much of her childhood was beyond her control- that she had a role to play that was beyond her making. She was treated unfairly by Conway not because of who she was, but because she reminded him of who he was. Conway's resentment and rejection of Fern was only a reflection of his own self-loathing. Conway pushed her away because of shame, but it was shame of himself- his own history- that he refused to face, and therefore could not bring himself to face the innocent daughter who resembled him in so many ways.

In her own hand. Fern began to express self- acceptance, and then, remarkably, she began to value herself. She learned that she was not a mistake, but like everyone else, she had certain qualities that could be used to fulfill her "calling" in life, or to be part of her demise.

Fern had been given personal power, which, like a thunderstorm, could cause people to either be awestruck or afraid. She could be terribly intimidating, often frustrating, but always elicited strong feelings from others. Some people wanted to be around her, to witness her excitement. Others wanted to conquer her. She was overwhelming in her intensity and she made people feel uneasy, and yet she was lively, exciting, and passionate. Fern learned that none of these qualities are shameful, but rather, they cause those who are afraid of their own feelings, their own intensities, to loathe her because she was stronger than they were.

As I poured over her journals, I was awash with the sense of change overcoming my sister.Fern had started to remember herself. She remembered her desire for adventure, exploration, and even her desire for artistic expression that had long been suppressed.

I love the late summer weather in Eastern Nebraska. July is usually brutal, with triple-digit temperatures causing the heavy humidity to rise off of the Missouri River like steam. The air takes on a haze that seems to trap pollen and dust, which are then attached to any vulnerable surface.

Prior to the advent of air conditioning, folks would structure their days to avoid any serious work during the hottest hours. The heat was prohibitive and those of us with any kind of stubborn streak found ourselves vexed by the speed at which we lost our energy and determination. Even today, working outside is unwise unless one is fortunate enough to have a coveted air-conditioned tractor. The rest of us measure our activities according to the heat index.

A wonderfully cool daybreak finally comes after the first weeks of August. On the best days, the late-night temperature dips low enough to reach the dew point, which then invites soft rain to fall until mid-morning. Cool breezes come from the west, and the Eastern sun is slower in heating the air, which gives us a reprieve from the heat that sometimes lasts until mid-afternoon. I love these mornings most of all. There is something magical about the timing, the relief that arrives just at the point when we begin to fear it never will.

In her life, Fern had a habit of repeating the same cycle that I see in the late summer with the relentless heat finally being chased away with the rain. Fern could withstand misery longer than anyone I knew. I certainly didn't have the patience- or the determination- to suffer through men like Dewey Rue Wayne, for instance. But with Fern, it was as if she had to exhaust every last resource before she would resign and accept that things were not going to be as she wanted then without making changes.

His ears ringing with Linny's constant complaints about her, Conway became convinced that Fern was incapable of being a mother. Maybe. It could just as easily have been that he wanted to appease Linny, who wanted to raise Freshie as her own. Either way, Conway pressured Fern to assign him legal guardianship of the girl. When Fern resisted and began to talk about leaving with Freshie, Conway threatened to take Fern to court to get legal custody of his granddaughter.

Fern had begun making jewelry again, in the way she had been taught by Slade's family. She had also taught herself to weave and do beadwork, both of which resulted in quite beautiful pieces. At first, Fern sold her work through Toile's shop, and then she began to travel to various craft fairs that coincided with the rodeo circuit. Though her jewelry and beadwork were popular, and she was able to make some money, Fern knew that there was no way she could afford to engage in any kind of legal battle with Conway. What's more, Fern had been persuaded that Freshie was better off with Conway and Linny because they could give her stability, opportunity, and nearly anything her little heart could desire. Freshie Lynn seemed happy and in good care, and Fern realized that she had no place in that world anymore.

Finally, in 1965, Fern bought an old jeep and a small camper into which she loaded all of her supplies and her few other possessions, and took to the road. She kept in touch for a while. The last we heard, she had befriended a nice man named Ernie Twipps, who also sold wares on the rodeo circuit. Mr. Twipps had been quite successful, actually. He had a large Winnebago out of which he sold fine leather belts and boots, and beautiful buckles. He had been connected with the rodeo circuit for years when he met Fern, and he was dazzled by her beauty and by her talent. Ernie helped Fern to establish her business and served as a mentor. He kept his distance, though, because he was fifteen years older than she was, and was certain she had no romantic interest in him. And she didn't, at first. Fern didn't have romantic interest in anyone.

But Mr. Tipps's friendship made her happy. He helped her to feel successful, valued, and safe. They were friends, best friends, so much so that Fern hadn't realized that she had fallen in love. Ernie wanted nothing from Fern but her companionship. He encouraged her to maintain her independence and not compromise her freedom. Finally, someone saw Fern's untamed spirit and did not try to conquer or contain her. And finally, Fern accepted that she was not meant to be tamed. To remind her of that truth, Fern never did get rid of her old jeep and camper.

Freshie Lynn turned twelve in 1970. Linny had spent the past five years fulfilling her every wish. Linny seemed to believe that it was her role to ensure that Freshie's life was without strife. Linny would intervene in any circumstance in which she could save Freshie from experiencing consequences. Soon, Freshie became intolerable. As the summer breaks came to an end, teachers would dread seeing Freshie's name on their class rolls. Mothers would come up with any number of reasons their kids may be too busy to play with little Freshie Lynn.

Linny was no better, really. Her boasting only seemed to increase. She would tell anyone who listened how wonderfully caring she was, raising Fern's daughter as her own, sacrificing for the child as she had because Fern abandoned the poor, sweet baby. Freshie had been told since the day Fern disappeared that her "selfish" mother just left her one day, never to return. Linny's goal was not only to debase Fern, but elevate herself. Of course, as had been the case with Conway, Linny wanted Freshie to adjust to the idea that Miss Linny was much better suited to parent her.

Linny and Conway had done a pretty fair job of keeping Freshie away from my sisters and me. Of course, I was easiest because I was living in the city and really only sent notes and letters on holidays and her birthday. Toile and Vernie did not see much of Freshie because, as a youngster, she didn't have a lot of freedom to get around town. For her twelfth birthday, however, Freshie wanted to have a party at the Beaumont Boutique, where she and her friends could spend the afternoon trying on clothes and using Vernie's materials to design their "dream bedrooms." At first Linny thought she could talk Freshie out of her party, but true to form, Freshie insisted.

On the day of the party, Vernie and Toile were both on hand to help the girls. They were quite looking forward to spending time with their niece. With her usual dramatic flair, Linny sashayed into the store first, decked out in her heels, gloves, and sunglasses, followed by Freshie Lynn and four other girls her age. Toile and Vernie didn't even seem to notice Linny as they greeted Freshie and her friends.

It was ridiculous for Linny to expect a warm reception from Vernie and Toile. She was a ridiculous woman, however, so she wouldn't expect anything else. She had commandeered a child that was not her own, squeezed her way between Fern and our niece, and fully expected that we would be grateful for her efforts. Instead, she received nothing from Toile and Vernie but professionalism, which Linny found quite offensive. After a few minutes sitting nearly invisible amidst all of the pre-teen fray, Linny made up an impressive excuse for having to leave and proclaimed that she would be back in two hours to fetch the girls.

Freshie and her friends had been led first to the decorating section of the shop, where Vernie had accumulated every type of fabric and décor. Vernie showed the crew where they could find various decorating items and explained that she would be on hand to answer any questions they might have. While her friends had fun with all of the decorating props, fabrics and supplies, Freshie found herself mesmerized by Vernie. There was something so familiar, so comforting about her mannerisms, her presence. Freshie was puzzled for a while as she took in the scene, not knowing what it was about Vernie that tickled her memory. In mild frustration, she leaned back on the pillows on which she had been sitting and closed her eyes. It was then that Freshie realized that Vernie had a voice exactly like her mother's.

It had been almost five years since Freshie had heard her mother's voice, and the shock overcame her. She quickly removed herself from the group and found a corner in which to sit. For the next thirty minutes, Freshie sat amidst a pile of furry pillows, unnoticed in the commotion of teenaged excitement, with her eyes shut, desperately trying to hear the voice that could have easily been Fern's. As she listened, memories began to emerge in Freshie's mind. Instead of pushing them away as she had in the past, Freshie let them linger. She began to remember her mother's smile, her eyes, the way she moved. She remembered moments when her mother held her when she had been sad or afraid, or tired. At last, Freshie's mind became simultaneously overcome with her mother's scent- a blend of cedar and wildflowers- and the memory she had from long before, when she had been sitting in her mother's arms watching fireflies.

Freshie had not been aware of the tears that had been streaming down her cheeks, perhaps because she was so intent on capturing the memories of her mother. She had kept her eyes closed as she sat in the huge pile of pillows and had become almost cocooned in bittersweet recollection, so much so that she heard her mother whisper her name. Freshie listened intently to see if she could hear it again- and in seconds, she did. Then, the third time she heard her mother say, "Freshie? Are you okay?" she felt a hand on her shoulder and her eyes opened. Before her she saw Toile, her beautiful, kind face full of concern. Confused, Freshie looked away, and then realized in a flash that her mother and her aunts sounded exactly alike.

In the months following her party, Freshie found herself thirsting for contact with her mother's family. When she could get away, Freshie would ride her bike to the Beaumont Boutique and park it in the alley behind the store. Then she would sneak inside where she would spend time with Toile and Vernie. She listened intently to stories of their childhood experiences with Fern, and learned more about her mother's wild spirit. She learned about the daughter Fern had taken from her many years before, a girl named "Mina", a Lakota name meaning "eldest daughter". Vernie and Toile would gush about Fern's bravery, marvel at her adventures, and sometimes they would cry for her heartache. During it all, Freshie began to understand that she had not been allowed to know her mother as she truly was. She was not a sum of her bad choices, as Conway had maintained. And she was not a selfish, unsophisticated embarrassment as Linny would have had Freshie believe.

Freshie grew increasingly angry at Conway and Linny. For years, they had been telling her half-truths about her mother, manipulating her memories, causing her to question everything she thought was real. Moreover, they had hidden their involvement in her mother's departure.

At first, Conway and Linny thought that her ire was contributable to teenage moodiness. As time went on, however, Freshie's tone became more accusatory, especially toward Linny. In response, Linny became more desperate to win back Freshie's affections. She gave her anything she wanted- freedom to hang out with friends, endless new clothes, shoes, records, parties- and nothing seemed to work. Nothing seemed to bring Freshie back under Linny's spell

I don't know why people are afraid of their children. Maybe the fear begins when the children are young, and by the time the kids grow up, fear has become a normal response. I have seen it happen so many times- a parent wants for nothing more than her child to love her, so she gives the child everything she can, hoping that the return will be love, gratitude, respect, loyalty...

Children don't need gifts, accommodating or pandering. They need solid ground. They need rules, stability, predictability, safety. It is absurd to believe that a child who was brought up believing that she is the "exception" to somehow learn respect and gratitude. Frankly, that makes as much sense as expecting someone to know Latin because they took a few swimming lessons.

And so, the absurdity continued in Conway's house. Conway opened his wallet, Linny shopped and spoiled, and Freshie rebelled. Freshie had lost any sense of enchantment she had ever felt toward her grandfather and Miss Linny. Freshie saw Linny, an older, more pathetic version of the woman she once admired and she now witnessed and understood her feeble attempts to be relevant, and she simultaneously loathed and pitied her. It was as if her heart had been a pendulum, pulled to one side from the time she was 7- the side of Linny and Conway and all that they represented. Finally, the pendulum was set free and her heart swung as far as it could in the opposite direction. Freshie felt disdain, resentment, and rage toward Conway and Linny. In fact, Freshie had determined that she would find a way out from under Conway Duque forever.

Though he was very adept at creating the image of a strong, successful, intelligent man, Conway Duque was terribly insecure. He also found himself quite disenchanted with his granddaughter. Freshie had been spoiled, he knew, in her youth and now she disgusted him with her sense of entitlement and lack of gratitude for all that he afforded her. He blamed Linny, of course. Now as he watched Linny fussing over Freshie, trying desperately to win her approval, he found that she repelled him. The two females had their own orbit, and it certainly was not around him.

He had been with Linny now for around twenty years, and had been relatively faithful to her. For years, she had been cautious, too, being sure to accompany him on as many out-of-town trips as she could. She also had made quite a habit of checking in on him at work, keeping her eye on his female employees. Conway was aware of her efforts, and as long as he was happy with her, Conway didn't seem to mind Linny's hovering. Frankly, he didn't see the benefit of what would certainly be an inconvenient sexual relationship with anyone else, until now. Now Conway was bored, tired and increasingly resentful, and Linny was otherwise occupied.

It was not as easy to find a good woman as it had been. He was also not nearly as young as he had been, but even at seventy years of age Conway was strikingly handsome. For a while, Conway had a series of flings with lesser known women. Then, one day in 1974 Conway left the house early to avoid yet another benign conversation with Linny who seemed desperate to cram words into his morning routine. (She would have to wait another few hours for Freshie to show herself.) He climbed into his F150, rolled the window down and breathed in the fresh morning air. Conway was in no hurry to get to the office, so he lazily trolled the neighborhood, his arm resting on the door frame soaking up the sunlight as it peeked through the trees.

The older neighborhoods in town had wide avenues, some even bisected by flowery medians. There was a different air about them than the newer developments with their flat lawns and seedling trees. Conway was driving down one of the more established, coveted streets when he caught site of the moving truck in front of a little white bungalow. He was familiar with the house. It belonged to a widow whose husband owned the local newspaper. Even in her later years, this woman prided herself on her beautiful gardens with extraordinary lilies, roses, hollyhocks and daisies. In the shade, she grew ferns and Hosta. Along the fence in the backyard grew wild strawberries and black raspberries. This day the yard looked as beautiful as ever, and yet it's beauty was nothing compared to the newly arrived woman who emerged from the front door.

Marlene was a sexpot. She had russet hair that was long, layered and wavy and her skin was golden tan- maybe just a bit olive. She must have been around fifty-five because she had the confidence of a mature, experienced woman, and yet she had the tight, rounded derrière and smooth legs of a twenty-year-old, which she highlighted in fashionable shorts and wedged espadrilles. Conway hurriedly parked his truck in the street and tumbled out, rushing to make an introduction. In a matter of moments, he was smitten.

Within a few days, Tarford Flats was agog with speculation about Miss Marlene. Men talked about her as if they were back in a Freshman locker room, and the women both feared and despised her. Baseless scandal grew about Marlene, her marital state, and her associations. Women and their sheepish husbands tended to avoid cavorting with Marlene and Conway because the new woman in town was rumored to be at the very least, sexually progressive.

I guess it was because divorce was still such a rarity in our small town that suspicions grew so wildly. Marlene was a knockout, so it was hard to imagine her husband may have abused or rejected her. He was supposedly a mid-level executive in the Union Pacific railroad which had operations out of Omaha. Because railroad men are known to travel, folks speculated that Marlene must have gotten bored, or lonely, and taken up with another man. That would certainly have been the only reason a red-blooded husband would turn his back on a woman like that.

Conway was intrigued and excited at the idea of being with Marlene. He found her experience and maturity to be a welcome change. And of course, he would not forget how she looked in shorts and heels. He was also fascinated by the way she smelled. He told my sisters and I on several occasions how nice Marlene smelled. It was a huge selling point, he figured, in convincing us of her qualities.

Conway was not interested in upsetting Linny. Perhaps he felt some measure of loyalty or responsibility toward her. In any case, he continued to see Marlene while Linny lived in his home. Folks who knew him well did not find this behavior surprising. Conway was not in the habit of taking much responsibility when it came to dismantling relationships, and public opinion was that whoever wanted a relationship with the man did so at their own risk. So, when Linny finally learned about his affair, folks didn't feel much sympathy. In fact, they had found Linny so irritating and entitled, they watched the drama unfold with fascination and a sense of retribution.

Marlene was very pleasant. She had made her acquaintance with Toile and Vernie soon after she moved into the bungalow, and my sisters genuinely liked her. Her relationship with their father was puzzling, as Marlene seemed too…smart, cultured, confident…. too good for him. And she did smell fantastic. In fact, at her request, Toile started carrying Marlene's favorite perfume in the Beaumont Boutique. It was called "Diorella," and it was quite pricey compared to the more popular "Love's baby soft", "Jean Nate" and "Charlie" brands, but Toile sensed that stocking the perfume would pay off when furtive husbands found out that their wives could smell like Miss Marlene, the sexpot.

She was right. Before long, several women in town smelled fantastic, and Toile's cosmetics counter was never busier. In fact, Toile's store had increasing sales of sexy lingerie, high heels and nail polish. Unwittingly, Miss Marlene had rejuvenated the intimate relationships of several couples in town.

The relationship between Conway and Linny, however, had never been so dull. Maybe she had been preoccupied with Freshie, maybe she had become utterly complacent in trying to maintain Conway's interest, or maybe she suffered from simple denial, but it was surprising how long it took Linny to figure out that Conway had been philandering. To his credit, he was quite adept at sneaking around with women.

Linny's epiphany finally arrived when Conway flew to Denver on a business trip. One of the newer girls in his office seemed surprised to see Linny at the market that weekend, and questioned if she was unwell. At Linny's obvious bewilderment, the young woman tried to explain that she knew it was none of her business, but that she could not conceive of a reason Linny would not be enjoying every amenity at the Broadmoor Resort with Mr. Duque. Linny was well aware of the Broadmoor. It was a glorious retreat for those who could afford it, and an unforgettably romantic experience to share with someone special. Yet, Linny was in Tarford Flats, alone.

Of course, she verified his reservation by calling the Denver hotel. The upbeat desk clerk on the other end of the line delivered the death blow in her well-crafted, overly polite tone.

Linny knew then that her time with Conway Duque was coming to a close. She was furious, of course, but her instinct to survive superseded her need for revenge. Immediately, Linny began to flip through her mental lists of other moneyed men in town to whom, like a dislodged deer tick, she could reattach herself.

There was one "unattached" man in Tarford Flats who met Linny's income standards. His name was Evan and he owned the corner drug store in town. Evan had never been married, and as far as Linny could learn, he had never had anything more than a congenial relationship with anyone in town. Evan was nearly 50 years old, but he looked much younger. It was not, however, because he was in wonderful physical health with a zestful countenance. Evan was a tall, slim, pale man with graying hair, hazel eyes and soft, thin skin. He actually looked like he hadn't spent any amount of time in the sun- even as a youth. He had no freckles, no markings or scars, and the only wrinkles he had presented themselves when he was deep in concentration.

Evan was considerate, intelligent and particular in his work. In the drug store, he comported himself in silence, and seemed desperate to avoid any contact beyond a simple business transaction.
I remember meeting Evan on a few occasions, and at those times I felt compelled to treat him as I would a field mouse hiding under a parked car. At first, he tried to process the interaction, and then, if things became overwhelming or somehow signaled danger, Evan would retreat to his shelves as a field mouse might hide near a tire.

The thing about mice- and Evan- and nearly every creature that is wired to be afraid is this: If a fearful creature is caught hiding under a tire, for instance, there must be a complete absence of threat for that creature to remove itself from the precarious spot. I am sure more scared creatures have allowed themselves to be crushed to death by a tire rather than summon the courage to get out from under it.

Such was the case with Evan. Looking back with the knowledge I have now, I could assume that Evan was a high-functioning Autistic man, but in the 1970's in a tiny town like Tarford Flats, Evan was just labeled "odd." That label, however, did not seem to interfere with his ability to run a drug store- with a little help from his parents- and it certainly did not impair his ability to get a druggist's license. Evan just happened to be in the perfect spot for a man who loved Chemistry and Biology and could earn a handsome living from behind a glass wall.

One day there appeared in the drug store window a sign indicating employment available at the soda counter. The soda counter in the drug store was a popular after school hang-out for kids. Evan's mother, Edna, was a cheerful, pleasant, rounded woman who seemed to love the teens who stopped in for a snack. Edna, however, was quite old and easily exhausted by late afternoon, so she convinced Evan to try to hire someone to fill in for her. Because he was so easily overwhelmed by loud noises and crowds of people, Evan knew he needed to find an assistant.

Toile and Vernie encouraged Freshie to apply for the job. Freshie was naturally beautiful, but in no way overwhelming. Her beauty was more warming, and familiar- and completely safe. Her voice was clear but gentle, and slightly deeper than her peers. Her movements were like her mother's: fluid and strong. She would be someone Evan could trust.

In the years since she discovered the lies about her mother, Freshie became surprisingly adept at reading people. Perhaps she was able to tap into the natural abilities that seemed to run through Mama and her daughters, or perhaps it was out of sheer resolve never to be fooled again, when it came to ferreting out a con artist, Freshie was as good as any seasoned detective. Similarly, she was also keenly aware of people who may fall prey to such manipulation.

When she met Evan, Freshie was instantly aware that he was a kind, nervous, honest man who, if anything, was in need of protection. It may have seemed a strange friendship to one who didn't know them well, but Evan was naïve, and terribly vulnerable and Freshie felt compelled to shield him. Freshie had spent the better part of her childhood watching Linny Spitt and Conway Duque. She knew every trick ever tried to swindle a gentleman.

The two got along famously. Freshie was mindful not to allow too much noise or drama to filter back to Evan's area, which he appreciated greatly. Edna appreciated Freshie too, and found her to be surprisingly dependable. Freshie would come to the drug store directly after school and stay until it closed in the evening, and spend most of the day on Saturdays there too. When things at the soda counter were slow, Freshie would help to clean and organize the shelves of the pharmacy, arranging the first-aid section, the cosmetics, stationery, and small gift items. Evan and his mother recognized the value of Freshie's input on new fads among young adults and eventually asked Freshie to help them keep their merchandise up to date.

Freshie loved her job. She loved how she felt when she was at work. Things were so different in the drug store than they had been in every other area of her life. Communication with Evan, Edna, and their customers was real, honest and sincere. She felt appreciated, valuable, and part of a unified team. Freshie felt respected and honorable, which she grew to cherish more than anything else.

In the time she spent with Edna and Evan, Freshie became more like herself than she had been in years. She was friendly with customers, caring with Evan, she joked wonderfully with Edna, who so appreciated the way Freshie could bring levity to the tense moments in which Evan struggled. Freshie was becoming centered, less affected by petty things- and she was becoming adventuresome, kind of like her mother. Freshie let her hair, golden like Fern's, grow long and wavy. She tied it up in a loose bun on top of her head (much like the modern girls do these days.) More significantly, Freshie began to allow that love and appreciation she felt from Edna take hold inside of her. Strangely, that love slowly changed the burning resentment of Conway and Linny, their duplicity and their selfishness, into pity. Freshie began to see them as they had become- small, desperate, insular.

Linny was certainly small, and she was certainly desperate. Her objective to ensnare another host to support her lifestyle was the only thing on her mind.

The day that Linny Spitt chose to make her move on Evan could not have been more perfect. (At least that was how Freshie saw it when she shared the story with her aunts). Evan had just returned from spending a few days in Omaha. He and his mother had attended "market," where retailers go to see new items available with which to stock their shelves. The event had been chaotic and loud, and the weather in Omaha had been unseasonably warm and heavy with humidity. Evan's senses had been completely overwhelmed with the barrage of perfume spritzes, hair crème samples and the like. All he wanted was to go to a cool, quiet place away from the crowd-somewhere he could find peace and a sense of order again.

Edna sensed that her son was not completely recovered from the fracas the next day, a least enough to go back to work, however, Evan insisted he would be fine. With his nerves still a bit frayed, he stayed behind the glass wall as much as he could and tried to avoid unnecessary human contact. The day had become another muggy, hot mess discouraging many folks from venturing out from their homes. The drug store had been empty all morning, so by early afternoon Edna felt confident she could step out for a bit. She grabbed her handbag and announced that she needed to walk to the Post Office, leaving Evan unattended. Linny had been waiting outside the drug store in her bright yellow convertible for several minutes, trying to come up with the perfect conversation starters. As soon as she saw Edna bustling away, Linny descended like a bird of prey on Evan's store.

Linny Spitt did nothing quietly, and her introduction to Evan was no different. She trounced into his store wearing her typical tight pants and ridiculous heels with her hair sprayed until it was stiffly formed- like rusty cotton candy- in an "up-do." On her tan arms were scores of thin metal bracelets that clanged like chimes with her every move. Linny had applied more make-up than usual this day. Her eyelids just under her dramatically penciled eyebrows looked like they had been coated with milky lithium grease. The area closer to her eye was a metallic blue, followed by a royal blue so dense it could only have been applied wet, like paint. She had bright pink Bonnie Bell lip gloss and hot pink nail polish that matched her shoes and her patent leather bag. The most noticeable feature, however, had to be her perfume. Linny had bathed in some kind of floral mix which smelled as if it had soured, like an odor emanating from a dumpster behind a flower shop.

She was so intent on making an impression on poor Evan that Linny failed to notice an acorn that had been kicked in from the sidewalk onto the floor of the drugstore. In one move, Linny set the ball of her foot on the acorn, which threw off her balance just enough to send her toppling over into a precariously arranged display of feminine hygiene products. The display collapsed, causing a downpour of boxes of feminine napkins, belts, cleansers and sprays which seemed to last for a full minute, punctuated by a stream of obscenities let loose by Linny and her perfectly glossed lips.

When Edna returned from the post office, a bedraggled Linny pushed past her, still cursing and stumbling over feminine products. On her last stomp in the store, Linny managed to stab her heel through a full bottle of Massengill Douche, which remained wedged onto the four-inch spike, leaving a trail of liquid behind Linny as she staggered to her car.

Edna did her best to clear a path through the tousled and torn boxes and bottles to prevent any further accidents with customers, and finally, after a brief search she found poor Evan, cowering and skittish in a corner behind the glass wall. Miss Linny Spitt had quickly proven herself too much for him to handle.

CHAPTER 9: DARREN

"One of the many truisms I have found in working with couples and individuals is this: whatever worth you see in yourself as a member of the human experience is directly proportional to the treatment you expect from others. If a person feels truly and intrinsically valuable, he or she will live and comport his or herself in such a way that mistreatment will not take hold in his or her life. Conversely, (barring mental illness) if a person feels as if he or she has little worth, he or she will accept that same regard from others. It is nearly impossible to change the relationship a person has with the world and others in it if there is not a change in self-concept first. In short, the level at which we esteem ourselves predicts our relationships with others. Good or bad, we will continue to involve ourselves in relationships that mirror our sense of self-worth."
<u>Creating Healthy Relationships the EZ Way with Jessie Duque</u>

His self-image had always been spectacular, maybe because he knew he was the most handsome man Tarford Flats had seen since Conway Duque, or maybe because his mother filled his head with endless ideas of grandeur. Darren Turnbull had an air of confidence and a jovial manner that drew almost everyone to him. He was six foot four, lean and muscular with broad shoulders, narrow hips and strong, athletic legs. He wore designer boots, Levi's 501's with one of several heavy silver belt buckles, and an ivory Stetson hat that matched his perfect teeth. His powerful shoulders and torso were accentuated by the crisp button-down shirt he wore tucked in and "casually" unbuttoned at the top. On special occasions when Darren dressed up, he wore even nicer boots and sleek, fitted polyester pants instead of his usual jeans.

At every moment, he was flawless. His nails and cuticles were supple and gleaming as if freshly buffed. His naturally wavy chestnut hair was just long enough to make him look hard-working yet respectable, and the way it curled at the top of his starched collars made him seem adventurous, youthful and exciting. And he smelled amazing. I would not have been surprised if Darren had found some eager perfumer to create a custom cologne that combined the scents of freshly washed laundry, rosemary, leather and cinnamon that left many admirers woozy in his wake.

In the few years he had been involved with the family business, Darren had created a farm implement empire. Turnbull Farming Equipment dealerships could be found in most sizeable towns east of North Platte. With the level of inventory he was able to move, no small-time dealerships could compete with his prices and service programs. Because he had businesses in so many areas, Darren had a direct line with lenders in most small towns. It was during a "donut and coffee session" with such lenders at a small-town bakery that Darren heard about a loophole in Nebraska tax law that stated if a property owner was behind in tax payments, another citizen could pay those tax bills, effectively putting a lien on the property. If, after a few cycles of this practice, the property owner had a series of missed payments, and the other party had made those payments, the other party could legally assume ownership of said property. Never one to ignore opportunity, Darren set his mind to accumulating that property.

Darren instructed the finance manager of each of his dealerships to notify him if any implement accounts fell into default status. Economic times had been tough in the 1970's- especially for farmers. Darren knew that as farmers missed payments on their equipment, chances were that they were missing their tax payments as well. At first, Darren dug into the family fortune to finance his acquisitions. Next, he took advantage of government programs that pay the farmers not to produce. Finally, he formed yet another branch of Turnbull Enterprises which chose the very best of his properties to transform into magnificent estate developments.

As Darren began boasting about his upcoming tracts of country estates, he drew the interest of many of the old-moneyed folks in town as well as folks who were looking to move out of Omaha to a more peaceful existence.

Before long, Darren Turnbull had achieved what he had been looking for years ago in California. He was becoming famous. Soon his name began to appear on sponsor lists for member-guest golf tournaments in Lincoln and Omaha, and on the donor boards for the zoos and museums. He was appointed a Knight of Ak-sar-ben- an Omaha philanthropic group- and used that connection to involve Toile and the Beaumont Boutique in helping to prepare for that year's annual Aksarben Coronation Ball. Darren loved the life of a public persona. Being Darren, he also loved the trappings of such celebrity. He was at his best when people were watching.

It was at one of the Aksarben events that Darren met his future wife. She was a tall, lithe, graceful debutante- and much like Darren's mother had been, she was the daughter of a successful politician. Her name was Cecelia and she was 6 years younger than Darren. She wasn't blonde, tan and voluptuous like Darren's many other women had been. Cecelia was more aloof, thin and pale. She had fine features and a reserved manner, which was in considerable contrast the gregarious Darren. In his much-practiced manner, however, Darren was able to sweep Cecelia (whom he adoringly nicknamed "Cece") gently but swiftly off her feet. He did the same with her overtly discriminating parents, and within months, Darren and Cece were married in a lovely ceremony held in one of Omaha's most established churches, with nearly three hundred people in attendance.

Leona Turnbull made sure everyone knew that so many people wanted to attend, the seats were filled thirty minutes before the wedding. The others had to stand in the choir loft or out in the foyer trying desperately to witness what was dubbed in the Omaha Herald society section the "wedding of the year."

Almost perfectly timed with the ringing in of each new year, Cece had given birth to a series of sons. They had five in all, each one named for a county in Nebraska. By the time 1975 rolled around, Darren and Cece and their children were living in a beautiful newly built home in one of Darren's developments. Although it was well known that they had hired help, Cece rarely left the house to venture out and socialize with the other ladies of Tarford Flats. It was rumored that she struggled with exhaustion.

When it was incumbent upon her to accompany her husband to campaign events and fundraisers, Cece dutifully stuck right by his side with a pleasant smile pasted on her pallid face. Of course, Cece had been raised amidst the culture of politics. As the year of campaigning and hobnobbing, bootlicking and glad-handing went on, however, she seemed to appear with him less often. Folks assumed that she was perhaps tired, or visiting family, or quite likely pregnant again.

In contrast, Darren seemed to be seen everywhere. He had begun to campaign for a seat on the State Legislature, and frankly, he was expected to trounce the competition. With the exposure he had to the Hollywood culture, and the anemic morality of those involved, Darren had been able to develop an effective political persona. He was a natural- an incredibly hollow-hearted, smarmy success.

Some evenings, when Darren wasn't prepared for the demands of a wife and five boys, he would steal away a few hours at an out-of-the-way bar on the county line. The campaigning was intense, and Darren had found himself trying to remember the myriad vows and promises he had made to constituents. Remarkably, even Darren, who thrived on the attention of inspired followers, needed an occasional escape.

This place was perfect. It was situated by a small lake, behind a thick grove of trees and it could hardly be seen from any paved road. It had been built decades before for use as a supper club, complete with a stage for performers and a large dance area with polished parquet flooring. Over time the live musicians had been replaced by a jukebox, and the dancefloor was used only sparingly by older couples who carefully shuffled their way through bygone dance steps.

More often the bar and adjoining restaurant were used by bird hunters who liked to debrief the day's hunt over a glass of scotch whiskey or a cold can of beer.

It was still months before goose season would be in full swing and Darren knew this place would be as safe as any he could find to have a few unfiltered moments to himself. Even a stray reporter would have trouble lurking around this place thanks to the owner's massive Saint Bernard who alerted anyone within earshot of an oncoming stranger.

Darren liked to sit in the corner, his back to the windows that faced the river. His habit was to get change at the bar when he ordered his first beer, then make his way to the jukebox where he would select every song by Don McLean, Jim Croce, and Gordon Lightfoot he could find. Then he would settle back in his seat, waiting for the waitress to bring him subsequent beers and a relish tray complete with pickled herring and goose liver pate.

When Darren got his first look at Linny Spitt that evening he had already had four beers and his table was littered with empty cracker wrappers. Linny was up to her usual presentation of tight pants and high heels, although she had acquired some new wedged heels that complimented her sheer bohemian top and ornate "folk-art" earrings.

She strolled over to the empty bar where she ordered a glass of Rose' wine and sat on a barstool. Darren watched as Linny sat, her right shoulder to him. He looked at her pretty ankles and caught a glimpse of her reflection as she used a pocket compact to check her lipstick. Coyly, Linny slid off the barstool and carried her drink over to the jukebox where she began to wag her hips ever-so-slightly to the music. The last of Darren's selections came to an end, which prompted Linny to set her half-empty glass on a nearby table and begin to look through her purse for a quarter.

Darren rose from his seat and in smooth, heroic fashion, approached Linny with a stack of quarters in his outstretched hand. Together, he and Linny programmed the Jukebox to play their favorite songs. After making several selections, Linny looked up at Darren, who was being typically charming. Linny giggled and swayed toward him, ultimately losing her balance on her less familiar wedge heels.

As Linny reached out to brace herself, her purse swung just enough to tap the half-filled wine glass, which threatened to tip over and spill its contents on the table. Darren swiftly swooped up the glass with one hand and Linny with the other. Linny, embarrassed, exclaimed that she must not have eaten enough before drinking her wine.

Gallant as ever, Darren led Linny to his table and asked her to enjoy his relish tray while he refilled her drink. It appeared that she had composed herself by the time Darren returned with a fresh glass of Rose'. Linny smiled gratefully as she twirled a carrot stick between her manicured fingertips. She explained without prompting that she was expecting to meet a girlfriend that night, and realized after she had gotten her wine that she had mistaken the day. She finished her sentence with "so...." and raised her eyebrows in obvious flirtation.

Darren had been in this situation many times before. Even if he was unfamiliar with Linny Spitt, he was aware of her reputation. What's more, he was familiar with many women just like her. Darren knew from the moment Ms. Spitt walked into the bar that she would be his. He knew she would leave the bar a few minutes before him, that she would find her way into the bed of his big, beautiful pickup truck with the custom camper shell on the back. And he knew he could claim her in the parking lot without anyone being the wiser. Everything that transpired between Darren and Linny, everything that took place between the barstool and the truck was just a game to him. It was a game he always won.

Linny took their interactions to be far more serious than a game. Over the next few months, Linny put every effort toward keeping this new man interested in her. Linny spent more time sunbathing and having her hair and nails done, she updated her wardrobe and read any articles she could find about the art of seduction. Linny planned to invest everything she could in her relationship with Darren Turnbull, and she expected a huge return. History had evidenced to Ms. Spitt that relationships are little more than transactions, and that she had something to sell. Linny imagined herself a prize to any man, even one who was already married. The way she saw it, a man like Darren would relish having a frisky sex-kitten at the ready to counter-balance his stressful campaign and squeaky-clean family-man image. Hadn't his eager response to her flirtation at the bar been proof enough that he was interested? Linny was convinced that she had Mr. Turnbull under her spell.

But Darren Turnbull was an ass. After a few months of fooling around with Linny Spitt he lost interest and stopped taking her calls. He was handsome, arrogant, entitled, rich… and he lived by certain creeds: First, why buy the cow if you can get the milk for free? And second, wealthy men don't buy dairy cows- especially old, dried up ones. Wealthy men buy thoroughbred horses and go on to sire thoroughbred colts. As far as Darren was concerned, he had acquired an exceptional thoroughbred mare when he married his wife. Her lineage was supreme, and he intended to weave himself inextricably into that bloodline. He had no intention of giving Linny anything but a few rolls in the hay- a quick scratch of an itch-and putting her out to pasture.

When Linny realized she had been used in such a way, she confronted Darren. It happened after a late summer campaign rally in the park. Darren was usually surrounded by his family and various campaign staffers at these events, but on this particular day Linny got lucky. His wife and boys were visiting family in Omaha and several of his staff were involved in steering the crowd. Linny quietly approached Darren from behind and tugged at his sleeve, her face already posed with a juicy pout and wide, mascara laden eyes.

Darren's reaction was jarring. His instant fury caused her eyes to widen even more and brim with frightened tears. Linny's hand sprang from his sleeve to her face as she tried to shield herself from his anger. Like a viper, Darren seem to coil over her as he spit his venomous words into Linny's horror-stricken face. Darren made it clear that she was not, nor would she ever be, someone he valued. He seethed as he warned her not to stand near him, touch him, speak to him, or attempt in any way to contact him again. She was anathema to him. She was nothing at all and he turned his back on her.

Angry, confused and deeply wounded, Linny tried to salvage some control over the moment, to strike back at Candidate Turnbull. Impulsively, she threatened him: "What do you think people around here would say if they knew what you done to me?"

She grew to regret her words as she watched Darren inhale deeply, square his shoulders and turn around to face her. By the time his face met hers his expression had grown cold and terrifying. His eyes looked like those of a predator- completely devoid of sympathy- of any human emotion at all. Darren Turnbull stepped menacingly close, leaned over her and hissed, "Are you really that stupid? Who would believe you? What could someone like me, with my life, my wife, my future, possibly want from someone like you?"

Linny's face was burning and her ears were ringing as she watched Darren turn from her and put his hand on the shoulder of one of his many buddies. She watched him give a hearty laugh, motion with his head in her direction and thought she could see his mouth form the word "gross…" Then Darren broke into another grin, another laugh, another shoulder slap and was swallowed by the crowd.

Returning to Tarford Flats had been unsettling for Texas. The smaller things- those under the surface- were so different, yet on the surface it all looked the same. Texas remembered a time when beavers had built a large enough dam to interrupt water flow to the Platte river. As the water level fell, folks began to see a surprising amount of debris that had gathered and dispersed along the river bottom. There were several old tires, a rusty cattle grate, an ancient icebox, yard and farm tools, and plenty of mysterious pieces he could not identify. It was a strange realization that so many unwelcome things could accumulate in a river forming, over time, various eddies, holes, and entrapments and changes in current that can be quite treacherous yet are imperceptible to one casually looking over the water's surface. This thought stuck in his mind as Texas tried to reconcile the thoughts and feelings of his boyhood with the understanding he held now as a more worldly, experienced young man.

When he first returned from Columbia in 1973, Texas lived with his parents. Toile always kept her home beautiful and comfortable, yet Texas quickly began to feel edgy, confined when he was there. Of course, it is completely normal for a young man to want to leave home and make his way, in the same way a young lion leaves the pride of his father to begin his own.

In the Spring of 1974, Texas procured a pop-up camper from a friend needed to sell it fast and for cash. The camper was set up next to the Turnbull's barn which sat embedded deeply within K.C.'s fields. In the heat of the summer, the camper was kept on the North side of the barn, which shaded it throughout the day and kept everything inside surprisingly cool. At least, this was the reason Texas gave to anyone who asked why he wanted to sleep in a camper by the barn. This, and the fact that he loved the sounds of the wildlife in the fields and trees at night.

As the sun set, the darkness would come alive with coyotes yipping and howling, foxes "gekkering", and the strange emanations of tree frogs, toads, crickets and owls. Occasionally, raccoons would venture out to investigate any new scent of food or garbage that was yet undiscovered. The noise and activity were not unsettling, however. In fact, to Texas it was remarkably calming. Texas welcomed the distraction from his internal noise, his worries about his parents, about his crop, about enchanting Lucia and how he longed to see her again.

Most useful of all, the ambient sounds of nature provided a reverse alarm system. Most animals are keenly aware of the presence of humans, especially those who are unfamiliar. When a stranger arrives to the area, the usual sounds of nature are silenced, which can be as alarming as a blaring siren to someone who is habituated to the nighttime noises. And Texas definitely needed to know if anyone came near the barn.

While he had been working with his father, Texas slowly took over the management of the barn along with the lesser fields. Ken Cash had come to realize that he enjoyed the big, predictable, well-mapped plots and it was on those he planted the most uniform, predictable crops with the best consistency year after year. It was the smaller, asymmetrical plots- laid upon odd drainage patterns or among groves of trees- that drove him to despair. He was relieved when Texas asked to take them over. Texas had wanted to experiment with unconventional farming techniques, crop engineering and so forth.

When his son approached him with the idea of splitting up the farm in such a way, K.C. felt as though he finally had a way free of the torment, he had experienced in trying to force the natural land into a perfect system. K.C. gladly handed over the plots with the joyful expectation that he would never have to look upon them again.

Texas immediately started tilling up the dying crops and laying out new planting designs. Unbeknownst to any of us at the time, Texas had managed to break down the process of cross-engineering Marijuana with psychedelic mushrooms- and it all started with corn smut.

Corn smut is awful stuff. It is a fungus that infects the roots and stems of the plants, but isn't outwardly manifest until the corn is nearly mature. It is then that a darkened bulb of fungus, like a grey sack of spores begins to emerge in the place of a kernel in the ear of the corn. Then another kernel begins to change, becoming gray and swollen. Before long the entire tip of the ear can become infected, bursting with gray sacks filled with smut spores. The most difficult thing about corn smut is not the ruined cobs, but the soil, which by the end of a season of corn smut has been completely contaminated with the stuff. And, by cruel design, even the coldest winter will not kill the fungus off once it is in the ground.

The only way to respond is to treat it with fungicide for a season- and during that season either risk trying to plant a different type of crop entirely or nothing at all. This is the true cost of the havoc brought upon by corn smut. It is a total loss of at least two years' harvest.

Texas had figured out how to deliberately saturate the soil with another kind of fungus- one extracted from high-grade psychedelic mushrooms. Moreover, he designed his precariously lain plots in such a way that the fungus would refresh through trickle-down irrigation.

It was an ingenious plan, really. Each plot of land was arranged on a slope, with rows of marijuana plants growing in horizontal lines, interspersed every few rows with a furrow of spores. The larger plants would shade the fungus, allowing it to grow even in sunny areas. The spores would ride the water droplets to the base of each plant, becoming absorbed in the soil. Texas would occasionally rejuvenate the spore population at the uppermost rows of the plot and allow gravity and water flow to disperse the new spores to the plants below. By the end of his first harvest, Texas had perfected the system and had an outstanding marijuana crop.

True to his intentions, K.C. had kept his distance both in the fields and in the barn. The old barn made him crazy anyway, especially now that Texas was sharing in its use. Texas did not value fastidiousness the way his father did. Tools had been put in the wrong places and were sometimes put away dirty or broken. More often than not, the barn floor was littered with used rags, sloppily folded tarps and a variety of spilled fertilizer pellets. There was a rickety staircase along the south wall that led to a large hayloft, however over the past few years, Texas had begun to store a collection of tin buckets, half-used oil or fuel cans, and tractor hitches along the bottom steps, making the climb upward nearly impossible.

The barn itself was inconveniently located. It sat at the end of a poorly graded dirt path that was lined with scraggly Russian olive trees that grew wild in the region. Anyone with a nice car tended to avoid driving down paths like that, where a wayward branch with several well-hidden thorns could do quite a bit of damage to an expensive paint job. The road itself was miserable to drive. More than once a sedan was high-centered on a ridge between dried mud-tracks. In truth, by this time hardly anyone besides Texas and his father even remembered that the barn was there. And now K.C. refused to step foot in it.

Of course, this was all by design. Texas was well aware of the repellant nature of a messy barn where his father was concerned. He knew that eventually K.C. would avoid the place altogether and would rather send Texas to fetch whatever he might need. This allowed Texas full and unrestricted access to use the barn however he needed, and he needed to dry out his crop.

Just out of view from the main level, Texas had filled every foot of the hayloft with drying racks for his marijuana plants. When space grew scarce, he expanded by running wires between the trusses of the barn and hanging plants on those too.

With his first year completed, Texas had already made a surprising amount of money. He squirreled half away in an old root cellar near the barn. The other half he sent to Daniel and his family in Columbia. He felt indebted to his friend and hoped to reunite with him soon. He also hoped this gesture would remind Lucia that he hoped for a future with her. Growing even more wary of small-town gossip, Texas also knew that acquiring a sizeable bank account so quickly after starting to farm would draw all sorts of curiosity and speculation. No place was truly "confidential" in Tarford Flats.

Knowing this, Texas resolved to continue to toil away in his fields on his own. He could not risk anyone realizing his ingenious engineering, especially as it had proven so incredibly profitable. The only partner he trusted was implementing Texas's system in his own fields, twenty-four hundred miles away on the mountainsides of Eastern Columbia.

Daniel and his family were having success similar to that on the Turnbull farm. In fact even better because their plants did not have to contend with the strong winds that graze the surface of the Nebraska plains. With the money Texas had been sending, they were able to build stronger supports for their soil that might be otherwise washed down the slopes. There were also increased security measures, better quality fertilizers and pest control, and finally, the construction of a climate-controlled shelter for drying the marijuana.

Because the neighbors were curious and close by, Daniel and his family were careful not to show any outward signs of increased wealth when it came to their home. As tempting as it was to enlarge their home or increase their conveniences, they knew that to improve their situation would spur speculation that they could not afford. So things appeared quite unchanged for Daniel and his brothers.

Lucia, however, continued to change, to mature, and to realize the feelings that had taken root deep inside of her for the young American farmer she had known. In reflecting on the time she spent with Texas, Lucia felt she had been foolish, preoccupied with childish things, trivial in the things she had said. She vowed that if she were to have another chance to see him, Lucia would confess her love for Texas, hold him tightly and breathe in his scent deeply enough that it would be a part of her forever and she would never forget it.

_____

When Linny entered the big stone house she was completely downtrodden. She had been mocked and humiliated by the man on whom she had hung her hopes. Her sole focus had been Darren Turnbull, whom she was sure could pull her out of her spiraling situation with Conway. As she made her way to the Master bedroom, she heard Conway summon her from the den, which was toward the rear of his home. His tone was stony and left her with chills. Linny was suddenly filled with dread that he had learned of the scene in the park that morning. Linny had not yet considered the number of people who might have witnessed the exchange between her and Darren- and had no doubt that many of them would have enjoyed upsetting her- or Conway- with the exposure.

Conway was seated in a large leather chair in the corner of the den. The curtains were heavy and kept the room quite dim. There was a single lamp lit on the small round table next to Conway. On a larger coffee table in front of him sat a dark green metal box that appeared to have a broken lock. The box was sitting with the lid open and it contained only a few paper scraps.

Genuinely puzzled, Linny looked to Conway for some explanation. Seething, Conway explained that he had gone down to his "gun room," which was locked up tight, because he was going to pull some money out of his safe. Conway explained that the safe was closed and locked, but he found the now broken cashbox on a workbench next to the safe. It had been emptied of roughly twenty-five thousand dollars.

Seeing Linny's shocked expression only infuriated Conway, who was convinced that she was trying to trick him. As she stood trying to make sense of his words, he charged across the den and tightly gripped her arms. With a darkened countenance that terrified her, Conway spat his contemptuous words at Linny.

"I know it was you. I know it. Only a wretched, ungrateful wench like you would steal from a man who has given her so much."

Confused, Linny struggled for words but none came. She could have told him that nearly everyone who had visited the house knew where Conway had kept the key to his gun room, that they were often next to him when he pulled if from its hiding spot so that he could show off his rare guns or knives.

She could have reminded him that he kept the combination to his safe in a notebook on the shelf of the workbench, and that it would have taken a person less than five minutes to find it. But no words came. At least not from Linny's mouth. Conway, on the other hand, managed to spit a few more from his. Specifically and without hesitation, he directed Linny to pack whatever of her possessions would fit in that nice car of hers and to be out of his house in forty-eight hours.

Linny tried for a while to organize herself and find some way to begin packing her things. After an hour or so of staring into various closets, she was overcome with a need to escape her dismal reality, if even for a while. Conway had left after their confrontation and now the house was dark and ominously silent. Growing increasingly frantic, Linny increased her pace as she made her way to the front door. She found her purse and keys where she had left them on the entryway table, and grabbed for them mid-stride. She couldn't shake the dread she began to feel in that place.

Within a few minutes, Linny emerged from the supermarket with a six-pack of Coors, a bag of fresh popcorn and a grocery bag filled with a pack of cigarettes, toiletries, a bottle of orange juice and a half-dozen cinnamon rolls. She drove to the DeLux Motor Inn where she gave the clerk a phony name and paid cash to rent a room for the night. Without taking a moment to put her things in the motel room, Linny climbed into her long, yellow convertible and started to drive.

At some point Linny found herself out near the Turnbull farm, on the south edge down close to the river. She had been listening to The Eagles on the 8-track tape deck Conway had installed for her years before. She turned onto a narrow dirt road, killed the engine, and watched the last moments of the sunset. As the sky turned purple, Linny could feel the humidity, which is at its peak on the hot August afternoons, begin to lift, allowing the cool breeze to brush across her face and shoulders. The fireflies came out, one by one, until the air around her sparkled. Unlike most folks, Linny did not enjoy a sense of peace and calm as evening fell. It was as if the cool air caused her heart to harden, erasing whatever warmth she had left to feel. Very soon, Linny began to seethe with iced fury as she replayed the events of the day, the events of the past months and years.

It is an interesting thing how people are able to gather evidence to support an idea, even if that idea is without real foundation. They come up with a belief about their behavior, the behavior of others, a belief about why things are the way they are..., and then they conform the truth like warm, moist clay into whatever shape it must take to fit that belief.

Such was the case with Linny as she reflected in the dark fields that night. She was so very angry. She was angry that she ended up in a backward place like Tarford Flats, angry that Conway never saw fit to marry her, angry that she had been used by so many men- men of wealth and power- who should have shared more of that with her. She was jealous of Toile and K.C, who had so many things handed to them, jealous of Vernie, Georgeanne, even of Fern, who got to escape the demands of motherhood and put that responsibility directly on Linny's kind shoulders. She wanted what was due to her and was tired of waiting and hoping that someone else would give it to her.

And so it was that in the midst of dazzling fireflies and star-filled skies that Linny, cold and livid, conceived of a thought to get her revenge. She started the car, and carefully backed out of the field. With the top down and speakers playing "witchy woman, she's got the moon in her eyes...", Linny set her jaw and headed for town, straight for Evan's drug store.

CHAPTER 10: THE COMEUPPANCE

"It is difficult to say how any one person would respond to enormous stress, whether that stress is internal or external. We know that when the brain becomes overstressed, the frontal lobe where rationality prevails becomes, in a way, overridden, and the brain relies on primal instinct. This is when reactions rather than actions rule behavior. Often, you will see one of three responses to the overly stressful situation commonly referred to as: Fight, Flight or Freeze. "Fight" often looks exactly how one would expect, with clenched fists, heightened awareness, increase vocal volume and aggression. "Flight" can be either a physical effort to get away from the situation, a cognitive break ("disassociation") in which a person's awareness is removed from a situation, or seeking to alter one's state of awareness through substances or other addictions. Finally, "Freeze" can be observed when a person shuts down functioning, cannot speak or react, or such reactions are incredibly slow. Many instances of a person "freezing" are mistaken for that person being deliberately noncompliant. In any situation involving the override of the frontal lobe, it may take several minutes after the high-stress situation has ended for the person to become cognizant again.... It is a rare person indeed who can fully function under extreme stress. These people are those who make ideal soldiers, firefighters, law enforcement and others who have had intense and consistent training in such high-stress situation, Living with Anxiety the EZ Way with Jessie Duque

Linny was feeling wild. As she drove her convertible along the dark country road toward town she vacillated between rage and excitement. She experienced intermittent flickers of self-congratulation and concern that she may be going crazy. The further along she travelled down that road, however, the more resolved she became. She just needed to figure out the details of her plan.

After rolling onto main street, Linny found a spot to park that was just obscured enough to give her a view of the drug store without being seen by anyone inside. The lights were on and a few customers sat at the soda counter. Freshie looked to be alone in the place, cleaning the counters and preparing to close up. Eventually, the folks at the counter finished their drinks and left payment by their empty mugs. Freshie smiled, thanked them, and cordially walked them to the door which she locked after they walked out.

As she watched Freshie tend to her closing tasks, Linny was again filled with anger- and envy. Freshie was so youthful and pretty. Her skin was flawless- including the freckles that fell lightly across her nose. She was kind and graceful- both traits of which Linny realized Freshie had not learned from her. As much as she had tried, Linny had not been able to remove Fern, Georgeanne, or any of the Duque women from Freshie. Even restricting their access had not worked. Freshie had become like them anyway.

It was then that Linny knew that her suspicions about Freshie and her family were correct. Conway had told her for years that his former wife had tricked and betrayed him, how she was just interested in his money and wanted to take as much as she could get, all while making him suffer. Because even the most absurd statements can seem true after they're heard enough times, Linny had chosen to believe Conway. She wanted to see him as flawless, and faultless, and maybe someone she could save from his horrible ex-wife. So, she accepted everything he had said about Georgeanne, even as the rest of the world disagreed. Linny concluded that she and Conway were all the wiser for seeing through that façade. Now, as she looked through the lit windows of the corner drug store, Linny was convinced that the young woman inside had created the same kind of façade.

The drug store's lights went off. Freshie emerged from the back entrance and began the task of unlocking her bicycle. Fueled by a sense of injustice, Linny strode toward Freshie. Unable to cover her surprise in seeing a figure approaching her in the dark recesses of the alley, Freshie recoiled and let out a yip. Linny figured it was the slip of a guilty conscience that caused the girl to be defensive. Being convinced as ever that she had been wronged at every turn, Linny proceeded to unleash a tirade of blame and accusations.

Strangely, Freshie was not afraid as Linny's rage continued to hurl toward her. In fact, she seemed to transcend it all, moving her consciousness away from the storm outside of her, to a place separate from it all, where she found herself sitting in fresh grass, aware of the tender blades tickling the soft hair on her skin, feeling the warmth of the sun. Freshie took refuge in this moment, in this memory. She had been here before, she knew. It was long ago, Freshie remembered, and she was playing with a ladybug.

Calmly, and without any noticeable change in her affect, Freshie brought herself back to the alley behind the pharmacy. She had no idea how long Linny had been carrying on. Freshie felt surprisingly removed from Linny and her tantrum. How strange it was that she had no love for this woman who had played "mother" to her for so long. It was betrayal, Freshie concluded, that had caused her feelings for the wretch to morph from love to anger, then ultimately to pity and aloof disgust.

Freshie's attention awakened when Linny became quiet. The change was sudden, like the end of a monsoon, leaving just the slightest rainfall to finish out the storm. Linny had composed herself and spoke in a quiet but very serious tone. Linny began to reveal her intentions to exact revenge on Toile and Vernie, K.C and Darren Turnbull, and anyone else Linny held responsible for her misery. She then leveled a threat directly at the young woman standing before her: "Freshie, you are going to do exactly what I tell you, or so help me, I will do everything in my power to make sure everyone knows it was you that stole that money from Conway."

Summer sidewalk sales were huge annual events in Tarford Flats in the 1970's and 1980's. On a Saturday near the end of August, wares would appear to spill out of the stores that could contain them any other day of the year. Tables that lined the street were covered with great buys from shoes to novelty pencils, music books to stained glass décor. The streets were blocked to traffic and people could mill about between shopping and snack stands for block after block on Main Street.

It was a day-long affair that attracted over three thousand shoppers from Tarford Flats and neighboring towns. Stores stayed open later than usual, finally closing around 7;00 p.m. Then would begin the judging portions for the BBQ contests and chili cook-offs. The Lutheran Ladies League would host a fundraising bake sale, offering assorted pies and goodies. Finally, as the sun began to set, the street dance would begin. As the live music began to play, eager dancers would gather in the dancing area, while older folks and those with small children would find a place to sit at one of the many picnic tables around the perimeter. The dance and festivities drew a huge, fun-loving crowd from around the county and often lasted until well past midnight.

The morning of the sidewalk sale of 1975, Freshie packed her backpack with essentials and left early for work. She rode her bike first to the Beaumont Boutique where she found Toile and Vernie giggling about things they should not put out on the tables for everyone to see. Toile had just gotten a shipment of bras with extra firm cups, and had suggested that Vernie could fill them with potpourri from her decorating stash. Vernie, in turn, suggested that they might start a new line of dual-purpose undergarments, filled with an assortment of useful items including hard candy, salt and pepper packets, and sewing kits.

It warmed Freshie's heart to see her aunts that morning. She found their laughter reassuring after the fretful night she had just had. As Freshie approached them, Toile and Vernie could sense that she was struggling. They put down their projects and came to Freshie's aid. Freshie began to tell them all that had transpired regarding Linny's affair with Darren, his rejection of her, Conway's stolen money and his accusations, Linny's rage toward Conway, Georgeanne, Toile, Fern and Vernie and, finally, Linny's awful desire to get revenge.

Neither Toile nor Vernie were very surprised. Living in the wake of our father's lifestyle had exposed us to the deleterious nature of certain people in the world. The addition of desperation just removes their sense and inhibitions.

Toile and Vernie comforted Freshie and were sure to tell her everything she needed to hear- that everything would be okay, that she would make it through this without injury or worse, that she will have their support. And everything they told her they believed to be absolutely true. Rarely do major social coups take place in small towns. The gossips in town would be on duty to circumvent any surprise attack.

Freshie pedaled her bike the few blocks to the drug store where Edna was busy at work setting out toys and candy to lure children and their parents over. Freshie began to arrange the giant twisted lollipops in heavy blue and red glass vases, creating eye-catching bouquets of tempting sweet treats and soon became consumed with excitement over the sidewalk sale festivities.

As expected, Darren Turnbull spent much of the day rubbing elbows with the folks on Main Street. Throughout the day, he had visited each store, spoken with the owners and clerks, tried all of the food offered by various venders, and sampled BBQ from contest entrants who were all eager to please. He even made a brief campaign speech over the loudspeaker just before the street dance began.

Darren seemed to be having a grand time. His brother and city councilman Ken Cash was there too. In fact, it was K.C., not Darren, who was elected to judge the chili cook-off. Darren, of course, was happy to offer his opinion. Ken Cash, gracious as ever, awarded even the worst chefs with "honorable mention" certificates in specific categories from "Chili my Mom would Love" to "Most Colorful."

In truth, Texas won the day with his chili. Of course, K.C. did not award him "Grand Champion," to avoid any appearance of favoritism, but there was no doubt that Texas had an expert knowledge of spices and herbs and his methods for soaking and slow-cooking the beans were nothing less than brilliant. One could taste the passion Texas felt for Central American cuisine.

The second-best chili chef, and the one awarded top honors, was, of course, Jeffrey Buck. When the announcement was made, Vernie beamed with pride.

As the shops began to close at the end of the day, and the streetlamps came on, illuminating the congregants at the street dance, Toile and Vernie made their way to Vernie's place to relax and sample some of Jeffrey's hand-rolled sushi, his newest culinary interest.

Down the street, Evan and his mother closed down the retail portion of the drug store. The extended store hours left Evan exhausted and quite unsettled. He was anxious to leave and return to his usual nighttime routine. Edna called to Freshie that they were turning in for the night, and reminded her- as she did every night- to turn off the lights and lock up tight.

The soda fountain counter traffic had slowed quite a bit after the music started. There were several food vendors nearer to the crowd that offered cold drinks on this warm evening. With no one in the store, Freshie was hopeful that she was off the hook for the night, that Linny's nefarious plan would not come to pass. Then the bells hanging over the door began to jingle. Freshie looked up from her chores and her hope evaporated. As Linny predicted, Darren Turnbull had come into the drug store and found a seat on one of the padded stools at the counter. K.C. was there too, and smiled widely when he saw Freshie.

"Freshie Lynn! About to close up shop?" He chided. "We don't mean to keep you too long! Just thought we'd escape the crowd and get some root beer floats, unless you have something stronger." He and Darren bumped elbows a few times as they continued joking around. Freshie explained that she had to retrieve more ice-cream from the back.

On her way to the back room, Freshie carefully opened the door to Evan's pharmacy area. It was unlocked, as she assumed it would be. Evan usually had trouble collecting himself and taking care of even the littlest things when there was a change in his routine, and Edna was in a rush to get him home.

Out of sight from the soda counter, Freshie slyly located the stock bottle of Phenobarbital and quietly extracted four tablets. She then placed the bottle on the shelf exactly as it had been and hurried to retrieve a gallon of ice cream. When she returned to the counter, Freshie put two scoops of ice cream into each chilled heavy glass mug. Making sure her actions were concealed, she then put two tablets into each mug, and before anyone spotted the pills, she pulled the fountain tap and filled each mug with frothy root beer. The tablets dissolved quickly amid the carbonation and foam, and their transformation was imperceptible with all the activity that comes with a freshly poured root beer float. Freshie slipped straws into each mug and turned to present them to her uncle, K.C. and his brother.

Freshie didn't care much for Darren. She really didn't mind drugging him, truth be told. She felt that it was almost an act of Karma. Darren seemed the same sort of man as her father and grandfather-lots of bloviating about importance and success, with absolutely no trace of integrity. She knew he needed a comeuppance.

It was betraying her uncle K.C. that really got to her. Freshie appreciated her uncle and did not wish him harm. It was, however, just as Linny said it would be. In order to fulfill Linny's demands and deliver Darren into her hands, K.C. would have to be contained. Freshie thought it would be better to drug him into oblivion than to test Linny Spitt's resolve. That woman could very well have the inclination to silence K.C. permanently if he were to get in the way.

The brothers continued to guffaw and make sophomoric jokes for several minutes while Freshie snuck away to call Linny. The clerk at the motel where Linny was staying finally answered on the seventh ring. In a bored tone, he asked Freshie to hold while he rang the room number she had given. Linny picked up right away. Freshie reported that Darren was there, and told Linny how long it had been since she had given them the drugs. Without so much as a goodbye, Freshie hung up the phone and returned to check on Darren and K.C.

Her uncle appeared preoccupied with trying to line up his spoon and napkin with the edge of the counter. She had seen this kind of thing with Evan. Freshie knew that nervous folks often get more nervous when they don't feel quite right, so she left K.C. alone for the time being. Freshie looked at the clock. It had been twenty minutes since she made that phone call. Linny would be here soon and Freshie had a lot to do. She counted the money in the register and filled out the deposit slips, which she then placed with the deposit envelope on Edna's desk in the back room. Freshie cleaned all the dishes, the glass and the counter before Darren started to slide off his stool.

With all of her strength, Freshie held Darren upright and led him to the back entrance. She tried to lean him against the wall, but he proved too heavy for her and slid down into a heap on top of some empty cartons. Freshie returned to the front to find that K.C. had gotten off his stool and was carefully trying to make his way to the back room, steadying himself with both hands on the counter. Freshie locked the front door and returned to her uncle. Gently, she draped his arm over her shoulders and led him to the spot where his brother sat, then she quickly returned to the soda counter to make sure all traces of her last customers were wiped away.

Seconds later, Freshie opened the back door where she found Linny waiting. Linny took K.C.'s keys from his belt, left and returned again with his reliable Ford truck. She backed it up to the pharmacy, and with sheer determination, Linny and Freshie loaded the massive, limp bodies of the Turnbull men in the back.

Freshie had never been so worried as she was when Linny drove Ken Cash's pickup truck away from the pharmacy. She was sure they would be noticed, and worse, that they would be recognized. Linny kept the lights off until they turned off of main street and then found the least travelled roads to get them where they were headed, which happened to be the old barn at the Turnbull farm.

Linny had come prepared. In her satchel she had a liter of whiskey, an aerosol canister of "chemical mace", a second-hand army blanket, two dozen candles and a Polaroid camera with two boxes of film. In a larger duffle bag, she had stuffed everything else she had with her during her motel stay. Linny knew that if her plans fell through, she would have to stay out of sight for a while and come up with another scheme. As her nerves peaked, so did her determination to make this opportunity one that would pay off.

Freshie had never seen this barn from the road and was surprised when they came upon it. She was even more surprised that Linny knew it was there. Linny didn't seem the type to hike around in the backwoods looking for old buildings. She certainly wouldn't have driven her long convertible down these washboard roads, much less tried to venture out in her usual heels and adornments. Linny was familiar with this barn, however. It was one of the places she would go with Darren when he didn't want to be found. She knew that there was an old sofa in the back, covered with Mexican blankets and a few bales of hay that would serve as an adequate platform for adult activities. Linny also knew that there was no electricity in this barn, leaving a person to rely on kerosene lanterns or plenty of candles.

After parking the truck near the barn door, Linny instructed Freshie to guard Darren and K.C. Freshie knew that most people are out for a few hours after taking Phenobarbital, but Linny's expression kept her from saying a word. Linny shoved the mace into Freshie's hand and told her to spray either of the men in the face if he moved. Freshie put the canister in her pocket and waited for Linny to return with more orders.

After several minutes, Linny approached the truck, unlatched the tailgate and climbed into the bed. She grabbed K.C. by the ankles of his jeans and pulled him to the edge of the bed, then hopped down herself and resumed pulling him until his legs dangled over the edge. Linny motioned for Freshie to come over and put Ken's right arm over her shoulder while Linny threw his left arm over her own shoulder.

Together they struggled to drag K.C. into the back of the barn where they positioned him on the old couch. Without a moment to catch their breath, they returned to the truck to retrieve Darren. Freshie struggled under the weight of the younger Turnbull brother. As she and Linny approached the hay bale platform, Freshie slipped on some loose hay on the ground and pitched forward, landing on her knee and losing her grip on Darren. Linny barked angrily at Freshie, who was quick to respond. Freshie fought through the pain of her stinging, bloody knee and helped to hoist Darren's body onto the platform.

Finally, when both men were in the barn and situated to Linny's liking, Freshie chose a bale on which to sit and tend to her injury. She found a rag and wiped away the dirt and grime from her wound as best as she could. The blood continued to trickle down her leg in drops, but seemed to be slowing as she tried to elevate the wound. While seated, Freshie took a moment to look around. She saw several bales of hay stacked along the back wall and loose hay scattered about the floor. Along the walls hung a variety of ropes and tack which looked at first to be moving. Freshie then realized that the movement was caused by shadows cast by the many flickering candles Linny set about the scene.

Linny had already stripped down to a tank-top and panties and was working to relieve Darren of his clothes as she began to bark instructions to Freshie. Freshie was supposed to load the film in the Polaroid camera, which she had mastered after helping countless customers at the drugstore to do the same. Freshie, however, took her time. She wanted as little actual involvement with this step as possible. She had seen Linny's increasingly maniacal expression, which only caused Freshie to freeze up and respond more slowly.

Frustrated, Linny snapped at Freshie, telling her to get started, then positioned herself next to a naked Darren on the bed of hay bales. As Linny pretended to be having her way with him, Freshie began taking pictures. The more she heard the "Snap-ziiiip" of the camera, the more excited Linny became. At one point she decided to pose while pouring whiskey down her chest. Soon, with the aroma of hay, sweat, perfume, whiskey and fire, the barn smelled like an Old West whorehouse. Linny felt further inspired. Her original plan had been to blackmail Darren with the threat of publishing the photos as his campaign was picking up speed, but now Linny realized there was far more to gain if she were to include K.C. in the scandal. If Linny could document having a threesome with both Turnbull brothers, there would be no limit to what they would be willing to pay for those pictures.

Restating her threat to accuse Freshie of theft, Linny coerced the girl into moving K.C. yet again. Freshie and Linny loaded him up on the bed of hay and Linny began unbuckling his belt and wrestling with his boots. As she watched her unconscious uncle lying there being tugged here and there by the crazed woman, Freshie ached with guilt. Her thoughts flashed to Toile, her gentle, beautiful face- then to Vernie, with her contagious laughter and happy spirit. Freshie did not want Toile to suffer. She did not want to hurt her family. She could not let Linny hurt them either.

As Linny continued to struggle with Ken Cash's boots, Freshie pulled the mace canister out of her pocket. Trembling, she flipped the safety cap and quietly stepped toward Linny. Teeming with frustration, Linny glanced up to bark orders at Freshie when she was hit square in the eyes and nose with Mace- and not a little. Freshie emptied the entire canister into Linny Spitt's face.

The adrenaline may have helped stave off the initial pain that came with being sprayed, but Linny was overtaken none the less. It was as if all of her inhibitions evaporated and she was driven by absolute fury. Coughing and unable to see, Linny lunged at the spot where Freshie had been standing. Freshie had moved out of the way and began yelling for help. Again, Linny lunged in Freshie's general direction. This time, however, Linny swept through several lit candles, which toppled over onto a bevy of flammable materials including dried hay, dripped oil, and fertilizer pellets. Before Freshie could gather her senses, flames began to lick up the three walls nearby. The front of the barn, however, had not yet caught fire. Like a banshee, Linny's screaming could be heard through the night as far away as Vernie's cabin.

Texas, whose camper had been moved away from the barn by about 100 yards, thought at first that the sound was a scream of a vixen, or female fox in heat. Then he smelled the smoke and sprang into action, pulling on his boots and racing toward the fire. Freshie had pulled K.C. to the front of the barn, about 10 feet inside the entrance and had gone back in to retrieve Darren. Linny, who face was streaked with chemicals, soot and tears, growled when she saw Freshie return. Linny pulled a hatchet off the wall and charged for Freshie with every manner of a wild animal. Freshie froze, too horrified to move. Then Freshie heard a loud "thunk" and Linny crumpled to the floor. Texas Turnbull had whacked her good with an iron fence post driver.

Freshie's eyes were stinging and she could barely see. The barn had quickly filled with smoke and she fought for each breath. She pointed to the place where Texas would find his uncle Darren, and shook her head when Texas asked if there was anyone else in the smoke-filled barn.

Freshie then made her way for the entrance. She managed to pull K.C. the rest of the way to safety before she collapsed. Texas followed shortly after with Darren slung over his shoulder. Darren, K.C. and Freshie were 5 yards away from the barn, all three passed out in the grass. Texas turned toward the barn for one last run, hoping to get in and save Linny Spitt. She was still lying in a heap, and the flames were getting ever closer to her. Unbeknownst to Texas, she was also saturated with 120 proof whiskey. Texas was one yard from the barn entrance when the flames reached Linny. The last he saw of Ms. Spitt was a white and blue "poof" of flames, then the entire barn came down.

Toile and Vernie had been sitting outside on the cabin porch, watching the swallows swoop from the tallest trees to snatch up insects over the lake's surface. Vernie loved the swallows, with their speed in flight and acrobatic skills. They also seem quite aggressive and unafraid. Flying swallows, at twilight can be mistaken for bats because of their sweeping motions, quick turns, and aggressive nature. Swallows, however, are cute. Vernie said they looked like small bird-soldiers, holding themselves at attention with their dark feathers smoothed perfectly back, ready for inspection. Their little faces appeared masked across the eyes, implying that they were prepared for a serious, top-secret mission.

Vernie was an interesting romantic. She often assigned romanticized behaviors to animals. It was easy to do, of course, because animals don't practice betrayal. They don't defy laws of nature, and they don't set nefarious plans. Animals can be trusted to be what they are without deception or pretense. They are safe. It was easy to see, once I understood how Vernie sees the world, how much she loved and needed Jeffrey. He was like those swallows: mission-focused, honest, and completely aware of who and what he was.

Vernie and Toile were startled by the loud slam of the screen door on the other side of the cabin. Someone had come in and done so urgently. Toile's nerves were immediately on edge. Since they'd spent the evening on the porch, there was no need to turn on any lights. Now the cabin behind them was dark. They could only see the outline of a large, muscular figure coming toward them through the house. Vernie recognized his movements, and sighed, "It's Jeffrey." The women relaxed, but only for a second. Jeffrey's face conveyed his urgent concern. He quickly explained that he had seen smoke in the west as he was driving toward the cabin. It was about a mile away, he reported, in the direction of K.C.'s fields.

Toile, Vernie and Jeffrey piled in his Jeep Wagoneer and tore toward the direction of the smoke. The skies were quickly getting dark save for a few lines of bright fuchsia and purple along the horizon, the lingering effects of the sunset. Toile could see the billowing smoke against the beautiful backdrop of the darkening summer sky. As they drew closer, she knew that it was the barn that had caught fire. The trees in the area were too green and there had been too much rain for anything else to burn with that intensity.

Jeffrey's Jeep skidded to a halt just upwind from the flaming wreckage. Texas had already pulled his cousin, uncle and father out to the same dirt path on which Jeffrey's Jeep was parked. Jeffrey kept his lights on low beam, just enough to give him a view of the injured. Ken Cash and Darren were sitting upright, dazed and in obvious discomfort. Vernie and Toile quickly rushed over to help them, providing each with sips from a water canteen Jeffrey always kept filled in the jeep for emergencies.

Jeffrey found Texas kneeling over Freshie, using his shirt to wipe the soot away from her blackened nose and mouth. She was unresponsive to his touch. Immediately, Jeffrey checked her for a pulse and found one. Her respirations were also present, but very weak. As the adrenaline began to wear off, Texas's hands began to shake. Jeffrey moved himself into position and began to administer CPR to Freshie as he reassured Texas that he would do his best to save her. Texas turned to Jeffrey, his expression pained and his face streaked with soot and tears. His voice trembled as he confessed his sense of guilt: "I should have noticed… I didn't hear them. I was too late."

CHAPTER 11: THE DOZIER BOYS

"It is remarkable how the human spirit seeks to connect with others. Often, the strongest bonds develop from complimenting states of vulnerability and empathy. In our culture, we tend to believe that we need to present ourselves as strong and independent in order to prove our worth to humankind, and yet, in doing so we nearly repel others from connecting with us. I have found that all people- whether they be those who are struggling or those who witness the struggle- transcend pettiness, jealousy, pretense and condemnation when they allow themselves to feel true charity for one-another. There are few opportunities for such charity as are present when we allow others to see us as our genuine selves."

Creating Healthy Relationships the EZ Way with Jessie Duque

There is something about youth that allows for grand ideas, bold actions, defining loyalty and spirited resolve. Mama certainly had it, and, if "loyalty" is defined loosely, so did Conway. Darren Turnbull had it when he left for California. Texas had it when he left for Columbia, and still when he returned. Now it was Freshie's turn.

As she lay on the dirt road, unconscious, the breeze lifting the smoke away from her, Freshie had a vision. She saw the face of Linny, twisted with anger, the ropes and chains on the wall, the raging fire inside the barn. Then, as if watching from above, she saw herself being moved away from that place. Suddenly there was a dazzling white explosion that vaporized the scary face, the fire, and the ropes and chains which then floated through the air like glitter. The scene soon cleared, and Freshie saw herself in her grandfather's back yard. Conway appeared to be standing alone in the empty pool, surrounded with boxes or gifts that had been opened and tossed into a large pile. Freshie recognized her first fancy robe, her shiny new shoes and matching handbag, her toys and a few crumpled shoeboxes, some of which held money, and other things which she could not reconcile but made her feel very sad. Freshie heard her name and turned her head to see that there, beyond the pool, beyond the yard and house, stood her mother, smiling.

Fern was joined by Edna, Toile, K.C, Vernie, and Jeffrey, and a stranger whom Freshie did not recognize. The stranger was familiar, however. It could have been something as simple as the way she moved, or stood, or a look in her eyes. The stranger came close to Freshie. She was stunning. She must have been in her twenties, just a few year older that Freshie herself. She was tall and lithe, like Fern, and seemed very strong. She held her head up with quiet confidence. Her skin was the color of natural honey; her hair was long, smooth and dark. And her eyes were a brilliant emerald green. She knew this young woman... but how? The young woman held both arms out, as if inviting an embrace. Freshie was compelled to go to her, to speak to her, and yet as she drew her breath,

Freshie began to sputter and cough. She then became aware of Jeffrey, who had appeared before her face and whispered her name, "Freshie." She felt his grip on her shoulder and again, he whispered more insistently, "Freshie!" Everything before her disappeared, and Freshie opened her eyes to the dark night sky.

———————————————

There had been no sighting of Linny Spitt following the barn's collapse. Texas was the last one to see her before her alcohol-soaked body met the flames. As the fire died down, those who remained- K.C., Texas, Darren, Freshie, Jeffrey, Vernie and Toile- quickly devised a plan and put it into action.

Texas and Darren loaded into Texas's single cab pickup and stopped first at Vernie's cabin. There they quickly cleaned the soot off their faces, necks and arms. Then Texas drove Darren back to town, where, if anyone were to see them and smell their smoke-filled clothes, they could easily explain that they were clearing off the branches using Texas's burn-pit. The street dance was still going full force and the side streets were dark. No one noticed that Texas stopped around the corner from Evan's drug store where Darren slid out of Texas's truck and into his own, then headed for home.

K.C. stayed near the barn, making sure the blaze remained contained. As he did so, he cleaned out his truck and the surrounding area, removing any trace of the evenings' debacle, and more importantly, any trace of Linny Spitt.

Jeffrey, Toile, Vernie and Freshie climbed into Jeffrey's jeep and headed to town. Their first stop was Jeffrey and Vernie's bungalow which sat at the very edge of Tarford Flats. Freshie's eyes were stinging and Vernie insisted that she Jeffrey should look her over carefully in a well-lit house. Vernie also had something she needed to show Freshie and she wanted Toile there to help.

When they arrived at the bungalow, Freshie took a quick shower and emerged from the bathroom in a pink oriental robe Jeffrey had given to Vernie. She then sat at the kitchen table and Toile combed out her freshly washed hair as Jeffrey listened with his stethoscope to Freshie's heart and lungs. Vernie, who had gone quickly to her bedroom upon arriving at the house, finally emerged carrying a set of clean clothes for Freshie to wear and Vernie a stack of letters bound with string.

Within a few minutes, Freshie was dressed in the clothes Vernie had given her, drinking a refreshing glass of iced herbal tea and eating some of Jeffrey's handmade sushi as Vernie and Toile told her stories about her mother. The women laughed out loud as they recalled Fern's antics and adventures, and became so compassionate when they talked about Freshie's older siblings, Danny and Mina, and the heartache of Fern's relationship with Conway. As Freshie watched her aunts talk so easily about their sister, she became keenly aware of their bond with Fern, and with each other. Freshie yearned for such a bond, the kind of bond that could withstand heartbreak and tumult, the bond of sisterhood.

Soon enough, everyone loaded again into Jeffrey's Jeep Wagoneer. Jeffrey then proceeded to drive the group to Evan's drug store, behind which he parked the Wagoneer. Freshie directed Jeffrey to the location where she kept her bike and he immediately began the chore unlocking and taking the tires off of Freshie's bike to fit it into the back of the Wagoneer. Freshie, who still had her key to the drug store, quickly went in to retrieve her backpack and to leave a quick note to Edna. She then heaved the backpack up and over her shoulder, turned off the lights and locked the door on her way out.

After mentally retracing her steps to make sure she had done all she should, Freshie handed the drugstore key to Jeffrey who had promised to return it to Edna. Freshie then turned to her aunts and, with tears streaming down her cheeks, she said goodbye. Toile and Vernie nearly crushed Freshie as they embraced her and, for the longest time, showed no intention of letting go. Finally, Vernie peeled herself away from Freshie and said, "Freshie, you are strong, and you are smart, and you can do anything you set your mind to."

Toile took Freshie by the shoulders, and said, "We love you to the ends of the Earth, Freshie. And when you finally meet your sister, tell her we feel the same way about her."

With that, Freshie made her way to the bus station, where she bought her one-way ticket to Grand Forks, North Dakota. She sat with the stack of letters Vernie had given her- letters written over twenty years from Mina to Fern. Soon Freshie, with her backpack full of Conway's money and a newfound sibling connection, would be on her way to the University of North Dakota, where she, like her older sister Mina, would soon become a "Fighting Sioux."

Toile and Vernie had yet one more thing to accomplish before the night was over. First, they had to figure out how to hotwire Linny's car.

It has always been true with my family that even in times of extraordinary stress, we tend to find humor in stupidity. I would love to pretend that my sisters were proficient, or even barely competent at hotwiring a car, but of course, that was not the case. Jeffrey had given them clear instructions before he pulled away toward the spot where they were supposed to meet after their job was done.

Vernie and Toile proceeded to encounter several mishaps. First, when Vernie struggled to pull away the heavy casing that held the ignition wires within the steering column, her long hair got tangled around the gearshift. Crawling across the passenger side of the front seat, Toile tried to come to her aid only to knock the gearshift from "park" to "neutral." This caused the car to lurch forward, hitting the curb and knocking Toile into the passenger foot well where she became wedged, bottom first, with her hands and feet reaching skyward. Vernie's head, still affixed to the gear shift next to the steering wheel, was propelled forward by the force of the lurch and hit the steering wheel dead center. This resulted in a jarring blare of the horn reminiscent of a massive and unexpected fart during a church service.

Regardless of the years of training to comport herself with poise and grace, this moment found Toile with nothing to do but laugh. Like an upended June bug, her arms and legs flailing uselessly, Toile was completely stuck,

Eventually Vernie was able to collect herself enough to untangle her own hair from the gear shift. She sat up, put the car in parking gear and successfully ignited the engine. When she looked at her sister, Vernie realized Toile was not going to get out of the foot well without help. It was not until she opened the passenger side door and helped Toile to wrench herself from her compact position that Vernie realized Toile had been laughing so hard she wet her pants, and not just a little.

After a few minutes of digging through Linny's messy trunk, Vernie announced she had a perfect solution! She and Toile crouched behind the massive car painstakingly peeling off Toile's wet pants. Giggling like scheming sisters do, Vernie insisted that Toile's only option was to cede to Vernie's idea. Moments later a daring Toile emerged wearing a pretty floral beach towel, wrapped around her lower body and secured just below the waist with a black rubber bungee cord. Toile rolled up the wet pants so that only the dry areas were exposed and carefully situated them in her purse. It didn't take much convincing once Toile realized the totality of her choices. The only thing Toile considered more mortifying than her beach-towel-bungee skirt was to be seen anywhere near Tarford Flats in those urine-soaked pants.

Given the many delays, it was quite late by the time Vernie and Toile pulled Linny's convertible up to Conway's house. By all appearances, he was either out of town or out for the night. The Lincoln had a smooth engine and made very little noise as it coasted up the driveway and into the back yard. Vernie cut the engine about ten feet from the pool and she and Toile quietly got out, softly shutting the doors behind them. Vernie moved the gear shift to neutral one more time, and she and Toile gave the car a great shove. The sleek yellow convertible glided forward obediently, as if it had accepted its fate. When Linny's once-coveted carriage finally hit the water, the splash was less impressive than the sisters had worried it might be. In fact, the car gingerly settled into the water as a tired old body might lie back into a warm bath.

Jeffrey was ready and waiting to collect my sisters when they appeared around the corner from Conway's street. As a man practiced at seeing women in uncomfortable circumstances, Jeffrey knew not to say a word to Toile about her new "skirt." The three rode back to K.C.'s barn in without much shared conversation. Instead, each worked to reconcile the events of the evening, the probability that Linny was dead and the hope that the sunken Lincoln Continental would cause Conway to react as predicted. Only Jeffrey seemed to notice the music coming through his AM radio. As they came nearer to the barn, he began to hum along with Eric Clapton's "I Shot the Sheriff."

Raymond Dozier was a quiet man. He was unusual in that he truly enjoyed his own company. Raymond was large and muscular, yet so gentle and soft spoken he often went completely unnoticed. His was a simple, unassuming soul and, although he kept his comments to himself, he had remarkable insight into the lives and ways of others. Much of his knowledge could very well have been a result of his work.

Raymond was the operator of the landfill used by the county. It was tucked over the hill, just west of the Turnbull farm. Raymond, "Ram" to his friends, knew more about the residents of Tarford Flats than anyone cared to imagine, I'm sure. Seeing how strangely people in small towns can behave, Ram chose to remain on the periphery. By his own design, people from town only really interacted with Ram if they were either coming to the landfill with an unusually large haul of waste that couldn't be burned in their burn-pits, or they were looking to hire Ram or his brothers for bulldozing, back-hoe or construction work.

Ram was the first of his siblings to arrive in Cass County. In fact, he was the first in three generations to leave his family's Amish community in Illinois. Over time, Ram was joined by two younger brothers, Dirk and Garth. The younger Dozier boys became quite well-regarded for their carpentry skills. Not only were their products of wonderful quality and workmanship, but they were finished with impressive speed.

They were a peculiar lot, even by the conservative standards of the 1950's when they were still considered "mysterious newcomers." They were known to be very religious, reserved, and maybe a bit suspicious of most townspeople. None the less, they were quite nice to look at. It wasn't that they were striking, but more that they seemed fresh and clean, unpolluted by the world. Their wholesome appearance was what one would imagine of folks who learned early to eat the healthiest of food, abstain from tobacco and alcohol and work hard using every bit of muscle and strength the Good Lord had given them.

An occasional sighting of one or more of the brothers would start an excited wave of interest and speculation among every young woman in town. The Dozier boys did not date and were never spotted at social events. Even when they did come into town, they went about their business without much conversation with other folks. They were certainly polite- more than that, their manners were exemplary. They were kind, honest, genuine, considerate, moral men. In fact, aside from their strong bodies and handsome faces, they were completely unlike Conway Duque.

By the time Vernie graduated from school and started to work on the cabin, Dirk and Garth were known to be very honest and reliable construction professionals. She consulted with them on several occasions, and the two younger brothers even helped her find lumber and supplies at greatly discounted prices. Vernie learned that they had a younger sister near her own age who remained in Illinois. Vernie always figured their kindness toward her must have been in part because she reminded the Doziers of the sister they missed so dearly. Vernie had struck up as much of a friendship as anyone could with Dirk and Garth. She always talked about the two men with great affection, and was quick to stamp out any rumors that might be making their way through the gossip mill of Tarford Flats.

The first time Vernie met Ram Dozier in person was the morning after the fire. She, Toile and Jeffrey had procured a clean pair of jeans for Toile before making their way back from town. Now the three was doing what they could to load any debris that had survived the blaze into K. C's truck bed. Suddenly there appeared in the distance a pair of headlights. They looked as if they were attached to a pickup truck that was bouncing as along the dirt path leading to the barn site. Alarmed, the group stood close together dreading an encounter with the Cass County Sheriff. Vernie was the first to recognize Garth Dozier's vehicle and assured the group that they had no cause to worry.

As the truck rolled to a stop, the brothers stepped out and waved the friendly, nonchalant greeting common among farmers and country folk. Shortly after their arrival, Ram appeared on the bulldozer. His approach had been quiet until he crested the last hill. At that moment, however, the dozer let out a growl, making Ram's arrival like that of a mythical hero mounted upon a massive wild beast. The impression he was making by such an arrival would have been appalling to Ram. He was embarrassed by the growl of the machine, and was loathe to be the center of attention. Garth and Dirk, however, would not let the matter rest. They teased him mercilessly for several minutes afterward.

As she watched the blushing older brother, something in Vernie's memory nagged at her. She was certain she had never made his acquaintance, and yet, she couldn't reconcile the familiarity she felt. He looked quite different than the younger Dozier boys. Garth and Dirk looked very much like brothers. They both had curls of blonde or strawberry blonde, freckles, bright smiles and eyes that always seemed to reveal an inner prankster.

Ram, on the other hand, was more subdued in every way. His hair was chestnut, cut closer to his head and curled just behind his ears. His face and neck were clean and tan with no hint of freckles. His eyes were also darker, more thoughtful, and with a sudden flash of remembrance, Vernie realized his eyes were kind.

It had been ten years or more, yet her mind was filled with the image of Ram Dozier, the gentle man on the bulldozer, readying the ground for Conway's pool. His was the kind face looking up at her as she stood in the window of Conway's big, cold house. How often had Vernie reflected on that moment: the contrast between kindness and cruelty, the warmth of a stranger that cut through the despair and loneliness that hung in Fern's dark room?

Vernie stood confused as myriad feelings continued to well within her. Her stillness gave no indication of the torrent in her chest. Anger, fear, sadness, resentment- all the things she had come to experience with Conway- wrestled with grief, guilt, regret, shame-all the things she had laid upon her own shoulders. It was the desire for comfort, the craving for appreciation, connection, that rose to the front of her mind, however, and Ram Dozier, the stranger, seemed to understand. He approached Vernie, holding her gaze with his, and held out his hand. Instinctively, Vernie put her hand out and it was swallowed up in his warm, strong, fleshy grip. As he gently shook hands with my sister, Ram reached out with his left hand, laid it on her shoulder and gave it a gentle squeeze. Then, with a smile and genuine affection, he said, "It's good to see you again, Vernie."

Vernie turned to watch him as he continued toward the space where the barn had been. She felt a true connection with this man, a mystic bond as if, in another life, he could have been her older brother. Fresh tears of joy ran down her cheeks as Vernie marveled at the unlikely kinship she felt with Ram and his brothers. She felt extraordinary gratitude for them, for their ease and their genuine nature and for their awareness of her.

The Dozier boys approached K.C. and Texas to offer their help. K.C. politely turned them down, explaining that he didn't want to impose. After Ram explained that they had participates in several quick "barn-raisings" in their previous community, K.C. happily accepted the Dozier's offer. The Doziers immediately got to work. Plans were quickly laid, and assignments were given to all present. Ram and his brothers, K.C. and Texas began their tasks of leveling the area and rebuilding the Turnbull barn.

Most of the Nebraska landscape is flat and without any apparent end. There are a few areas where the wild grass grows taller than others, and other spaces are strangely bare, giving the impression of an awful haircut. The State is roughly four-hundred miles across, and I have heard it said that you can drive three-hundred and fifty of those on the interstate without making a single turn. The Platte river runs along the center of the state from Wyoming all the way to the Missouri river. Little towns have sprung up along the river both because of the proximity to the water, and because the river valley, as slight as it is, offers a bit of protection from the harsh winter weather that can tear through the plains from November to March.

Gradually, going from west to east, the land becomes more visually pleasing. Fields appear more fruitful and the grass along the highways changes from pale blonde to healthy green. Finally, as one continues eastward toward the Missouri river, the land comes alive with trees, small lakes and ponds, rolling hills and valleys.

In and around Tarford Flats, the hills, valleys, lakes, rivers and the prairie winds often combine to create areas of inversion, or fog clouds. Tarford Flats, like the other little towns across the state, is nestled in a bit of a valley, and has certainly had its share of early morning fog.

The morning after the fire, in the first light of dawn, there appeared a heavy cloud of fog over the town. Toile noticed it first. She had been sitting on a bench near Texas's camper drinking a strong cup of coffee K.C. had percolated over a campfire. Vernie was inside the camper sleeping.

Toile stood to get a better view of the cloud. Something about this particular fog concerned her. It was dirty. As the sunlight continued to illuminate the landscape, the strange cloud appeared larger, thicker, and browner than it had before. Toile called for Vernie, who emerged a moment later wrapped in an old quilt. She and Toile agreed that the fog was troublesome. They hastily made their way to the others.

The scene in the field that morning was surreal. It had been almost eight hours since Linny and Freshie brought K.C. and Darren to the barn. In that space of time, the barn had burned to the ground, Darren scampered home, Freshie left town, Linny's car was returned to Conway's house, debris had been cleared away from the burn site, land had been bulldozed, and, according to Texas, Linny had probably exploded.

As they neared the small group of men who stood drinking coffee in the pale light of early morning, Vernie and Toile saw that a brand-new barn had been built in place of the old one. Well, it wasn't entirely new. The wood was clearly retrieved from the stockpile of lumber at the dump. But it was a beautiful piece of work, none the less. It was similar enough to the old barn as to not raise any questions, but the workmanship was superb. It was clear that Dirk and Garth were gifted engineers in addition to being skilled builders. Every door closed perfectly; every corner was square. This barn could easily stand for a century barring, of course, a strong tornado- or another fire.

Toile and Vernie never did get a definitive answer when they asked if anyone found any remains of Linny Spitt. K.C. and Texas feigned ignorance. Jeffrey busied himself with one task or another. Dirk and Garth shared a shrug and a hint of a smile. Finally, Ram looked over at the newly built barn and the smooth, packed dirt apron that surrounded it and said, quietly, "I don't think Ms. Spitt will be causing any trouble around here again."

Upon seeing the miraculous barn, Toile and Vernie had completely forgotten about the fog hanging over Tarford Flats. The group had been enjoying the peaceful sounds of morning when K.C. blurted out, "What the...."

Everyone turned toward K.C., then followed his gaze toward town. The cloud was still there, but it was clearly not fog. It was smoke. The dirty air mass appeared to be slowly losing density, revealing patterns of airflow that are more consistent with smoke than with mist.

"Where on Earth did that come from?" Asked Jeffrey, concerned that there may have been another fire in town. He and K.C. discussed the lack of sirens and the lack of movement in the air over town that would come with the heat of a large fire. The Dozier boys joined the conversation and all six men began hypothesizing about the source of the smoke. When Garth suggested that the direction of the wind last night could have carried smoke from the barn fire over town, Texas let out a dreadful sigh, "Oh, crap." He said, "I know what that is."

Texas estimated that there were about three hundred pounds of dried psychedelically engineered marijuana hanging from the rafters of the barn just before the whole thing burned down. Strangely, he hadn't really thought much about it until now. It could have been that the smell of grass, hay, fertilizer, engine oils and so on was strong enough that Texas didn't smell the marijuana. It could have been that he didn't smell it because it was burning in the loft, and the smoke was quickly carried away to the east by the night breeze. It could have been that he was so engrossed in making sure everyone was okay that he didn't give it a second thought. At any rate, there came a point at which Texas realized that there was nothing he could do to stop the marijuana from catching fire. He had to accept that over $100,000 of his crop would literally go up in smoke.

No one would have anticipated that the smoke would accumulate and settle over Tarford Flats. And yet, that is exactly what happened. The smoke blanketed the center of town, subtly at first so hardly anyone noticed. After a while, many folks assumed that the accumulating smoke was from the barbeque pits or from a dry ice smoke machine used to add to the ambiance of the street dance. The cloud lingered amidst the crowd through the late night and early morning hours, and yet when it was all over, there was not one person who seemed keen as to what had really happened. In fact, much of the night was a blur to everyone who had been present at the street dance.

This year's festivities lasted longer than they ever had before. Even those who felt tired resisted going home until dawn. The dance on this night was phenomenal.

There was something about the music they found mesmerizing- the drumbeats echoed in their chests and they could nearly taste the notes. Songs revealed colors and patterns in the minds of those who heard them. The dancing was natural, freeing. Old and young alike took to the street, twirling and swaying, letting their necks become loose, allowing their arms to reach far above their heads, feeling the breeze as if it were for the first time. Colors were spectacularly rich and full. Lights were stunning, glimmering.

The street-side vendor's drinks were heavenly. With so much dancing, people were parched. The ice-cold water and soda served that night had never tasted better. Some people exclaimed that they could feel every carbonated bubble burst on their tongues. Others believed they could feel the icy sensation of the chilled water coursing through their veins.

Oh, and the food! Never before had it tasted so good. Before long, vendors ran out of their offerings. Then in wave after wave, the people of Tarford Flats descended upon the bake sale put on by the Lutheran Ladies League. It started just before 11:00 p.m. as the last shift of women planned to pack up. Ironically, up until that point, sales had been less fruitful than years before, and the Lutheran Ladies were feeling a bit downtrodden. Then, at 10:55 there began a considerable upswing in business. It started with lemon bars. The crowd bought all forty batches. Next went the cookies, dozen upon dozen. There were snicker doodles, gingersnaps, oatmeal raisin-even the colorless, undercooked chocolate chip cookies disappeared from the tables. These were followed by turnovers, brownies, muffins, coffee cakes, sweetbread, dinner rolls, strudels, apple crisps, fruit pies, crème pies, pecan pies, Bundt cakes, fruit cakes, rum cakes, carrot cakes and spice cakes. Groups of men and women gathered together, sharing the various baked goods, laughing together, scooping the moist goodies out of the pans and eating with their hands.

Gone were the constricting social tensions, the condemnation and disapproval that so often turns the air acrid in small towns. This night was filled with friendship, community, and the faint scent of burned sugar.

By morning, the cloud had lifted a bit and its effects on the crowd had faded. Relaxed and contented, the townspeople went home and went to bed. The Lutheran Ladies had never before experienced such fun at a fundraiser, nor had they ever sold so many baked goods as they did the night of the Street Dance of 1975.

That same night, on a much smaller scale and in a much quieter place, Toile experienced her own cosmic awakening. She had finished gathering the debris she could find to load in K.C.'s truck. Walking around the passenger side of the cab, Toile spied an old quilted flannel shirt K.C. often wore when he went pheasant hunting. It was crumpled and half crammed in between the seatback and the bench. Finally giving a thought to the falling air temperatures, Toile snatched up the shirt and wrapped it around her shoulders. The fabric was well worn, and it smelled like her husband.

Toile had watched K.C. as he interacted with Texas and the Dozier brothers. K.C. was, as always, affable, friendly, and trying to make the best of a most bizarre situation. Toile watched as he bellowed in laughter at something Texas said, and then gave his boy a good-natured slap on the shoulder. She watched her son's shoulders relax as he talked with his father about Freshie and Linny, about his fears when he thought Freshie wouldn't survive, and most remarkably, how he was able to engineer his "crop" that way that he did. Toile watched as her husband brought Texas back into the comfort of his father's safe and steady guidance, not criticizing or condemning, but eager to listen and bring levity.

As she watched her husband, Toile's gratitude for this man grew, and so did the shame she felt at her foolishness with Eric. Soon the crushing regret fell upon her in that dark night. After K.C. had discovered the letters, Toile was sure he would bring it up, sure he would use it against her somehow. K.C. surprised her, however. He surprised us all. He made efforts to reconnect with Toile and with Texas. Over time, K.C. was able to let go of many of his rigid ways and soften himself toward those he loved.

This is the man Toile watched now, comforting his son, reassuring those around him that things would indeed be okay. Toile brought her arm to her nose, once again reminding herself of the comfort of K.C.'s scent. As she sat, watching her husband, K.C. glanced up, flashed a smile and a wink at his wife, and my sister's heart melted.

CHAPTER 12: CONWAY

"The clinical Narcissist is quite often a product of one or more narcissistic parents. This is because the primary relationship between parent and child is meant to teach the child of their place in the world. When a parent is a narcissist, however, they are incapable of empathy and tolerance. This manifests itself with the parent appearing painfully judgmental, impatient, critical and self-absorbed. A parent who behaves this way toward a child will leave that child emotionally incomplete, desperate for love and attention but believing that they must be extraordinary to achieve loveable status. The child may learn narcissistic tendencies as a way to cope with the emotional pain they experience in their formative years (i.e. overcompensation manifesting in aloof, elitist social behavior) and in an effort to understand the" rules" of showing and deserving love. Of all of the personality disorders I have worked with, narcissism is easily the most destructive to families. Narcissists tend to believe they are truly special, extraordinary, and deserving of praise and deference. A narcissist is often driven to success, achieving wealth, status and influence, which in turn creates the social admiration they are seeking. With societal reinforcement of the worth and value of a successful person, that person, if a narcissist, will have evidence of their flawlessness. Moreover, the narcissist will create relationships with others that support the idea that he or she is above the common masses. Therefore, anyone in a relationship with a narcissist will be convinced that if there is strain in that relationship the fault must lie with themselves. For how could a blameless, superior being be at fault? This is where we see a sophisticated system of emotional abuse in which the narcissist becomes ever more self-serving and the "other" in the relationship becomes more shamed, humiliated, and convinced of their worthlessness. If a person in such a relationship resists the notion of the narcissist's perfection, that person is castigated and removed from the relationship." <u>Creating Healthy Relationships the EZ Way with Jessie Duque</u>

Conway was seething when he called me. I could feel his fury reaching through the phone's receiver. He had to tell someone what had happened, and he couldn't get ahold of Toile or Vernie. Because I was the first to answer the phone on that Sunday morning following the street dance, I was first to hear the story of how he went into the back yard to check on some sprinklers and found Linny's car on the bottom of his pool.

He was convinced that Linny Spitt, in a petulant fit of entitlement and self-righteousness, had lashed out at him by dumping the car in the pool and leaving town with his money. He told me all about finding his empty cashbox and knowing that Linny had been the culprit. Conway conjured up a story of their confrontation in which he had been reasonable and willing to work with Linny, but that she became hysterical and moved out of the house.

This was a standard form of historical revision for my father. He was never the one to blame. Instead, he justified his behavior as a reasonable reaction to a hysterical woman. He tried it when Georgeanne divorced him and it did not work out as well as he had planned.

This same scenario worked out really well with the disappearance of Linny, however. When people acquainted with Linny would inquire about her absence, Conway would embark on a rant with such vitriol that they would dare not ask again. He would tell anyone who would listen how he couldn't believe the way she had treated him after all he had done for her. He was shocked at her ingratitude and her willingness to ruin the nice car she had just to spite him. He denied stepping out on Linny, and instead said that she had been completely unreasonable, jealous and paranoid about any friendships he might have with other women. Conway did all he could to paint Ms. Spitt in a terribly negative light. Little did he know he was creating the one rational explanation for her absence that didn't somehow end in foul play.

Of course, no one argued with him- especially any of his daughters. To anyone who would listen, he would go on and on about how Linny was a thief. Why would Toile or Vernie correct him? So that he could go after Freshie to get his money back? No, Conway had taken enough from that poor girl. Besides, Toile and Vernie found great relief that he finally had someone else to complain about instead of our mother.

To be completely frank, Linny Spitt was missed in Tarford flats as much as a summer cookout might miss a swarm of flies. Everyone was relieved she was gone.

Like a fish jumping in a still mountain lake, Linny's disappearance made but a small ripple, and the force of small-town homeostasis made sure that ripple was short-lived.

Freshie's absence, however, was noticed keenly by those who knew and loved her.

Jeffrey kept his promise to return the keys to Evan's drug store along with Freshie's heartfelt farewell. Edna was surprised at Freshie's last minute decision to go to college, but Edna knew that spirited kids like Freshie love the idea of adventure and, unlike her sweet boy Evan, Freshie would blossom if given the freedom to discover her passions. Of course she was talking with Jeffrey and Vernie, who completely understood both passion and the lure of faraway places. And why would anyone expect anything different from Freshie? We all knew the love of adventure was in her genes.

Freshie Lynn did great things with Conway's money. We all figured she would, given her experiences and her strong constitution. She enrolled at NDSU where Mina was a graduate student. With wise guidance from her older sister, Freshie eventually earned two master's degrees- one in Social Work and another in Business Administration. She went on to create a non-profit organization to help victims of domestic violence to discover their passion and find a way to an education and a better life for themselves and their children. She called it "Mother's Garden" in honor of my sister, Fern.

There were things that were utterly predictable in Tarford Flats following the annual sidewalk sales and street dance. The Lutheran Ladies continued with their charitable works and a new Country Club was built north of town with plenty of input from the Roane crowd. Darren Turnbull was elected to State Senate with an impressive 70% of the vote. He remained in the state senate for two terms- enough to become known throughout the state, then attempted a run for U.S. congress and was soundly defeated. Darren came back to manage the more lucrative and high-profile entities within Turnbull Enterprises for roughly six months of each following year. He and Cece managed to break away from their dealings in Tarford Flats and attend to their Arizona home during the colder months between November and March. Then, in the summer they traveled to Cece's family's resort in Estes Park, Colorado. In the end, Darren still managed to live the life of a true politician.

Vernie and Jeffrey remained in Tarford Flats for another fifteen years or so. Finally, at fifty-eight, Vernie agreed to allow Jeffrey to plan their next big adventure. Vernie had plenty of help in her decorating shop, what with all of the junior decorators she trained through the years. They had reached a point in their lives when they could finally travel the Orient, experiencing all of the foods, designs, culture and history they could find. Vernie returned an even richer person, not monetarily, but richer in perspective. As they had with Jeffrey over a decade before, the Eastern philosophies spoke to her, helped her to find the sense of inner peace she had been seeking since she was a little girl. My dear sister, once so eager to hide away from the risks of the world, found her innate courage and learned to be bold beyond her size.

Jeffrey suffered a stroke when Vernie was 70 years old. The two had been active and in good health, so his stroke was completely unexpected. Vernie brought Jeffrey back to the bungalow in Tarford Flats after he was released from the hospital. The brutal winter storms were over and Vernie looked forward to taking Jeffrey out to their garden in the spring. On a chilly night in early March, Jeffrey suffered another stroke. This one was massive, and he died in his sleep snuggled next to my sister.

Vernie lasted a few more years, filling her time with letter writing and meditation. I was with her when she died. Lying in her quilt laden bed, Vernie was surrounded by people who loved her, yet she seemed restless and impatient. As her spirit left her little body, I realized that it had been excitement she had been feeling. Vernie was excited to reunite with the man who changed her world; a strong, gentle soldier and midwife who had been the love of her life.

Distressing news reached Texas a few months after the fire. It came by way of a letter from young Filipe in Columbia. Apparently, the Columbian drug trade was growing evermore violent as the cartels moved in on private farmers. Many of the more successful farmers had been targeted for extortion and strong-armed into handing over their profits or, in some cases, their land. Daniel, who was as much a rebel and a natural leader as his father had been, fought against the tyranny he saw taking hold over his culture. The cartel responded by making him an example to anyone else who might rise up in insurrection. In retribution for Daniel's resistance to the cartel, the family's fields were burned. When Daniel set out to save his crops he was ambushed and taken hostage by local thugs. During the several days he was held captive, Daniel was summarily beaten about the legs and head with pipes, leaving him hobbled, concussed and permanently blinded. The family was now without his direction and they needed a leader they could trust. Feeling compelled to help, Texas immediately made arrangements to return his part of land to K.C. and started the process of returning to Columbia, this time to stay.

Now in his late twenties, Texas had made plenty of money during his time in Tarford Flats. His uncle Darren had also been quite generous toward the nephew who had saved his life. Upon learning of his nephew's intentions, Darren gave Texas a few lessons in being a shrewd businessman. In the end, Texas sold all property relating to his hybrid marijuana product to another former Peace Corpsman for a small fortune.

Surprisingly, Daniel's family was not devastated by the losses they had recently suffered. Even Daniel was in good spirits when he received his dear friend. Texas was overwhelmed with relief to see that his ambitious young friend still had his wits and his humor about him. With Daniel's help, Texas convinced the brothers that the drug trade, although profitable, was too volatile for their family to survive. Instead, Texas had some ideas about coffee (and, of course, engineering hybrid strains that would be the strongest, most productive, most consistent while being infused with the richest, fullest flavor.) After witnessing Texas's success with marijuana, the family enthusiastically agreed to follow his recommendations.

With that, Texas was returned to being one of the family with five boisterous brothers whose love for him they did not hide. Even when teased mercilessly by Texas for his changing voice and odorous teen body, Felipe, now thirteen, beamed with joy and affection.

Of course, it was Lucia who still held Texas's heart. At eighteen, she had become a strong, self-assured woman. Texas found it baffling that she could be even more beautiful than he remembered. Lucia remembered him too, and with great affection. It seemed understood by all that their future was bound together.

Texas did exactly what he set out to do when he left the second time for Columbia. He and his new brothers were wonderfully successful with their coffee crops. They even did something magical with the addition of some part of the Mexican vanilla plant. For the remainder of his life, K.C. expounded to anyone who would listen about the exquisite coffee his son sent to him each month. Toile relished in her husband and how proud he was of his son. She felt such joy in being a part of a truly loving, truly complete family.

Toile did not favor Texas's coffee as much, although she admitted it was delicious beyond compare. Instead she preferred the stuff K.C. made over an open fire. She said it reminded her of wild adventure and appreciating every moment with the man she loves.

The cabin has grown chilly again. Every room has a lovely quilt draped over a chair just in case the fire hasn't chased out the cold. The morning light reveals beautiful patterns of frost on the windows, a gentle reminder that heavy snowstorms are not far away. I have recently hired a very polite young man to deliver dried wood for the fireplace, which he does once a week. He is a handsome young man, beaming with health, strength and a very kind spirit. I suspect that he might be the grandson of one of Vernie's Dozier friends. His seems to be the only soul I see around here.

I know there are several hunters along the river. I hear the reports of their shotguns just after dawn. It is goose season again and people come from across the country to take their chances at getting a bird. Goose hunting has become a growing business in Nebraska. We have more than a few fancy hunting lodges that provide hunting licenses, rent guns and gear, and will furnish all the trappings of a sportsman's resort for those willing to pay. The hunters awaken before sunrise, set decoys on and around the frozen water, and warm up their quality underground blinds with propane heaters and a few hotplates on which they may cook eggs, bacon and sausage. Then the real hunt begins. Men dressed in waders- a pair of chest-high neoprene pants connected to a pair of rubber boots to ensure the hunters stay dry as they traverse the river- hats, flannel shirts and jackets sit hip-to-hip waiting for the geese to arrive.

The sounds of the hunt travel for over a mile. I can hear the less experienced hunters trying their hand at calling geese for a few rounds until they realize they're scaring the birds away. Anyone who really wants a goose learns quickly to cede to the best caller to bring the gaggle into shooting range.

My father was that man. He was notorious for his skill with a goose call. He was also known for having the best trained water dog, being the best shot, and having the nicest goose pit in which to wait for hours at a time to lure the perfect prey. It seemed like everyone wanted an invite to hunt with Conway. His misbehaviors were overlooked, forgotten and he was deemed a generous, considerate host, and a friend to many. He was a man who knew how to treat his friends well.

There were several instances in which the father I saw was not the father I knew. My sisters and I did not know our father to be a generous man. When it came to his family, he sent us to ask our mother for everything because she "had taken all of his money." His anger toward Mama never did abate. We merely learned that if we didn't want to witness his ire, we should not ask him for things. It was a strange juxtaposition then, to hear stories of his eagerness to open his wallet to others.

To us it wasn't about the money. We were raised to be self-starters and self-reliant. We could, and would, make our own way in the world. No, we didn't covet his money for money's sake. Instead, we understood that money and gifts were the manifestation of his affection. Those were the commodities by which he garnered love from Linny, from his friends, and also by which he expressed love to those same people. For some reason, our father did not seem to seek after love- or offer his- where his family was concerned.

At first, I was angry- or confused- at the lack of what I had understood to be loyalty to his family. I believe it would have been easier if he had proved to be incapable of loyalty altogether. Maybe I could attribute it to a neurological or developmental issue- anything to explain away what otherwise looked like deliberately hurtful behavior. I had been kidding myself, however. Conway knew how to express loyalty and he did so quite often. He had been loyal to Linny, to his various other girlfriends, to some of his friends, and to himself. He just wasn't loyal to us.

Upon the heels of that realization there arrived the conclusion that we just must not be worthy of his loyalty, of his attention or efforts. What else were we supposed to think, as we watched our own father and his stream of girlfriends, some with their children, all lining up to receive his love and attention?

Again, looking back, I question- was I just being petty? Do I remember clearly enough the many times he would surprise his girlfriends and their children with trips to Disneyland or money for college? Our father went to great lengths to keep knowledge of these things secret from his daughters, whom he reminded time after time to blame their mother for their own removal from his good graces?

Once, shortly after Linny came to town, I got a phone call from Toile. She was furious. She told me that she had just run into our father and Linny during the summer sidewalk sales. Conway might have known Linny for a month at most, and yet as he introduced her, he praised Linny's many positive qualities as if he had known her since childhood. He went on to endorse Linny as one of the hardest workers he had ever known. He went on and on, praising Linny's positive attitude, her sense of style and her wonderful personality. Conway then suggested that if Toile wanted to bring some fresher ideas into her shop that Linny would sure make a good hire. Normally, one who was not aware of how Conway operated would see nothing amiss in that exchange. To Toile, however, it was as if he had shoved a spear through her heart. Conway had never extolled such compliments on Toile, or any of us, for that matter- and yet, about a woman without any modicum of achievement, he gushed.

That was how he did it, though. There was no question that Toile and Mama had worked tirelessly to create the Beaumont Boutique, and that, thanks in part to Uncle Buddy, it was always at the peak of fashion. It would have been nearly impossible to find harder workers than Mama, Toile, Vernie- any of us- and yet, that is how Conway kept us believing that we were not quite good enough. We had to work harder, be prettier, have a more positive attitude than anyone else if we were even to dream of receiving his compliments- the compliments he doled out so eagerly on anyone else. The feeling of inadequacy haunted all of us. We each carried the belief that there must have been something we could have done to change him. We also carried the belief that we failed.

There is still a part of me that wants to believe that he was a good father, or at least that he desired to be. I want to believe that he did feel fatherly love toward his children, that somewhere in his mind we were valued.

My experiences might prove otherwise, however. What I want to believe were sincere efforts always had another purpose. A frustrating example might be the time he took me skiing in Colorado.

He was heading out to Cheyenne and invited me along. I was in Junior High at the time, and it was a special treat because I was allowed to miss school. We stopped in Cheyenne where Conway met up with a girlfriend and her daughter who happened to be a year younger than me. After spending the night at their apartment, the four of us traveled a few hours to the Loveland ski area in Colorado where, unbeknownst to me, Conway had leased a condo for four days.

We went shopping for food, ski outfits and cold-weather gear that evening and my father generously picked up the tab for everything. The next day he bought 4 three-day passes and rented the ski equipment for all of us.

It was strange to be a part of that situation for so many reasons. Most obvious was the assumption that he could place me in a new, makeshift family unit without considering how I would be affected. I had a very close relationship with my mother and sisters, and had never met these people before. As a thirteen-year-old, I still wanted a relationship with Conway, wanted to spend time with him, and so I played along. Looking back now I realize that I was a pawn meant to play a position. If this woman had to bring her daughter along on some winter rendezvous, clearly it would be best for him to bring along a playmate to keep her occupied. I had been a tool.

This was not the first nor last time I had been used by Conway to achieve something he wanted. There were many girlfriends to impress, many of their children to entertain. For a long time I felt compelled to play along, either because I did feel a duty to represent my mother and sisters well, or because I still harbored some hope that it would one day be proof enough that I was lovable.

Now that I have had children and grandchildren of my own, I find that the contrast in my memories of my father fills me with sadness. There is some poignant recognition that the relationship I thought we had- even during the few years when I thought things were going well- was false. Conway was not interested in me, my thoughts, my life, but was using me to fulfill a role, to benefit his own agenda. And yet, for most of my adolescence he never had to convince me to accompany him. He knew I would go. He was fully aware that I desperately wanted to spend time with him, to somehow earn his approval. If I ever did have the opportunity to talk with him, to share a conversation he was often distracted- so much so that he wouldn't even hear me talking. I didn't seem to be that interesting to him.

As I grew older, I became more acutely aware of his philandering and bullying behaviors among the working people of Cass County. A clammy sense of dread would fill my chest when people would connect me to Conway Duque. At first, it was rather subtle, the way people would mention his name and his activities. Tarford Flats is a small town, and he was always up to something. That had become the norm for me. Moreover, I was still naïve enough not to grasp the depth of his iniquity. As I grew and gained a more complete understanding of right and wrong, I began to cringe when I sensed conversations lead toward the topic of my father.

As an adult I tried constantly to distance myself from him, proving that I was not like my father. Conway would not have understood that at all. I believe he truly felt justified in using people to feed his own needs and appetites. He was a vain, proud, accomplished man who was loathe to apologize or admit wrongdoing.

This, we concluded, was left to us. Believing that our father's notoriety had reached every corner of Tarford Flats, his children and their families readied themselves for any kind of surprise confrontation. For each of us, the chance of running into someone whose life or family had been ravaged by Conway's appetites seemed likely. Uncompassionate peers and teachers had made snide comments about our father as far back as elementary school. As a result, Toile, Vernie and I would feel compelled to apologize for his behavior, assuming he had been a party to infidelity that ravaged their family, or that he had intimidated them somehow. Among the people of Tarford Flats we would often go out of our way to show kindness, charity, and sincerity in a near desperate effort to undo the moral wrongs committed by our father.

I remember on multiple occasions when I came to visit my sisters, Toile would quietly point out a young person whose parents nearly divorced because Conway seduced their mother. Occasionally, we might see a man on the street who had stood up to our father, and we would watch him walk by, admiringly estimating his courage and fortitude.

Overall, though, the people of Tarford Flats were kind to us. I dare to hope that it was due to the efforts of our mother, to Toile, Vernie, Jeffrey and K.C.

Relief came when Conway was finally deemed incapable of living on his own. Leading up to his placement in a nursing home, Conway fought like hell to prove he was as sound of mind as he ever had been. He refused to consider moving out of his giant home, refused to stop driving around town. And he refused to let my sisters and I make any decisions on his behalf. He had several minor car accidents, which he either denied or blamed on someone else, and he became increasing agitated and confrontational with his neighbors. Finally, the county sheriff got involved, and Conway was put in a nursing home.

Finally Conway had been contained. The scope of his hurtful antics had been miraculously reduced to the square footage within the "Darren and Cece Turnbull Special Care Unit" in the Tarford Flats Nursing Facility.

What a knotted mess of guilt, shame, sadness, frustration and jealousy had become of our relationship with Conway. Each of his daughters have suffered in our own way and according to our own understanding. Shockingly, we have not become like him, although maybe that would have been easier to bear. Instead, we vacillate between our pain and some sense of compassion for a man who had been damaged long ago.

When my father relocated to the nursing home, my sisters and I had to clear out his big stone house to get it ready for sale. Most of his fine household items were donated to those whose homes had recently been destroyed by flooding or tornadoes. In the locked "gun room" in his basement, we found a trove of memorabilia we had never before seen. The three of us spent an entire day going through pictures and letters that, when pieced together, gave us new insight into the mind of our father and his origins.

My grandmother, Doris Duke, was not a nurturing woman. Conway had admitted as much. We knew that she had divorced his father when Conway was young. We were surprised and disturbed to learn, however, that following the divorce Conway was left for several months in a children's home, then called St. Bartholomew's Orphanage, in St. Joseph. Vernie had uncovered an ancient court document placing custody of Conway with the Nuns of St. Bart's due to immoral behavior on the part of his parents. It wasn't until Doris married the man from her boarding house and could prove he had a stable income that Conway was returned to her home.

Sitting in his basement amidst boxes of paperwork, letters and photos, my sisters and I pondered at that secret he kept from all of us. How clear it became that his understanding of family, parenthood and loyalty had no foundation! I was awash in sadness, frustration, regret, and fury without knowing whom to blame.

That same afternoon in that same basement room my sisters and I learned for the first time that we had an aunt. Our father had a sister about six years his senior. Although Conway never mentioned her, he did save letters sent to him from a Charlotte Duke, her name later changed to Charlotte Mensing, from Chicago, Illinois. In her letters, Charlotte was always loving and kind, and interested in her brother's well-being. Why he never mentioned her, we could not understand, until Toile found the most tattered letter in the stack. When she realized what she was reading, Toile told Vernie and me to hush, then began again from the start, this time reading aloud:

My Dear Connie,

I have long considered how I might explain to you my absence from your life those last years in St. Joseph. I don't know what mother told you, but I can only assume she sought to sully my name and reduce my character in your eyes. I understand how hurt and confused you must have felt when I left without explanation. You and I were such friends, and you know I adored you so. How would I explain to you, in your naiveté and innocence, the reason for my departure? I had cared for you when Mother was absent from us, I taught you to read and to tie your boots. I showed you how to sweep the floor and to feed the chickens without getting pecked. But I couldn't tell you why I was made to leave.

Mother would never have allowed it.

When Mother became involved with our stepfather (whose name I will never write nor speak), her eyes seemed to be closed to his designs. Even before they married, the man began seeking physical familiarity with me.

When I tried to tell Mother she fell into a fit, accusing me of ill intent and expecting that I was scheming to keep them apart. That man went on to convince Mother that I had been seeking out his attentions, and that he supposed I was keen on him.
Connie, I promise you I wanted nothing to do with that old man! I swear I was not keen on him. The mere sight of his smarmy face made my stomach turn. I was a pretty young girl. I certainly did not want his affections!

After their wedding, Mother's husband made his way into my room. He told me that I had better not make any mention of what he was doing to me because he could put us all out on the street if I squealed. Even worse, he said that the judge would take you away from us again.
I didn't want to let him at me, Connie. I even began to block my door at night as best I could to keep him out, but he would still find a way to get to me.

In due time I became pregnant by our Mother's husband. When I confessed it to her, she flew into a rage. Mother accused me of trying to steal away the affections of her husband. She called me all manner of foul names, the least of which was "liar."

Mother and her husband tossed me from our home and gave me just enough money for bus fair to Kansas City where there was a well-reputed home for unwed mothers. They were very clear about two things: I was no longer welcome in Mother's home, and I was no longer allowed to contact you. That was the worst punishment, Connie. Not knowing what else I might do, I left you in that home to fend for yourself.

I am so sorry, my dear Connie. I should have had more courage. I should have been stronger for you and fought to remain a part of your life. I feel ashamed and very sad that you experienced abandonment at my hands. I don' t know how I could ever fix the heartbreak I have caused you.

Please forgive my weaknesses, my brother. I will always love you.

Your ever most devoted sister,

Charlie

Toile lowered the tattered pages and stared at the floor. Vernie and I also felt completely awash in unexpected information- and then came the waves of anger, betrayal and disgust.

So much about our father began to fall into place; his distrust of women, his preoccupation with what he perceived as abandonment or betrayal, his need to maintain control over everything in his life...
And how would he not experience these things? Conway Duke was raised by a self-serving woman and a sadistic stepfather. The loss of the one person in his world who truly cared for him must have been more than he could bear.

When we got him, our father was already broken.

Healthy boundaries are good things. In my professional life, I did a lot of work with boundaries. It is the ultimate goal in relationships to have healthy mutual boundaries with others in our sphere. Sometimes, we are so desperate to create boundaries with those who hurt us, we can only do that by physically removing ourselves from them. Vernie did that when she moved into the cabin. Fern did it when she left with Ernie Twipps. I now realize that I also protected myself from the pain that spread like a fungus through the wife and children of Conway Duque. It is a common phenomenon that people become "super reasonable" to separate themselves from pain. It is also an easy reaction to defend, because of course, who can argue with reason? After growing up in Tarford Flats I moved away to attend college. I met and married my husband in a small ceremony far from home. We raised our family and made the respectable number of visits to see my sisters and sometimes my father, but those visits were out of duty and produced lingering pain. I now realize that I learned early that it felt much better to take on the role of an observer rather than a participant in much of my upbringing. It should not come as a surprise that I ultimately became a behavior scientist and a family therapist. I have no doubt that I could have accurately diagnosed any of my family members, and confidently predict their reactions to various stressors, but I could not give them what they needed from our father, Conway. It was just not meant to be.

When my father died, we decided not to have a funeral or memorial service. We tried to phrase his obituary in a way that he would have appreciated, detailing his hobbies (except philandering), his interests and affinities (except anything related to women), and some nice things he provided to the community. We didn't include anything about our mother or their marriage to spare her any resurgence of gossip. It was her idea, really, as she considered the period of their marriage one of her hardest times. We briefly listed his daughters, their husbands and children, there was no mention of Linny, or Marlene, Bunny, or the countless women strewn along his life's path. We just wanted some end, some punctuation, like the final "stop" on a telegraph to signify the end of the pain and betrayal.

I have thought often about Conway's death- and why I longed for it. What an awful thing to want! Still, I longed for it because I thought maybe it would bring some peace, or at least, closure.

Even after he was diagnosed with Alzheimer's disease, I found myself hoping that someday Conway would have some epiphany- some change of heart- which would lead him to treasure his family. Alas, to no avail. As his mental state deteriorated, Conway tried desperately to cling to thoughts and memories that connected him to his past, to the world. The thoughts he happened to cling to, however, were thoughts of anger and blame, things my mother had done or said in moments of anger, suspicions he held about each of us deep in his heart. His feelings of victimization ran long and deep.

In the end, he died alone. As with narcissists, their biggest fear is to end up alone, and yet through the pain they inflict on those who love them, ending up alone is nearly inevitable. First to leave were those who sought after the things he could offer. He no longer had control over his money, so he could not give it away. His friends lost interest as he lost influence. Finally, those closest to him had to remove themselves to save themselves from his poisonous condition.

I received another Christmas card today. My boys have sent cards each year with pictures of their growing families. I expect to see many of them soon, as I have recently received a ticket to fly out of Omaha to spend time over the Christmas holiday in a warmer climate.

I heard from Freshie again this year. She is still blazing trails for displaced women. She has had some pretty interesting relationships, but has yet to feel the need to settle down.

Mina sent her annual letter, detailing the activities of her brood. Mina is a mother of three, all in graduate school at their mother's alma mater. She married a wonderful man of Scottish descent who has a gregarious nature and has cherished her unceasingly.

I used to hear sporadically from Fern, too. She always sounded hopeful, happy, and growing more and more weightless. By the time she passed away a few years ago, I believe Fern had finally shed the self-loathing and guilt she had carried from her youth.

I feel heartened when I think of my family, the way we have created our paths and found meaning, even with the struggles we have had. I find that I am most grateful for those who have had an abundance of gumption- or spirit- the sense to seek freedom from those who would seek to cause pain. I truly believe that we all must have an awareness of our worth, and that, as small as that speck of awareness might seem, if we stop and pay attention, we can feel it burn like a fire in our souls.

The envelope I opened this day had been sent via airmail from Santa Marta. Inside was a picture of a large family on the beach, looking out into the beautiful teal waters. There in the center stood my nephew, Texas, his arm around the waist of his beautiful wife whose hair has become streaked with glistening silver. With them were their three grown sons and their wives. Just off to the side of the adults stood an impish little girl of about six years of age. She looked strong and stunningly pretty, with fire in her dark eyes and a smart little smirk just like her grandmother used to wear. Her name is Lucy.

Made in the USA
Las Vegas, NV
21 January 2021